William I

The Episodes of Vathek

Translated from the French
by Sir Frank Marzials

Edited with an introduction
by Malcolm Jack

Dedalus

In Memory of Brian Fothergill

Published in the UK by Dedalus Ltd,
Langford Lodge, St Judith's Lane, Sawtry, Cambs, PE17 5XE

ISBN 1 873982 61 5

Distributed in Canada By Marginal Distribution,
Unit 103, 277, George Street North, Peterborough, Ontario, KJ9 3G9
Distributed in Australia and New Zealand by Peribo Pty Ltd,
58, Beaumont Road, Mount Kuring-gai N.S.W. 2080

This edition copyright © Dedalus 1994

Typeset by Datix International Ltd, Bungay, Suffolk
Printed in Finland by Wsoy

A C.I.P. listing for this title is available on request from the British Library.

The unnatural and the strange
Have a perfume of their own

Fernando Pessoa

Somos o outro dos
outros

Marco Aurelio

Malcolm Jack is an eighteenth century specialist;
his book, *Corruption and Progress: the
Eighteenth-Century Debate* was published in 1989,
he is editor of *Vathek and Other Stories: A
William Beckford Reader* (London: Pickering & Chatto,
1993) and a biographical sketch, *William Beckford:
An English Fidalgo* is at press in New York.

Contents

Introduction

When William Beckford began writing *The Episodes,*
he was still in his early twenties but he had already enjoyed
a long career as a 'poor Arabian storyteller'; indeed in
1782, he had written *Vathek,* his best-known Arabian tale.
The cycle of stories that led to these maturer works had
started as early as 1775 when the precocious fifteen year
old master of Fonthill was already composing plots that
display all the ingredients of the typically Beckfordian tale:
wayward passion, forbidden desire, fanaticism and high
drama, all wrapped in rich, oriental imagery. How did the
heir to a Wiltshire estate, an English adolescent acquire
such rare and exotic tastes?

Beckford's childhood, spent in his father's country man-
sion, *Splendens,* equipped with a superb library and boasting
unusual Eastern decor in some of its chambers, was a
protected, even isolated, experience. His father, a radical
Whig politician and friend of Wilkes, had died in 1770
leaving the nine year old William, his only legitimate
offspring, in the care of the dour and aristocratic Maria
Hamilton, his mother, and certain grandees, including the
Lords Chatham and Thurlow, who acted as his guardians.
His mother (whom he nicknamed the 'Begum', a Persian
lady of high rank) made a significant decision when she
decided not to send William to school, instead entrusting
his education to tutors. As a result the young heir stayed at
home on the estate in Wiltshire and escaped something of
the banalizing effects of a public school education. When
William was not actually at class, he spent his time brows-
ing in the well-stocked library or wandering in the leafy
glades of the considerable grounds at Fonthill.

While Beckford was in his early teens, the artist Alexander Cozens, then in his late fifties, arrived to become his
drawing master. Cozens' career had been distinguished; his

childhood spent in St Petersburg where his father had been master shipbuilder to the Czar, exotic. His influence on the imaginative young heir to Fonthill was considerable: not only did he inspire William with a love of art that lasted his entire life but he encouraged him in that forbidden taste for the oriental that his mother and guardians were so anxious to suppress. Under Cozens' direction, Beckford began to learn Arabic and Persian; his already fluent French enabled him to read the *Arabian Nights* which had been translated by Antoine Galland in 1704 and was among the collection in the family's library.

From Beckford's earliest writing, this Eastern influence is apparent. *The Long Story* (1777) is one of the earliest sustained attempts to amalgamate oriental imagery with a fast-moving narrative of mystery and imagination. The hero of the story has to cross a dauntingly lunar landscape where hideous reptilian creatures slink and squirm; he undergoes mysterious rites of initiation set by ghostly oriental figures in order to achieve knowledge and pleasure unknown to other Europeans. The scenery is by turns lush and grotesque; an insinuating sensuality lures the hero and the reader towards hedonistic delights of an unspecified nature.

Beckford's career as an oriental fabulist continued with a series of further tales, such as the *l'Histoire d'Al Raoui* and the *l'Histoire Darianoc*, several of which, were written in French. During this period we know that Beckford was also pouring over original manuscripts brought back from the East by Edward Wortley Montagu and may have been planning his own translation of the *Arabian Tales*. In the event, in 1782, as we have learnt, came *Vathek*, his chef d'oeuvre, which relates the story of the journey of Caliph Vathek to Eblis or hell. Told in the third person, *Vathek* is a complex, sophisticated narrative; its theme is damnation, a ruin that is visited upon the hero because of his impious desire for knowledge proscribed by the true religion of Mohammed. Caliph Vathek is an impetuous and autocratic ruler; careless of the welfare of his subjects, he embarks upon a fateful quest that can only lead to the incandescent chambers of Eblis. Even so he has some redeeming features and his evil is outdone by that of his mother, Carathis, a Lady Macbeth-like figure of ruthless and callous determination who exercises a fatal influence over her son. The frightful progress of these moral monsters toward ultimate destruction is lightened by occasional touches of humour and burlesque in the telling of the tale.

In his preparation for *Vathek*, Beckford had read widely on Eastern themes. As well as the *Arabian Nights*, we know that he made use of scholarly books such as B. d'Herbelot's *Bibliotheque Orientale* (1697) and J. Richardson's *A Dissertation on the Languages, Literature and Manners of the Eastern Nations* (1777) as well as the manuscripts of Edward Wortley Montagu. However, completing *Vathek* did not assuage his taste for the oriental tale; early in 1783, writing to Samuel Henley, his collaborator and author of the lengthy footnotes to *Vathek*, Beckford refers to 'other tales to which *Vathek* belongs' which he would also begin to write in French. His work on these other tales, *The Episodes,* was to continue for another three years, a period that was to prove the stormiest of his life. Personal disasters came apace: an accusation of sodomy (then a capital offence) forced him into exile on the Continent; while abroad his beloved wife, the young and supportive Lady Margaret died. Meanwhile, in London, Henley published *Vathek* against Beckford's specific instructions and without *The Episodes* which he had always intended to produce together with his major tale. Forced to publish his own edition of *Vathek* in Lausanne and another in Paris in 1787, Beckford advertised *The Episodes* but he did not produce them in the text. Between his two advertisements, the number of 'other tales' diminishes from four to three, the number that have finally survived. They were never published in Beckford's lifetime.

The Episodes are passionate, frightening stories. Like *Vathek*, they pursue the theme of damnation and retribution; indeed Caliph Vathek meets the heroes of these new stories bemoaning their fate in hellish Eblis. Less stylised and complex than *Vathek*, *The Episodes* are in many respects more terrifying; the analysis of evil contained in them is starker and more direct; the subject matter, including necrophilia and incest, as well as homosexuality, put them well beyond the pale until modern times.

Today's reader will be less shocked than Beckford's contemporaries by the overtly homosexual theme of the first of the three stories, The Story of Prince Alasi and the Princess Firouzkah. Indeed the initial impression the Prince gives out is not unsympathetic: Alasi dreads kingship because of the burden of duty that it places upon those who accede to it. He therefore comes over as a modest and respectful young prince. However, although certain imperious qualities appear once Alasi has become King, it is not until the appearance of the 'delicately fashioned' Firouz, a gamine-like adolescent, that we begin to encounter 'essential badness'. Alasi, like many of Beckford's other heroes, cannot resist the blandishments of a character more evil than himself; Firouz, young and impetuous as well as beautiful, exercises a total control over Alasi and is ruthless in sweeping aside anyone who gets in his way or diminishes his hold on Alasi. A feeling of foreboding hangs over the two friends from the moment of their first meeting; Alasi, besotted by his young, viperish companion exercises his princely authority imprudently and unjustly. His desire, carnal as well as emotional, is profane and alienates him from the religion into which he was born. It contributes too to a growing atmosphere of decadence and effeminacy that hangs over the story. While others suffer and die, the two protagonists indulge in sensuous pastimes, eating from tables covered in dainties and exquisite wines, served by nubile youths and maidens, garlanded in jasmine sprays. The revelation that Firouz is in fact a girl does nothing to dispel the atmosphere of moral corruption that has already been created. Indeed the only moral as well as significantly masculine figure in the story is the much-wronged Princess

Rondabah who nevertheless lives to see her enemies vanquished.

The story of Prince Alasi is not told without those recognizably Beckfordian strokes of humour and irony that we have already remarked upon in his earlier tales. When it comes to the second of *The Episodes*, The Story of Prince Barkiarokh, a study of unrelenting evil is still relieved by these lighter touches. Barkiarokh is technically more complicated than Alasi: Beckford uses the technique of ancient Arabic story-telling which enfolds one plot within another. Thus we have at least three tales related to us: there is the story of the peri (a superhuman being having magical powers) Homaïouna, the end of which merges into the tale of the jinn (a demon spirit); there is the the the story of Barkiarokh's younger sister-in-law and finally there is the story of Leilah, his daughter.

Throughout the adventures of all these actors, surrounded as they are by evil spirits (afrits), ghostly creatures and an array of eunuchs, negresses and priests always found in attendance in Beckford's stories, the progress of human evil is charted. Barkiarokh commits murder, indulges in necrophiliac passion and profanes, as Alasi had done, the name of the true God Allah. In seeking his ends, he is vicious and merciless: opponents are banished or killed; princely authority is once again abused. But Barkiarokh's obsessive pursuit of pleasure and new stimulation is a vain and unfulfillable quest: never satiated, he finally turns his lustful attention on his own daughter, Leilah. Like Alasi and the Caliph Vathek before him, his corruption is now absolute and hell can be his only refuge.

The last of *The Episodes*, The Story of the Princess Zulkaïs and Prince Kalilah appears to be unfinished, though its dark plot once again suggests an inevitable progress toward doom. Here we see an evil that is hereditary: Princess Zulkaïs' father, the Emir, is a man bent on controlling the future. Instead of accepting, as behoves a faithful follower of the Prophet, those burdens as well as benefits that life bestows, his ambition and vanity make him commit the 'unpardonable error' of opposing the decrees of heaven. Ignoring the teaching of the Koran, the Emir turns to the lore of the ancient Egyptians to support his impious plan to control the flow of the Nile. When a Holy Man, much in the mould of St John the Baptist appears to challenge his actions, he is summarily strangled and thrown into the river. Still influenced by these ancient and evil doctrines, the Emir has Zulkaïs and her brother Kalilah immersed in a magic bath after their birth so that they will assume the qualities of extraordinary beings. The result is an extraordinariness that no-one welcomes: brother and sister are bonded in an unhealthy relationship that makes them unable to bear separation or the lack of each other's caresses. The rest of the tale deals with the fated outcome of this unnatural and incestuous attachment which, like other moral heterodoxies, can only flourish in the evil underworld of Eblis.

Although *The Episodes* remained unpublished in Beckford's lifetime, their existence was known of and a few contemporaries, such as the poet Samuel Rogers, were privy to parts of them. Rogers had no doubt about the quality of what he heard read out to him when he visited Fonthill Abbey in 1817 but he came away with the impression that they displayed something of a 'diseased' mind in their author. That opinion may have made Byron, who had read *Vathek* with enthusiasm, even keener to read these 'other tales' but he was to be denied that privilege. The jibes Byron had made about 'England's Wealthiest son' in *Childe Harold* (1812) must have cooled any feeling that Beckford had for the poet: in the event he refused even to meet him. A talented young writer whom Beckford did meet and about whose work he expressed admiration was Benjamin Disraeli. Indeed Beckford regarded the flamboyant Disraeli as something of a spiritual heir, with a similar interest in all things oriental. Although their meeting was a success, years

14

of isolation made it difficult for Beckford to open up to a newcomer. Like Byron, Disraeli too was to be disappointed in his hope of reading *The Episodes*.

Beckford's reluctance to share his stories with his contemporaries arose from his realization that their autobiographical nature would be recognized. Personalities from his own life stalk the pages of the tales. In the Story of Princess Zulkaïs, the Emir, autocratic and frightening, represents Beckford's own father, the Alderman whose career as a rumbustious politician must have made him seem very remote to his young, sensitive son who was being brought up in the remote fastness of Fonthill. The Climber, a sinister and malevolent figure who turns out to be an agent of Eblis and who encourages Zulkaïs to rebel plays a similar role to Alexander Cozens' in Beckford's own childhood. That someone who was a friend and supporter should be so darkly drawn shows the extent of Beckford's insecurity and paranoia. However much Beckford feared that real persons from his own life might be recognized in the stories, his real dread was that his reader would see his own vices – impetuosity, violent temper, a curiosity that knows no bounds and an imagination that veers to the evil and perverse - represented in all his fictional heroes, drawing the inevitable conclusion that the Abbot of Fonthill, as Beckford sometimes styled himself, was a creature of satanic evil.

To the modern reader, inhabitant of the post-Romantic age of extreme individualism such personal embarrassments might be less disturbing than a moral dilemma that the author of *The Episodes* poses, unaware of how inescapable it would become for succeeding generations. If Alasi's homosexuality, Barkiarokh's evil and Zulkaïs' incestuous desires are implanted in their nature; if, in that way, these instincts are 'natural'; how can we expect these fictional characters to behave in any other way? By analogy, in real life, how can anyone, however morally repugnant his behaviour may be, be held responsible for actions which result from his nature? Sifting through the flotsam and jetsam of human existence, like the Decadents who were to succeed him, Beckford can find only a deep psychic malaise in individuals which reflects the absolute corruption of society. What started as the *moraliste's* jesting and jibing at the frailty of the human condition has become something much more threatening. Despite the lush, oriental dressing of his *Episodes* and the ironic tone of his story-telling, Beckford's voice in these tales is authentically modern: it is the cry of despair of a creature alienated and adrift in a cold and morally indifferent universe.

Malcolm Jack,
London.

Note on the present edition

The Episodes were written, in French, between 1783 and 1786. Although Beckford intended them as a continuation of the story of *Vathek*, *An Arabian Tale* (1786), they were not published until 1912.

The 1912 edition was prepared by Lewis Melville on the basis of a translation of the text by Sir Frank T. Marzials. That translation, with minor corrections and alterations, has been used for this edition.

Select Bibliography

1 Works of William Beckford Consulted

Life at Fonthill 1807-22, ed. Boyd Alexander (London: Rupert Hart Davis, 1957).

L'Histoire de Prince Ahmed, ed. D. Girard (Paris: Jose Corti, 1993).

Suite de Contes Arabes, ed. D.Girard (Paris: Jose Corti, 1992).

The Episodes of Vathek, trans. Sir Frank Marzials ed. Lewis Melville (London: Stephen Swift, 1912).

Three Gothic Novels, ed. P. Fairclough (London: Penguin, 1968).

Vathek, ed. R. Lonsdale (Oxford: Oxford Classics, 1983).

Vathek and Other Stories, ed. M. Jack (London: Pickering & Chatto, 1993).

Vathek, Conte Arabe, foreword by E. Bressy, preface by S. Mallarmé (Paris: Jose Corti, 1984).

2 Other References

Alexander, Boyd *England's Wealthiest Son* (London: Centaur Press, 1962).

Bishop, M., ed. *Recollections of the Table Talk of Samuel Rogers* (London: The Richards Press, 1952)

Byron, Lord George Gordon, *Poetical Works* (Oxford: Oxford Standard Authors, 1945)

Chapman, G., *Beckford* (London: Jonathan Cape, 1952).

Fothergill, B., *Beckford of Fonthill* (London: Faber, 1979).

Graham, K.W. ed. *Vathek & The Escape From Time* (New York: AMS, 1990).

Irwin, R., *The Arabian Nights A Companion* (London: Allen Lane, 1994).

Lees–Milne, J., *William Beckford* (London: National Trust Classics, 1990).

Sage, V., *The Gothick Novel* (London: Macmillan, 1990)

The story of
Prince Alasi and the
Princess Firouzkah

I reigned in Kharezme, and would not have exchanged my kingdom, however small, for the Calif Vathek's immense empire. No, it is not ambition that has brought me to this fatal place. My heart, so soon to burn in the fires of the divine vengeance, was armed against every unruly passion; only the calm and equable feelings of friendship could have found entrance there; but Love, which in its own shape would have been repelled, took Friendship's shape, and in that shape effected my ruin.

I was twenty years of age when my father died; and I regretted his loss sincerely, not only from natural affection, but also because I regarded kingship as a burden very heavy to be borne.

The soft delights of the harem had little charm for me; the idea of marriage's more formal bonds attracted me even less. I had been solemnly betrothed to Rondabah, Princess of Ghilan, and this contract, entered into by my father on my behalf, for the good of the two countries, was one which I could not lightly venture to cancel. All I could dare to allow myself was delay.

With this almost misanthropic repulsion from the ordinary ways of men, I had to ascend a throne, to govern a numerous people, to endure the ineptitude of the great, and the folly of the meaner folk, to do justice to all, and, in a word, to live among my subjects. But in those days generosity and virtue were not to me mere vague and empty words. I fulfilled all my duties exactly, and only from time to time indulged in the delights of solitude. A tent, disposed after the Persian manner, and situated in a dense forest, was the place where I spent these moments of retirement, moments that always seemed to pass too quickly. I had caused a considerable number of trees to be cut down so as to leave an open clearing of fair size, and had filled this clearing with gay flowers, while round it coiled a moat whose waters were as clear as those of Rucnabad. Near this bright spot, which I used to liken to the moon shining full-orbed in the dark blue of the firmament, I often admired the gloomy depths of the enfolding woods, and strayed in their recesses, to dream!

One day, when, stretched at length upon the moss, I was caressing a young deer that would come tame to my hand, I heard the sound of a horse galloping – not far distant; and soon after a rider came in view, who was unknown to me. His dress was outlandish, his countenance fierce, his eye haggard. But he did not long keep my attention. An angelic form, in a boy's dress, soon riveted my gaze. The stranger held this lad, who seemed most graceful, most delicately fashioned, clasped straight to his breast, and seemed anxious, as I thought, to prevent him from calling for help. Outraged by what I took to be an act of lawless violence, I rose, I barred the stranger's way, I flashed my sword in his eyes, and cried: "Stop, wretch! Do you dare commit this wrong in the sight of the King of Kharezme?"

Scarcely had I uttered these words, when the stranger sprang to the ground, without releasing his precious charge, and said, saluting me with every mark of respect: "Prince Alasi, you are the very object of my search. I wish to entrust to you a treasure beyond all price. Filanshaw, King of Shirvan, the intimate friend of the king your late father, is reduced to dire extremity. His rebellious subjects hold him besieged in the citadel of Samakhié. The troops of Calif Vathek are upholding them in their revolt. They have sworn the utter ruin of their sovereign. Filanshaw accepts undaunted the decrees of Fate so far as he himself is concerned, but anxious, if that be yet possible, to keep alive his only son, the lovely child whom you see here, he has commanded me to place him in your hands. Hide this pearl of incomparable price in your bosom; suffer its origin, the shell in which it was formed, to remain unknown, until such time as the years bring security. And so farewell. I fear pursuit. Prince Firouz will himself tell you all else that you may wish to know."

I had, while he was speaking, opened my arms to Firouz, and Firouz had sprung into them. We held one another embraced with a tenderness that seemed to fill the stranger with satisfaction. He mounted his horse, and was gone in a moment.

"Oh, take me hence," then said Firouz; "now indeed do I fear to fall into the hands of my persecutors. Ah! would they tear me from the side of the friend Heaven has given me – the friend towards whom my whole heart gives one bound?"

"No, dear child," cried I; "nothing shall tear you from my side. My treasures, my army, all I have, shall be used for your protection. But why hide your birth here in my dominions, where no harm can come to you?"

"Nay, it must be so, my most generous defender," rejoined Firouz; "my father's foes have sworn to extirpate his race. They would brave death itself in obedience to their oath; they would stab me in your very presence if I were recognised. The man who brought me here, and has guarded me through my infancy, will do all he can to persuade them I am no longer alive. Find some one to father me – it matters not whom – I shall have no other pride save that of loving you, and deserving that you should love me in return."

Thus speaking, we came to the tapestried enclosure that surrounded my Persian pavilion, and I ordered refreshments to be brought – but neither of us did more than taste of them. The sound of Firouz's voice, his words, his looks, seemed to confuse my reason, and made my speech come low and haltingly. He perceived the tumult raging in my breast, and, to appease it, abandoned a certain languor and tenderness of demeanour that he had so far affected, and assumed the childish gaiety and vivacity natural to his years, for he did not appear to be much more than thirteen.

"How," said he, "have you nothing here except books? No instruments of music?"

I smiled, and ordered a lute to be brought. Firouz's

playing was that of a master. He sang and accompanied himself with so much feeling, with such grace, that he raised in my breast another storm of emotion, which he again was careful to dispel by innocent mirth.

Night came on, and we separated. Though happy beyond what I had conceived possible, I yet desired to be alone. I felt the need of introspection. This was not at first easy: all my thoughts were in confusion! I could not account to my own self for the agitation of feeling I had experienced. "At last," said I, "Heaven has hearkened to my dearest wish. It has sent me the true heart's-friend I should never have found in my court; it has sent him to me adorned with all the charms of innocence — charms that will be followed, at a maturer age, by those good qualities that make of friendship man's highest blessing — and, above all, the highest blessing of a prince, since disinterested friendship is a blessing that a prince can scarcely hope to enjoy."

I had already extended beyond its customary term the time I devoted to seclusion and solitude. My absence, so short to myself, seemed long to my people, and a return to Zerbend became imperative. Some days before we left our retreat, I caused a shepherd living in the neighbourhood to be brought before me, and commanded him, on pain of death if he divulged our secret, to acknowledge Firouz as his son. This precaution seemed to reassure the young prince. He multiplied his marks of affection for me, and took more pains than ever to give me pleasure.

Friendship, as one may say, exercised upon me a humanising influence. I no longer shunned diversions and entertainments. Firouz shone in them, and was universally admired. His amenity and grace won golden opinions, in which I fully shared, so that I was not a little surprised to see him coming to me, one day, wild and furious. "King of Kharezme," said he, "why have you deceived me? If you were not prepared to love me, and me alone, you ought not to have accepted me as your friend. Send me back to the Mage, since the Princess Rondabah, who is instantly ex-

24

pected here, must, in the nature of things, take full possession of your heart!"

This extraordinary outburst seemed so out of place and unreasonable, that I assumed a very stern tone, and replied: "What excess of folly is this, Prince of Shirvan? How can my union with Princess Rondabah in any wise concern you? What is there in common between the affection I shall owe to my wife, and the affection I shall ever entertain for yourself?"

"Oh! it concerns me greatly," rejoined he. "It concerns me much that a woman, lovely and lovable, should also become your staunch friend! Is it not said that the Princess of Ghilan unites to the fortitude, the courage of a man, all the charms of her sex? What more will you want when you possess her? Where shall I stand then? Perhaps you imagine you will have done all I am entitled to expect at your hands when you have reinstated me in my dominions; but I tell you beforehand that, if you placed the world's empire at my feet in exchange for your tenderest friendship, I could only regard you as my deadliest enemy!"

Firouz knew me better than I knew myself. He played upon me as he wished. Besides, he had himself well in hand, knew how to act so as to excite my sympathy, and to seem yielding and amenable, as it served his purpose. He quieted down after this outburst, and resumed his ordinary playfulness.

Though he passed for the son of a shepherd, Firouz, being the son of the King of Shirvan, had a claim to my fullest consideration; and I would rather have been accused of a ridiculous partiality than that he should be treated without the deference due to his real rank. He occupied the pleasantest quarters in my palace. He had chosen his own attendants, in addition to two eunuchs, sent to him by the Mage on the very day of his arrival at my Persian pavilion. I had provided him with instructors in every kind of knowledge – whom he exasperated; with superb horses – which he rode to death; and with slaves – whom he ill-treated without mercy. But all this was hidden from me.

My boundless partiality gave rise to some murmurs, no doubt, but it prevented any direct accusation from reaching my ears.

A venerable Mullah, highly esteemed for learning and piety, was commissioned to expound, for his benefit, the salutary moral teachings of the Koran, and caused him to read and learn by heart a variety of its sacred texts; and of all my young friend's tasks this was the most irksome. But I attributed his distaste to any cause but the real one. Far indeed was I from suspecting that his mind had already been saturated with doctrines altogether opposed to those of Islam.

One day when I had passed several hours without seeing my amiable pupil, I went to look for him, and found him in one of the large halls, capering and dancing about with a strange figure grotesquely huddled up in an ass's skin. "Ah, my dear prince," cried he, running up to me open-armed; "you have before you the very strangest spectacle in the world. My Mullah is transformed into an ass – the king of all asses, since he talks even as he talked before!"

"What do you mean?" cried I; "what game are you playing now?"

"It's not a game," replied the Mullah, waving two false ears of an immeasurable length; "I am trying, in all good nature, to fully realise the character I am now personating, and I entreat your Majesty not to be scandalised and take my so doing in evil part."

At these words I stood confounded. I misdoubted whether I was listening to the voice of the Mullah, or whether I really had before me a donkey, which, by some miracle, had been endowed with the gift of speech. Vainly did I ask Firouz for an explanation. He only laughed immoderately and replied, "Ask the donkey."

Finally, my patience quite exhausted, I was about to order this disgusting buffoonery to be brought forcibly to an end, when Firouz assumed his most serious air, and said: "Sire, you will, I hope, forgive the innocent artifice by which I have endeavoured to demonstrate how much you, and other princes, are deceived as to the character of the people about them. This Mullah has, doubtless, been presented to you as a man of very superior merit; and, as such, you have appointed him to act as teacher to your friend and pupil. Well! be it known to you that, in order to obtain one of my most hideous negresses, with whom he is madly in love, he has consented to remain three days thus ridiculously accoutred, and so to be a universal laughing-stock. And, indeed, you must agree that he presents the form and figure of an ass in a highly satisfactory manner, and that his speech does no discredit to his outward appearance."

I asked the Mullah if what Firouz said was true.

"Not quite," he replied, stammering and stuttering in a pitifully absurd way; "the girl he is to give me, though black as night, is beautiful as day; the oil with which she makes her charms lustrous is scented like the orange-flower; her voice has the bitter-sweet of the pomegranate; when she toys with my beard, her fingers, which are prickly as the thistle, titillate my very heart! Ah! so that she may be mine, suffer me, suffer me to remain for three days in the form and figure of an ass!"

"Wretch, in that form and figure thou shalt die!" I cried, with an indignation I could not contain; "and let me never hear speak of thee again!"

I retired as I spoke these words, casting at Firouz looks of a kind to which he was in no way accustomed.

The rest of the day I spent in reflecting on Firouz's ill-nature, and the infamous conduct of the Mullah; but, when evening came, I thought only of again seeing my friend. I caused him to be summoned. He came at once, timidly and affectionately. "Dear prince," said he, "you don't know what grief I have felt all day at the thought that you seemed angry with me. In order to obtain forgiveness, I have lost not a moment in executing your commands. The ass is dead, and is buried. You will never hear speak of him again."

"This is another of your ill-timed jests," I exclaimed.

"Do you ask me to believe that the Mullah, who spoke with such vigour this morning, is dead to-night?"

"He is, and by your command," replied Firouz. "One of my negro slaves, whose mistress he wished to appropriate, despatched him, and he was buried incontinently and without ceremony, like the donkey he was."

"This is really too much!" cried I. "What! do you think you can, with impunity, assassinate a man whose head you yourself had turned?"

"I executed your orders," he rejoined. "I executed them literally. Surely the loss of so vile a creature is not to be regretted. Farewell, I go to weep over my own imprudence, and the fragile nature of your affection – which the slightest jar can shatter."

He was about to retire. I stopped him. The most exquisite viands, delicately served in plates of enamel, were placed before us; we began to eat together, and I was again weak enough, during our repast, to laugh at all his jokes and jibes upon the subject of the ass.

The public did not take the Mullah's death with quite so much equanimity. It was said that Firouz, in derision of the faith of the true believers, had administered some philtre to the holy man, causing him to lose his wits. An act so atrocious was naturally regarded with abhorrence, and I was accused of culpable partiality for a child of low birth and vile instincts. The queen, my mother, felt herself bound to bring these mutterings of discontent to my knowledge. She spoke of them openly, and in no ambiguous terms, before Firouz himself, so as to moderate his arrogance, if that were possible. For myself, I recognised the justice of her reproofs, which were at once affectionately expressed and reasonable; but my friend never forgave her.

He was specially outraged by the contempt heaped upon him because of his humble birth, and told me it was absolutely necessary his true parentage should be disclosed. I represented the danger involved, a danger that he had himself set before me in such strong terms, and entreated him to wait at least for the return of the envoys I had sent to Shirvan. But he was too impatient to wait, and, in order to overcome my objections, bethought himself of a device which I could certainly never have foreseen.

One morning when I was about to start on a hunting expedition, the Prince of Shirvan, who always gladly accompanied me on such occasions, feigned sickness. I wished to remain by him; but he urged me not to stay, assuring me that, with a little rest, I should find him, on my return, in a fit condition to share with me in such amusements as would be a pleasant relaxation after the fatigues of the day – amusements that he would himself devise.

Accordingly I did find, on my return, a superb collation, prepared and served in a little grove of trees, forming part of my gardens, and decked and illumined after a fashion all the prince's own – in other words, with the utmost taste and refinement. We sat under a kind of dais formed of the intertwining branches of pomegranates and oleanders. A thousand flowers, shed at our feet, formed a rich carpet, and filled the senses with their intoxicating fragrance. Unnumbered crystal vases, containing fruits perfumed with ambergris, and floating on snow, reflected the light of small tapers daintily set on the margin of a succession of fountains. Choirs of young musicians were so disposed as to charm the ear without interrupting our discourse. Never was eve more delicious; never had Firouz shown himself more gay, more amiable, more enchanting. His pleasant mirth, his wit, enlivened me even more than the wine, which he poured out freely. When the wily son of Filanshaw perceived that my head was in a whirl of pleasant excitement, he knelt before me on one knee, and, taking both my hands in his, said: "Dear Alasi, I had forgotten to ask you to forgive a wretch who has deserved death."

"Speak," I replied. "You know that from me you have but to ask in order to obtain; and, besides, I should be pleased indeed to find your heart sensible to pity."

"The matter stands thus," rejoined Firouz. "I was to-day in my apartment, surrounded by your flatterers, who at once hate me and seek to win my favour, when the shepherd, my supposed father, came in to kiss me, open-armed. At that moment the blood of Filanshaw surged rebellious in my heart. 'Hence, churl,' said I to the shepherd, 'go and stifle thy misbegotten brats with thy clumsy caresses! Wouldst thou have the unblushing effrontery to maintain that I am thy son?' 'That I am bound to do so, you very well know,' he replied firmly. 'I will maintain it with my life.' This reply of his was, no doubt, in strict accordance with his duty; but, curious to see how far we can really depend on those to whom we entrust our secrets, I ordered the man, who seemed so resolute, to receive the bastinado. He endured it but a very short time – he revealed all. After your express orders, and the punishment with which you threatened him, he is no doubt worthy of death; but I pray you to forgive him."

"The ordeal was severe," said I. "Will you ever be cruel? What irresistible power compels me to love you? Assuredly not the sympathy of fellow-feeling."

"It is most true," he rejoined, "that I do not endure mankind as patiently as you do. To me men seem as ravenous as wolves, as perfidious as the foxes in Loqman's Fables, and so flighty of feeling, so false to their promises, that it is impossible not to hold them in abhorrence! Why are we two not alone in the world? Then the earth, now swarming with the vile and wicked, might boast itself inhabited by two faithful and happy friends."

By such exalted and romantic outbursts of sentiment, Firouz brought me to tolerate this new proof of the essential badness of his heart. He had, indeed, not told me the whole story, as I learned on the morrow. It was by his own orders, and at his own suggestion, indirectly conveyed, that the shepherd had come into his presence, and accosted him as he had done; and, moreover, the poor wretch had had the fortitude to endure his punishment almost unto death before infringing my commands. I sent the unhappy creature a sum of money, and held myself most to blame for his condition.

As this transaction had filled all Zerbend with indignation, and seemed to reflect more blame on Firouz than he actually deserved, I publicly, and with some pomp, declared his real birth, and the reasons why it had been hidden. I also thenceforward surrounded him with regal state; and was not a little surprised to see that those who had hitherto been most bitter against him were now all eagerness to do him service. This made me somewhat mistrust their real intentions. But the Prince of Shirvan reassured me. "Don't be afraid," said he, laughing; "you can trust the care of my person to these people just as safely as to their fellows; there is nothing that really savours of treachery in their bearing; their affection has only changed with the change in my fortunes. I am now no longer the sly and cruel little shepherd lad, who, for his evil pranks, was sure sooner or later to be sent back to his hovel. I am a great prince, good and humane of disposition, from whom a thousand benefits may be expected. I am ready to wager that I could have the heads of five or six of them cut off daily, by lot, and that the rest, trusting to be more fortunate than their companions, would continue to sing my praises."

Such speeches – and I knew only too well how true they were! – served insensibly to harden my heart. It is a great evil to look upon mankind with too clear vision. You seem to be living among wild beasts, and you become a wild beast yourself.

I had thought at first that, in his new position, the Prince of Shirvan would yield, even more freely than he had done before, to his evil bent; but in this I was mistaken. He showed himself noble in manner and sensible in conduct, and his bearing towards great and small was affable and obliging. In short, he completely obliterated the bad impression produced by his former practices.

These days of quiet lasted till the arrival of Rondabah. I happened to be in Firouz's apartments when news was brought that that princess, attended by a retinue suitable to her rank, was only at a few parasangs' distance from Zerbend. Startled, I scarce knew why, I turned my eyes on my friend. His condition makes me tremble even yet, as I think of it. A deathly pallor overspread his countenance, his movements became convulsive, and at last he fell to the ground, senseless. I was about to bear him to his couch, when the Mage's two eunuchs took him from my arms, saying: "Leave him to our care, lord – and deign to retire. If, on recovering his senses, he were to see you at his side, he would instantly expire."

These words, and the tone in which they were uttered, impressed me so much that I could scarcely drag myself through the portal of the apartment. Once outside, I awaited the issue with anguish unspeakable. At last one of the eunuchs came out and begged me to re-enter. Firouz, leaning on the arm of the other eunuch, advanced to meet me with halting and trembling steps. I made him sit down on the divan, and, seating myself by his side, I said: "Friend of my soul, Fate alone can be answerable for the strange and unaccountable feelings of our hearts. You are, against all comprehension, jealous of Rondabah; and I, notwithstanding the engagements into which my ambassadors have entered, am ready to risk all rather than plunge you into a sea of sorrows!"

"Nay, let us go and see this redoubtable heroine," replied Firouz; "suffer me only to accompany you in this your first interview; at my age my presence cannot be open to objection. If you leave me here alone, I shall die before you return."

To this I had nothing to reply. The fascination he exercised upon me was extraordinary, to myself quite inexplicable. And I could but agree to his every wish. He resumed his ordinary spirits, and continued to repeat, as we went along: "Ah! if only this accursed princess should prove not to be beautiful!"

She was beautiful, however; but of a beauty that inspired awe rather than excited desire; very tall, of majestic port, her whole aspect proud and austere. Her hair, black as ebony, enhanced the whiteness of her complexion, and her eyes, of the same dark hue, looked commanding but did not softly allure. Her mouth, though graceful in its lines, had no inviting smile, and when her coral lips opened, the words were words of sense indeed, but very rarely moving and persuasive.

Stung, as it seemed, by my want of a lover's ardour, and offended because, contrary to all use and custom, I had come accompanied by my friend, Rondabah no sooner perceived us advancing than she turned to my mother and said: "Which of these two princes is the one to whom I am destined?"

"To both, if you please," replied Firouz unhesitatingly and mockingly, so that I almost burst out laughing. I restrained myself, however, with an effort, and was preparing to find some excuse for my friend's ill manners, when the Princess of Ghilan, after looking me over attentively from head to foot, and casting a disdainful glance at Firouz, remarked – always addressing herself to the queen: "Those who allow an insult to pass unnoticed deserve to be insulted; farewell, madam. And you, Kali," continued she, turning to the chief of her eunuchs, "make all the necessary preparations for my return to Ghilan this very night." Saying these words she retired, and the queen was not slow to follow her, only stopping to threaten us with all the calamities that must ensue from the offence given to Rondabah. But we were at that moment in no humour to listen. As soon as we found ourselves alone, we burst out laughing at the scene which had just taken place. "Is that a woman?" asked Firouz. "No, it is the ghost of Roostum, or of Lalzer – or may we not rather say that the spirit of some famous warrior, Rondabah's ancestor, has taken possession of that tall and stately form, which we are asked to look upon as hers? Ah! my dear Alasi, sharpen your sword, prepare to defend your life if you do not in all things exactly conform to the ceremonial enjoined by the all-powerful Kali, with his voice of silver."

We remained in this mood till the queen interrupted us. She had nearly appeased Rondabah, and wished me to complete her task. Her representations, dictated by all a mother's love, were strong and urgent, and I yielded to them.

On the day preceding that fixed for the marriage ceremonies, I rose earlier than usual. Anxious, agitated, I went down alone into the large gardens containing the funereal monuments of my ancestors. I wandered through the most sombre alleys, and entered at last into a grotto, through which ran a stream of water. The darkness was such in the grotto's deeper recesses that scarce a feeble ray of light could be discerned. I penetrated into the blackest shade, so as to be able to dream unseen and undisturbed. Soon, to my surprise, I saw a figure approaching that bore, in form and attire, a close resemblance to Amru, the son of my vizier. He went and seated himself in a part of the grotto where a little light was shining, so that I could see him while he could not see me. I spoke not a word, but saw with surprise another mysterious personage approaching, out of the very heart of the darkness; and this figure bore the likeness of Rondabah's chief eunuch. The second personage accosted the first, and I seemed to hear him say: "Son of Ilbars, too charming Amru, let your heart rejoice; it shall possess the object of its desire! Rondabah, my mistress, will come here this very night. The first of her love-vows will be yours. Only the aftermath will be given to the King of Kharezme to-morrow." Amru kissed the ground in token of submission, and murmured a few low words whose meaning was lost in the sound of the running water. They then left the grotto.

I was about to follow, and wash out the affront in blood; but a moment's reflection arrested this first impulse. I had no love for Rondabah. I was only marrying her for reasons of state, and out of pity. That there should be anything in what had passed to make me really unhappy was out of the question. I had only to bring her criminal perfidy into full light, and I should be quit of her, and recover my own freedom with all honour. These thoughts passed swiftly through my brain. I thanked whatever lucky star had led me in time to this important discovery, and

34

ran to impart it to Firouz. What was my dismay when, on entering his apartment, I found him in the arms of his two eunuchs, who were holding his hands and weeping and crying: "O master, loved master! What harm had your beautiful locks done? Why have you ruthlessly cut them off? And now you would gash your lovely white forehead! No, not if we die to stay your hands!"

This sight so moved me that I could not utter a single word. My speechless anguish seemed to quiet Firouz. He tore himself from the arms of his eunuchs, and, running to me and embracing me, exclaimed: "Calm yourself, generous Alasi! Is it my condition that troubles you? Surely it should cause you no surprise; but forget that you have seen me thus; notwithstanding these tears, this hair that I have given to the flames, notwithstanding the despair to which you saw me reduced, I wish you every happiness with Rondabah – yes, though it should cost me my life!"

"Ah," cried I, "perish a thousand Rondabahs if your nerves, so delicately strung, could thus be spared these terrible shocks and jars – yes, perish a thousand Rondabahs, one and all, even if they were as true as our Rondabah is false!"

"What!" cried Firouz in turn, "have I heard aright? Are you speaking of the Princess of Ghilan? For pity's sake explain yourself."

I then told him all that had happened in the grotto, and my determination to blaze abroad to all men the shame of Rondabah. He fully approved my design, and made no effort to hide his joy at the course things were taking. "I congratulate you," said he, adding in a whisper: "It has cost me my hair, but you have had a lucky escape."

We resolved not to reveal our secret to the queen, my mother, until the time came for taking her with us to surprise Rondabah.

The queen seemed more astonished than grieved when we went to her apartment and told her what had brought us thither so late. The affection she had at first shown for Rondabah had gradually cooled as mine had appeared to increase. Nevertheless, she had not been able to help respecting her, and never ceased, while following us, to express amazement at her shameless conduct. Firouz, on his part, laughed, and for more reasons than one.

We went down into the garden. A faithful slave, whom I had set to watch the place, came and told us that the two culprits had been in the grotto for some minutes. Immediately we entered, with torches, and in such numbers that those whom we thus surprised must, as one would have thought, fall dead for very shame. They seemed, however, in no wise disconcerted. I drew my sword in a fury and thought, with one blow, to send their two wretched heads rolling on to the ground; but my sword clove the empty air alone: they vanished from my sight!

At this moment of confusion a cry arose: "The Princess of Ghilan has forced the guard at the entrance to the grotto!" And she appeared before us. "King of Kharezme," she said in clear tones, modest but unabashed, "I am advised that a plot is being hatched in this place against my honour; and I am come to confound my enemies. What is going on here?"

"Fly, wretched creature," said the queen, "or my son will repeat the blow you have just evaded by your magic arts."

"I do not fear death," replied Rondabah quietly. "Alasi has made no attempt upon my life. If you have been misled by some seeming prodigy, I ask you to tell me what was its nature. I rely on the help that Heaven always extends to innocence, and have no doubt as to my ability to undeceive you."

Rondabah's proud and noble bearing, her looks, that commanded respect, all served to confound me. I almost doubted the evidence of my eyes and ears, when Firouz exclaimed: "Oh! we must indeed confess that the Princess of Ghilan's memory is of the shortest! We find her in the arms of her beloved Amru; she disappears with her favourite, and when, within a moment, it pleases her to reappear on the scene, she has entirely forgotten all that has taken place."

At these words Rondabah changed colour. The flush died on her cheeks, and left them deadly pale. She turned upon me eyes that were full of tears. "Oh, most unhappy prince!" she said, "I now see the full depth of the abyss yawning at thy feet. The monster dragging thee thitherward will not fail of his prey! The spirits of darkness are at his beck and call. I cannot save thee, and yet I shudder at abandoning thee to thy fate. Thou hast covered me with infamy, but it is thy ruin only that wrings my heart!" Having thus spoken, Rondabah retired with majestic steps, none daring to stay her.

We stood as if turned to stone, and looked fixedly at one another, unable to speak. "Surely we must all have lost our wits," cried the queen at last. "What! the cool effrontery of an unworthy magician would make us disbelieve the evidence of our eyes and ears! Let her go, and deliver us for ever from her hateful presence! Nothing could happen better!" I agreed, and Firouz, who seemed confused and frightened, most assuredly was of no other opinion. We each went towards our own apartments.

I left the place so troubled that I did not see Firouz was following close at my heels, nor could I altogether repress a feeling of horror when I found we were alone together. But ah! when the heart is evil, all presentiments are sent to us in vain!

Firouz threw himself impetuously at my feet, and said, sobbing: "Why, why, O King of Kharezme, did you give me shelter? Why did you not leave me to die with my father? I was then but a child; no one could have accused me of being a magician. Is it at this court of yours, and here by your side, that I have learned the art of conjuring up the Dives? And yet Rondabah, the wicked Rondabah, has almost persuaded you. Will she not also say I have gained your friendship by some evil charm? Alas! you know well enough that the only charm I have used is to cherish you a hundred times more than my own life!"

But why dwell upon this scene? All of you must foresee its inevitable end. Firouz succeeded in dissipating my suspi-

cions. Like the Calif Vathek, I had heard the voice of a
beneficent spirit, and, like him, I had hardened my heart
against its saving influence. Rondabah's words were forgotten; I disregarded the confused doubts they had aroused in
my mind. The Prince of Shirvan became more dear to me
than ever. That moment was the turning-point in my life.
It sealed my ruin.

We heard on the following morning that Rondabah had
departed during the night, with all her retinue. I ordered
public rejoicings.

A few days afterwards Firouz said to me, before the
queen, my mother: "You must see, King of Kharezme,
that war with the King of Ghilan is now inevitable. His
daughter, with her wiles, will easily persuade him that she
is innocent, and he will want to avenge her wrongs.
Forestall him; raise an army; invade Ghilan, and ravage the
country: you are the aggrieved party!"

The queen agreed with Firouz, and I assented. Nevertheless, I watched the war preparations with regret. I thought
the war a just war, and yet was troubled in conscience as
though it had been unjust. Moreover, the qualms I felt
with regard to my extreme attachment to Firouz grew
stronger day by day. The son of Filanshaw had learned to
read in my heart very clearly, and was in no wise deceived
by the pretexts I put forward for my misgivings, and
involuntary fits of perplexity; but he made as though he
accepted my explanations, and took occasion of my perturbed state to devise new pleasures and forms of
distraction.

One morning, as we were starting on a great hunting
expedition, we found, in the palace yard, a man who bore
a heavy chest, and was disputing with the guards. I inquired
what was the matter. "It is a jeweller from Mossul,"
replied the chief of the eunuchs. "He says he has certain
gems of the utmost rarity; but he is importunate, and
refuses to await your Majesty's leisure."

"He is quite right," said Firouz; "nothing that pleases
and amuses can ever come amiss; let us go back and

examine these wonders. The beasts of the forest are doubtless prepared to await our pleasure."

We retraced our steps accordingly, and the jeweller unclasped his chest. Nothing in it seemed worthy of our curiosity, till my eyes fell on a golden casket, round which were engraved these words: "PORTRAIT OF THE FAIREST AND MOST UNHAPPY PRINCESS IN THE WORLD." "Let us look at her," exclaimed Firouz. "The portrait of this beauty, doubtless in tears, will appeal to our hearts. It is good, now and again, to be moved to pity."

I opened the casket and was struck mute with astonishment. "What are you looking at in that way?" asked my friend. He looked in turn, was moved to indignation, and, turning to the eunuchs, exclaimed: "Lay hands upon this insolent merchant, and throw him, his chest, and all his wares into the river! What! Shall a wretch like this disclose to the whole world the face of Filanshaw's daughter – the rosebud that I pictured to myself sheltered from every evil wind beneath the humble roof of adversity?"

"Heavens!" I exclaimed in turn; "what do I behold? What do I hear? Let no one touch this man! And thou, friend of my soul, speak! Is this indeed thy sister – thy sister, featured like thyself?"

"Yes, King of Kharezme," replied the Prince of Shirvan; "you have here indeed the portrait of my twin sister, Firouzkah. The queen, my mother, saved her, with myself, from the fury of the rebels. When they separated us, and handed me over to the charge of the Mage, I was told that she would be hidden in some place of safety. But I now see only too clearly that I was deceived."

"My lord," then said the merchant, "the queen, your mother, has taken refuge with her daughter in a house of mine, near Mossul. It is by her orders that I carry this portrait through the divers countries of Asia, in the hope that Firouzkah's beauty will rouse the beholders to avenge the wrongs done to the king, your father. I have already travelled through various lands, and not without success; but the queen never told me I should find you here."

"Doubtless she knew it not," said Firouz, "and thought I was still with the Mage. But," he continued, turning towards me, "you are pale, dear friend; let us regain your apartments, and put off our hunting to another day."

I let him lead me in, and, having first cast myself down on a divan, did not cease to look at the portrait. "Oh, my dear Firouz," I cried, "these eyes, this mouth, all these features are thine. The hair, indeed, is not quite like thine, and I would it were; but this has taken the colour of camphire, while thine has the colour of musk."

"What!" said Firouz, laughing, "a pale cold picture can thus inflame with love a heart that resisted all the fire of Rondabah's charms! But calm yourself, my dear Alasi," continued he, more seriously; "the wife of Filanshaw will yet call you her son. I purpose sending the jewel-merchant back to her. He will tell her, from me, to accept no help of any prince save yourself – that it is you, my benefactor, my friend, who are the destined avenger of her wrongs. But let us first make haste to punish the Princess of Ghilan for the indignities she has heaped upon you. Let us anticipate the fury of her attack. How can you reconquer my kingdom while your own is in jeopardy?"

From the moment that my passion seemed to myself intelligible and normal, my heart regained its calm. Peace reigned in my breast. I gave strict orders that the preparations for our enterprise should be hastened, and very soon, with a numerous host, we were marching against the enemy.

The frontiers of Ghilan were undefended. We ravaged the marsh country without mercy. But Firouz's strength did not equal his courage. I spared him as much as possible, even at the risk of giving the enemy time to complete the full equipment of his forces.

One day that I had called a halt, in a valley clothed with fresh moss, and watered by a clear stream, we saw tripping by, not far from us, a doe whiter than milk. Immediately Firouz caught up his bow, and sent an arrow flying after the innocent creature. The shaft went home; the doe fell;

we ran to the spot. A peasant, perceiving us, cried: "What have you done? You have killed the holy woman's doe!" This exclamation seemed to amuse Firouz. But his mirth was of short duration. An enormous dog, the doe's companion, leapt upon him, dragged him to the ground, held him pinned down with heavy paws, and seemed to be only waiting some master's orders before putting its fangs through his throat. I dared neither to speak nor attack the dog, for fear of enraging it the more; nor could I attempt to shear off its head: the heads were too close to one another. At last, when I own I was almost terrified to death, I saw approaching a woman, veiled, who forced the dog to relinquish its hold, and then, turning to me, said: "I did not think, King of Kharezme, to find you here, in a place where I had come to bury myself alive. I have just, according to the divine precept, returned good for evil, in saving the life of Firouz. Do not you, on your part, return evil for good by destroying this people, who, far from seeking to avenge my wrongs, are quite ignorant of the indignities heaped upon me."

As she finished speaking these words she lifted her veil, and disclosed the majestic countenance of Rondabah. Then she turned on her heel, and retired with quick steps, leaving us in a state of inexpressible surprise.

Firouz was the first to recover. "Well," said he, "do you still entertain any doubt as to Rondabah's dealing in magic? What shall we do to protect ourselves against her arts? I know but one remedy: let us surprise her this very night; let us take a band of our trusty followers, and burn her alive in her retreat -- which we can easily discover by skilful inquiry; or else we may resign ourselves to being torn to pieces by the Afrites, who serve her in the shape of savage beasts."

"Shame!" cried I. "Would you thus repay the service she has just done us? Whatever she may be, she has this moment saved you from a cruel death."

"Too credulous prince," rejoined Firouz, "do you not see that the infamous sorceress defers her vengeance, that she is only fearful of losing its full fruition by undue haste? But what am I saying? I only am the object of her malignity; nor would I wish it otherwise. I only hope that after my death, she will spare your life and be satisfied with making you her slave!"

This speech produced its desired effect. I was not master of my own judgment when Firouz opened out a glimpse of danger to himself. I became as eager as even he could wish, in the execution of his black and horrible design. The flames that consumed Rondabah's rustic dwelling were kindled by my hands as well as his; and, notwithstanding the resistance of the peasantry – whom we slaughtered without mercy as a reward for their generous efforts on her behalf – we did not leave the spot till we had left Rondabah buried, as we believed, beneath a heap of smoking ashes.

A few days afterwards I wished to advance, with my army, into the interior of the country; but soon found my way blocked by the enemy's forces, under the command of the King of Ghilan and his son. It became necessary to offer battle. Firouz, notwithstanding all I could urge, insisted on fighting by my side. This did not add to the effectiveness of my arms. I thought less of attacking the foe than of parrying the blows aimed at my friend. He, on his side, threw himself in the way of those directed against myself. Neither suffered his sight to be diverted from the other. No one could doubt, seeing us, that each, in defending the other's life, was defending a life dearer than his own.

The prince of Ghilan had sought me out everywhere. We met at last, and, swooping on me with uplifted sword, he cried: "King of Kharezme, thy life shall pay forfeit for the atrocious wrongs done to my sister; had I known of them before, I should have sought thee out in thy very palace, and maugre all the spirits of darkness that dwell there!"

Scarcely had he spoken these words than the hand that held the avenging sword fell to the ground, struck off at the wrist by a back-handed blow from the blade of Firouz. The King of Ghilan hastened up, foaming with rage, and aimed at us two crashing blows. I avoided the one; the other went home on Firouz's shoulder. I saw him reel in his saddle. To send the old king's head flying in the air, to take Firouz on to my own horse, to spur out of the battle – all this was but the work of a moment.

The son of Filanshaw had lost consciousness. I was scarcely in better plight. Instead of returning to my camp, I plunged into a forest, deep and gloomy, where I did nothing but wander, almost aimlessly, like one bereft of reason. Fortunately a woodman saw us. He approached and said: "If you have not altogether lost your wits, and have no wish to see this young man die in your arms, follow me to my father's cabin, where you can get help."

I suffered him to lead me. The old man received us kindly. He caused Firouz to be placed on a bed, ran to fetch an elixir, and made him drink of it; and then said: "But a moment more, and this young man would have been dead. He has nearly lost all his blood. The first thing to be done was to repair that loss. Now we will examine his wound; and, while my son goes into the forest to find some simples that I shall require, you must help me to undress your friend."

I was doing this mechanically, and with a trembling hand; but came to myself with a start when, on opening Firouz's vest, I saw a breast which the houris might have envied. "Why, it's a woman!" said the old man.

"Now Allah be praised!" cried I, in a delirium of surprise and joy; "but what of her wound?"

"That is of no great consequence," replied the good man, examining it, "and when I have bound up the gash, she will soon come to her senses. Compose yourself, therefore, young man," continued he, "and be specially careful not to disturb the rest of one to whom, as I well perceive, you are passionately attached. Any emotion, at the present moment, would cause her to die before your eyes."

The transport of love and joy that filled my soul here

gave place to the apprehension caused by the old man's words. I helped him in silence to perform his kindly offices; and then, having enveloped the inanimate form of Firouzkah – for she it was – in a coverlet of leopard-skin, I waited, in mortal anxiety, till she should open her eyes.

The hope held out to me by the old man was soon realised. My well-beloved gave a sigh, turned her languishing eyes upon me, and said: "Where are we, friend? Is the battle lost, and are we..?"

"No, no!" I interrupted, placing my hand on her mouth; "all is gained since your precious life is safe! But keep still; you don't know how much depends upon your silence."

Firouzkah did not fail to understand the full meaning of my words. She spoke no more, and soon, from very weakness, fell into a deep sleep.

The old man watched her, well pleased; while my own breathing seemed to repeat every rise and fall of her breast, on which I had softly placed my hand. She slept for two hours, and never woke till the woodman entered abruptly into the hut. He did not bring with him the herbs for which his father had sent him, at which I expressed surprise. But Firouzkah, now restored by her slumbers, interrupted me, and said: "Thou hast news to tell us, hast thou not?"

"Yes, yes," said he, "and the very best of news. The army of the Kharezmians has been cut to pieces, and their camp pillaged. The victory would be complete if they could only catch those wicked princes, Alasi and Firouz, who have escaped, after killing the king and his son. But the princess Rondabah has ascended the throne, and is causing search to be made for them everywhere. She offers such great rewards that they must soon be captured."

"I am delighted at what you tell me," cried Firouzkah, without suffering any change to appear in her countenance; "we had been assured that Rondabah was burned to death in her woodland dwelling; and I had been most grieved to hear it, as I knew she was a most excellent princess."

"She is even better than you think," replied the wood-man, with a cunning look; "and that is why Heaven has kept her from harm. The prince, her brother, chanced upon her retreat, and took her away some hours before the perpetration of that wicked crime – a crime which, please God, will not long remain unpunished.''

The clod's tone sufficiently showed that he took us for what we really were; and he made signs to his father to follow him out of the room. They went out together. Afar we heard the trampling of many horses. Firouzkah immediately rose to a sitting posture, and, presenting me with a razor, which she took from under her dress, said in a whisper: "You see, dear Alasi, the danger we are in; cut off my hair, which, as you see, is growing again, and throw it into those flames. Don't answer a word. If you lose a moment it is all up with us!''

I could but comply with such a pressing command; and I did so. A few seconds later, a Dive, shaped like an Ethiopian, appeared before our eyes, and asked Firouzkah what she wanted with him. "I desire thee,'' she replied, "to carry me this very instant, with my friend, to the cavern of the Mage, thy master; and, as thou passest, to crush the two worthless wretches who are bargaining over our lives!''

The Dive needed no second orders. He took us both in his arms, sprang from the hut – causing it, with one kick, to fall on our late hosts, and then shot through the air so rapidly that I lost consciousness.

When I came to myself I was in the arms of Firouzkah, and saw only her charming face, lovingly near my own. I softly closed my eyelids again, as one does when wishing to prolong a pleasant dream; but soon I felt my happiness was real. "O wicked Firouz, O cruel Firouz!'' I cried. "What needless torments have you caused me to endure!'' Uttering these words, I pressed again and yet again, with burning kisses, those sweet and beautiful lips, that had themselves pressed mine while I lay entranced, and that now seemed to elude my own; when, suddenly recollecting my well-beloved's wound, I gave her time – at once to breathe, and to answer my anxious questions.

"There is no need for anxiety, dear Alasi," she answered, "I am perfectly healed, and all will shortly be explained to you. But lift up your head, and look around."

I obeyed, and thought myself transported beneath a new firmament, encrusted with stars a thousand times more brilliant and nearer to us than the stars in the natural world. I looked round on every side, and it seemed to me I was in a vast plain, and that round it were transparent clouds, which held enfolded, not only ourselves, but all the most beautiful and delicious products of the earth. "Ah!" cried I, after a moment of surprise, and embracing Firouz-kah, "what is it to us if we have been carried into Cheheristan itself? The true realms of bliss are in thine arms!"

"This is not Cheheristan," replied the daughter of Filanshaw. "It is only the Mage's cave, which an infinite number of Beings, superior to our race, take pleasure in decorating with a varied beauty. But such as it is, and whatever may be its inhabitants, everything will be done here to anticipate your wishes. "Is it not so, my Father?" continued she, raising her voice.

"Undoubtedly," replied the Mage, appearing suddenly before our eyes, and advancing towards me with a smile. "Prince Alasi will be treated here as he has treated my dear Firouzkah; and, moreover, the priceless jewel I confided to his care – Firouzkah herself – shall be his to possess for ever, if such be his desire. Come, let the marriage feast be at once prepared, and all things made ready for so great an event!"

He had no sooner spoken these words, than the cavern again changed its aspect. It assumed an oval shape, and diminished proportions, and appeared all encrusted with pale sapphires. Round us, on divans, were ranged boy and girl musicians, who charmed our ears with melodious strains, while from their heads, light-encircled, shone rays more pure and soft than would be shed by a thousand tapers.

We were placed at a table covered with excellent dainties and the most exquisite wines, and were served delightfully by Persian boys and by Georgian girls – all as white and graceful as the jasmine sprays engarlanding their fair heads. With their every motion the gauze robes, that half clothed half revealed them, exhaled the sweetest perfumes of Araby the Blest. Firouzkah, who could not at once forget her part as Firouz, sported with these children as they filled our cups, and indulged in a thousand pleasant pranks.

When the repast was ended, the Mage, first ordering the most profound silence, and addressing himself to me, spoke as follows:–

"You are doubtless surprised, King of Kharezme, that, with the power I possess, I should have taken the trouble to seek you out and obtain your protection for the girl-treasure committed to my charge. You must understand just as little why Firouzkah should have gone to you disguised, and have left you to the mercy of love-feelings, incomprehensible to yourself, which she might so easily have explained.

"Be it known to you, then, that the people of Shirvan, always a rebellious race, and inclined to murmur against their rulers, had begun to grumble because Filanshaw had no children. But when at last the queen, his wife, bid fair to become a mother, their insolence passed all bounds. 'She must have a son!' they cried round the royal dwelling; 'we will have no princess to place us under the yoke of some stranger prince. She must have a son!'

"The poor queen suffered quite enough discomfort from her condition without the disquiet of such alarming cries. She pined visibly. Filanshaw came to consult me. 'You must deceive these blockheads,' said I. 'Even that is much more than they deserve. If the queen has a daughter, pretend the daughter is a boy, and, in order that you may not be compelled to entrust the secret to her nurses, send the child here. My wife, Soudabé, will bring her up with a mother's care and affection, and, when the time comes, I myself will spare no pains in her education.' My proposal saved the queen's life. Firouzkah came into the world, and we called her Firouz. Under that name her birth was hailed with public rejoicings; and Soudabé, who received her from the king's hands, brought her to my cavern – from whence she was taken, from time to time, to show herself at court.

"We gave her the double education which, in view of all eventualities, it seemed desirable that she should have.

"She accepted Soudabé's instructions and mine, with an equal zest, and would seek relaxation, after her studies, in the company of the Dives, of every form, who haunt my cavern.

"These active spirits were so attached to Firouzkah that there was no whim of hers they were not ready to gratify. Some taught her such exercises as are common to either sex. Others kept her amused with pleasant games, or told her marvellous stories. A great number went the world over to find her rare and curious things, or interesting news. She never found time hang at all heavy on her hands, and always came back to my cavern with transports of delight whenever she had been obliged to pass a few days at Samakhié.

"The Princess of Shirvan had just reached the age of fourteen, when the Dive Ghulfaquaïr, being maliciously inclined, brought her your portrait. From that moment she seemed to lose her natural gaiety of spirits, did nothing but dream and sigh, and, as may be supposed, gave us great anxiety. The cause of her pain she carefully concealed, and the Dive took care to keep us in like ignorance. He was, moreover, pretty busy in following your movements, so as to be able to give her a report of all your doings. What he told her of your shyness, your insensibility to love, only served to further excite her passion. She burned with the desire of taming your mood, and bringing you under the sway of her charms; and soon the course of events was such as to add, to that desire, hope. The open rebellion of the people of Shirvan, Filanshaw's entreaties that I should so dispose of his daughter as to protect her from their fury, all conspired to embolden Firouzkah, and she spoke to me with entire freedom.

"'You, who have been a father to me,' she said; 'you, who have taught me not to be ashamed of the passions Nature has implanted in us, you will understand when I say that I love the Prince Alasi, King of Kharezme, and that I intend – however hard the task – to win his love in return. It is now no longer a question of hiding my sex so that I may reign over a people who have destroyed all my family, and whom I must ever hold in abhorrence. I shall now use my disguise in order to insinuate myself into a heart which soon, I hope, will be altogether mine. Alasi is insensible to a woman's charm. It is in the guise of friendship that I must make him feel a woman's power. Take me to him; ask him to protect me as the son of the King of Shirvan. He is too generous to refuse; and I shall owe to you a happiness without which life would be hateful!'

"I felt no surprise on hearing Firouzkah speak in this way. She was a woman; she wanted a husband; what could be more natural? I contented myself, therefore, with questioning her as to how she had become acquainted with you. She told me all, and spoke of you in such terms that I soon perceived any opposition would only make her unhappy. So I said, 'I will take you to the King of Kharezme, under the name of Firouz, because I feel I can rely on your prudence, and the strength of mind I know you to possess. You will need both; for by my magic arts I have discovered that you have a powerful rival, whose triumph would be your eternal despair. When, however, you are so pressed as to stand in need of supernatural help, burn your hair, and my Dives will instantly attend to receive your commands.' The rest, King of Kharezme, is known to you," continued the Mage. "Firouz has laboured hard in the cause of Firouzkah: *he* has won your heart by his gaiety, his light sportiveness; *she* must keep it by her love, and the prudence from which she has never deviated, even amidst dangers that would have daunted the courage of most women."

"Oh!" cried the Princess of Shirvan, "I ran great risk of losing the heart it had cost me so much to gain – and I should have lost at least a part of it if I had not, at the sacrifice of my beautiful locks, called up the helpful Dives who so effectually impersonated Rondabah, Amru, and Kali! What do you say, Alasi?"

"That I shall ever cherish the motives that induced you to commit that act of injustice," I replied, with diplomacy, and some misgiving.

"My daughter," said the Mage, "the word 'injustice', which Prince Alasi has just uttered, can only apply to your suggested doubt as to his constancy. For he must be aware that every being has the right, by all possible means, to remove hurtful objects from its path, and that the motives of anger or fear which impel us so to act are born of the living and self-preserving forces of Nature. But the hours are fleeting fast. It is time you should enjoy the happier fruits of your frequent sorrows. Receive, King of Kharezme, the Princess Firouzkah at my hand; lead her to the nuptial chamber, and may you there be endowed with a full share of the life-giving fire which the earth contains in her bosom, the same fire that nightly rekindles the starry torches of the sky!"

We stood in no need of the Mage's good wishes; the feelings that glowed in our hearts were all-sufficient for our happiness. Friendship, love – their transports were alternate, and commingled in an unutterable ecstasy.

Firouzkah had no desire for sleep, and related to me how, in a moment, the Mage had healed her wound. She vaunted his power, and advised that I should ask him to show me his Hall of Fire, confessing that she herself had been brought up in the religion of Zoroaster, and considered it the most natural and rational of all religions. "Think, then," she added, "if I could ever have taken delight in the absurdities of the Koran. Would that all your Mussulman doctors had shared the fate of the Mullah whose discourses wearied me to death! That moment was indeed delicious when I induced him to put on the outward seeming of an ass. I should have taken a like pleasure in plucking out all the feathers from the wings of the Angel Gabriel, and thus punishing him for having furnished a pen to the man who

50

wrote therewith so much nonsense, – if indeed I had been simpleton enough to believe that absurd story."

There was a time when such words would have seemed to me unspeakable for very wickedness; and in good sooth I did not like them much then. But any remaining scruples formed but a weak defence against the alluring caresses with which Firouzkah accompanied her every word.

A voluptuous sleep enveloped us at last; and we did not wake till the lively song of birds proclaimed broad day.

Surprised by sounds which I had no reason to expect in such a place, I ran to the grotto's entrance, and found it led to a garden containing all that is most delightful in nature, while the encircling sea enhanced the beauties which the earth exhibited to our gaze.

"Is this another illusion?" I asked, "for this, at least, cannot be part of the Mage's cavern?"

"It is one of its issues," replied Firouzkah; "but it would take you more than one day to explore all the beauties of the place. The Mage says that everything has been made for man's use, and that man must possess himself of everything he wants whenever the opportunity offers. He has spent part of his life in acquiring his power, and is spending the remainder in enjoying its fruits."

I did not fail to express to the Mage a very strong desire to see his Hall of Fire. "It will please you," said he, with a satisfied air; "but I cannot conduct you thither until you have visited my baths, and been invested with robes suitable to the majesty of the place."

To please Firouzkah I consented to everything that was demanded of me; and, for fear of offending her, I even refrained from laughter at the grotesque robes in which we were both ridiculously accoutred. But what were my feelings, on entering the Hall of Fire? Never has spectacle so filled me with surprise and terror – never, until overwhelmed by the sight that met my eyes on entering the fatal place in which we now are!

The fire that the Mage worshipped seemed to issue from the bowels of the earth and to soar above the clouds. The flames sometimes shone with an unendurable brightness; sometimes they shed a blue and lurid light, making all surrounding objects appear even more hideous than they actually were. The rails of glowing brass that separated us from this dread deity did no more than partially reassure me. From time to time we were enveloped in a whirlwind of sparks, which the Mage regarded as graciously emitted in our honour — an honour with which I would very gladly have dispensed. In the portion of the temple where we stood, the walls were hung with human hair of every colour; and, from space to space, human hair hung also in festoons from pyramids of skulls chased in gold and ebony. Besides all this, the place was filled with the fumes of sulphur and bitumen, oppressing the brain and taking away the breath. I trembled; my legs seemed to give way; Firouzkah supported me. "Take me hence," I whispered; "take me from the sight of thy god. Nothing save thine own presence has enabled me to endure *his* presence for a moment!"

It was some time before I fully recovered. In order to effect my restoration, the Dives introduced a fresher air through orifices in the vault of the cavern where we had supped the night before. They also redecorated the cavern itself in a novel manner, and prepared for us an exquisite repast. I was thus enabled to listen to the Mage with renewed patience. What my terrible host told me about his religion did not indeed possess the charms of novelty: I knew most of it before, and I paid small heed to this part of his discourse. But his moral teachings pleased me hugely, since they flattered passion and abolished remorse. He greatly vaunted his Hall of Fire — told us that the Dives had built it, but that he himself had supplied the decorations at the risk of his life. I asked him for no explanations on this point; I was even afraid lest he should give them unasked. I could not think of those skulls, of that human hair, of what he called "decorations" without trembling. I should have feared the worst in that dreadful place if I had not been so sure of the heart of Firouzkah.

Fortunately I was not called upon to listen to the Mage's discourses more than once a day. The rest of our time was spent in amusements and pleasures of every kind. These the Dives never failed to supply; and Firouzkah caused them to gratify my every taste by an infinite variety. Her assiduous care, her ingenuity of tenderness, made my every moment hurry by in such voluptuous enjoyment that I was never to measure the flight of time; and the present had so far obliterated the past that I never once thought of my kingdom. But the Mage put an end, all too soon, alas! to this period of delirium and enchantment. One day, one fatal day, he said to us: "We are about to separate, my dear children; the hour of bliss, for which I have sighed for such long years, is approaching; I am expected in the Palace of Subterranean Fire, where I shall bathe in joys untold, and possess treasures passing man's imagination. Ah! why has this moment of supreme felicity been so long delayed? The inexorable hand of death would not then have torn from my side my dear Soudabé, whose charms had never suffered from the ravages of Time! We should then have partaken together of that perfect happiness which neither accident, nor the vicissitudes of life, can ever mar in the place to which I am bound."

"Ah!" I cried, "where is that divine sojourn in which a happy eternity of mutual love and tenderness may be enjoyed? Let us follow you thither."

"You may do so, if you worship my god," replied the Mage; "if you will do homage to the powers that serve him, if you will win his favour by such sacrifices as he ordains."

"I will worship any god you like," said I, "if he will suffer me to live for ever with Firouzkah, and free from the horrible fear of seeing pale disease or bloody steel threaten her beauteous life. What must I do besides?"

"You must," replied the Mage, "cause the religion of Zoroaster to be received in your dominions, raze the mosques to the ground, erect Halls of Fire in their stead, and, finally, sacrifice without pity all whom you cannot convert to the true faith. This is what I have myself done, though not so openly as you can do it; and, as a sign of what I have been able to accomplish, see all these locks of hair that ornament my Hall of Fire – dear evidences that I am about to enter the gates of the only place where lasting joys are to be found."

"Quick, quick! let us go and cause heads to be cut off," said Firouzkah, "and so amass a treasure of human hair! You will agree, my dear Alasi, that the sacrifice of a whole tribe of crazy wretches who will not accept our belief, is as nothing if we can obtain thereby the supreme felicity of loving each other for all time!"

By these flattering words Firouzkah obtained my complete assent, and the Mage, having reached the height of his wishes, resumed: "I esteem myself happy, King of Kharezme, in seeing you, at last, convinced of the truth of my faith. Several times have I despaired, and I should certainly not have taken so much trouble about you if you had not been the husband of the daughter of Filanshaw – my friend and my disciple. Ah! what honour will be mine when your conversion is known in the Palace of Subterranean Fire! Hence, therefore! Depart at once. A ship, ready equipped, awaits you upon the shore. Your subjects will receive you with acclamation. Do all the good you can. Remember that to destroy those who are obstinate in error is accounted a great merit by the stern god you have promised to serve. When you deem that your reward is fully earned, go to Istakhar, and there, on the Terrace of the Beacon Lights, make a holocaust of the hair of those whom you have immolated in so good a cause. The nostrils of the Dives will be gratified by that sweet-smelling sacrifice. They will discover to you the steep and secret stairway, and open the ebony portals: I shall receive you in my arms, and see that you are received with fitting honours."

Thus did I yield to the last seductions of the Mage. I should have laughed his exhortation to scorn if my heart had not been so interested in the truth of his promises. For a moment indeed I did misdoubt them, and thought they might be false; but, nothing venture, nothing have, and soon I decided that, in view of the predicted reward, every hazard must be risked.

No doubt the Mage, urged on by ambition and an evil covetousness, had made a similar calculation, – to find himself ultimately deceived and cozened, as are all the miserable wretches who find their way to this place!

The Mage wished to see us embark. He embraced us affectionately at parting, and advised that we should keep in our service, as followers on whom we could always rely, the twenty negroes appointed to navigate our ship. Scarcely had we set sail when we heard a terrible sound – a sound like that of thunder as the lightning goes crashing among the mountains and heaping up the valley with ruin. Turning, we saw the rock we had just left crumble into the sea. We heard the cries of joy with which the exultant Dives then filled the air; and we judged that the Mage was already on his way to Istakhar.

Our twenty negroes were such good sailors, so adroit and alert, that we should have taken them to form part of the Mage's supernatural following if they had not assured us that they were simple Fire-worshippers, and no more. As their chief, Zouloulou by name, seemed very well acquainted with all the mysteries of the cavern, we asked him what had become of the pages and the little Georgian girls, for whom we had conceived a liking. He replied that the Intelligences, who first gave them to the Mage, had disposed of them, doubtless for the best, and that we could not do better than leave them in their hands.

My subjects celebrated my return, and my marriage, with such transports of joy that I quite blushed at the designs I entertained against them. They had found Firouz amiable as a boy; they found Firouzkah divine in the habiliments of her sex. My mother, in particular, over-whelmed her with caresses. But she changed her tone when we discovered that Motaleb, whom she had just established as her first minister, had thrown all the affairs with which he was charged into great disorder. She nourished a fancy for that ignorant vizier, and took it in very ill part that we should be angry with him. Firouzkah, who cared very little what she thought, would whisper in my ear: "Motaleb has a very good head of hair; let us cut off his head." But I was satisfied with deposing him from his office, and appointed, in his stead, a feeble old man who did everything as he was told, and never hesitated to cause the Great Mosque at Zerbend to be razed to the ground so soon as I ordered its demolition.

This revolutionary measure excited universal surprise. The queen, my mother, came in haste to ask what I meant by an act so impious and sacrilegious. "We mean," answered Firouzkah quietly, "never again to hear mention of Mahomet, and all his crazy dreams, and to establish, in Kharezme, the religion of Zoroaster, as being the only religion worthy of credence." At this reply the good princess could not contain herself. She overwhelmed me with angry words. She heaped upon us imprecations – which have been only too terribly effectual. I listened to her without resentment; but Firouzkah induced me to commit her to her apartments – where, not long afterwards, she ended her life in bitterness of spirit, and cursing the hour when she had brought me into the world.

Iniquity had now no terrors for me. I was resolved to stop at nothing if so I might allay the fear of an ultimate separation from Firouzkah – which fear an inordinate affection had implanted in my breast.

At first I met with so little resistance that Firouzkah, who saw how easily the courtiers and the army yielded to my wishes, would say: "Where can we get hair? How many locks I see would be of admirable use to us if only the heads that bear them were a little more obdurate! It is to be hoped there may be a change, or we stand in danger of never getting to Istakhar."

At last there came a change indeed! Most of those who frequented the Halls of Fire I had erected were only waiting for a favourable moment to rise in rebellion. Several plots were discovered, and then executions became frequent. Firouzkah, who wished to proceed with order and method, was fully acquainted with the zeal and qualifications of Zouloulou, and established him as her head missioner. She caused him to get up, every day, on to a tall stage, erected in the midst of the city square, to which the people most resorted – and there the brazen negro, vested in a robe of vermilion, his countenance assured, his voice piercing, would pour forth his orations, while his nineteen compeers stood ready, with drawn swords, at the bottom of the steps leading to the stage, and cut off the heads of all who refused to accept the preacher's teaching; nor, as I need scarcely add, did they forget to secure the hair of their victims.

Mine was still the stronger side. I was beloved by the soldiery, who generally care very little what god they serve so long as they are caressed by their king.

Persecution produced its ordinary effect. The people courted martyrdom. They came from all parts to deride Zouloulou – whom nothing disconcerted – and to get their heads cut off.

The number of deaths became at last so great that the army itself was scandalised. Motaleb incited them to rebellion. He sent secretly, in the name of the soldiers, of the nobles, and of the people generally, to offer the crown of Kharezme to Rondabah – inviting her to come and avenge the death of her father, and of her brother, and her own wrongs.

We were not without information regarding these secret machinations – for parasites seldom altogether abandon a monarch so long as the crown still glitters on his head; but we felt no serious alarm till we perceived that we were becoming the weaker party. My guards had already, on more than one occasion, suffered the negroes to be maltreated – at a cost, to Zouloulou, of his two ears. He was the first to advise us not to lose the fruit of our labours.

By the care and vigilance of this zealous follower, everything was soon made ready for our departure. In the middle of the night I left my kingdom, which was by this time in almost full rebellion against my rule – left it with a heart as triumphant as if I had been a conqueror instead of a fugitive!

Firouzkah persuaded me to allow her to resume male attire; and that is why the Calif Vathek mistook her sex. We were mounted, she and I, on two steeds, as swift, as superb, as Shebdid and Bariz, the ever-memorable coursers of Khosrou. The twenty negroes each led a camel. Ten of the camels were laden with human hair.

Though anxious to reach our journey's end, yet, in sooth, we did not hurry overmuch. It was, no doubt, by some true presentiment that we could not bring ourselves to finally abandon our present pleasures for those we had been led to anticipate. We used to encamp at night, and often stayed, for days together, at the places of delight that lay in our way. For half-a-moon we had been enjoying the beauty of the vale of Maravanahar when, one night, I awoke suddenly, under the oppression of a confused and fearful dream. What was my horror at not finding Firouzkah by my side! I rose, half beside myself, and quickly left our tent to seek her. She was coming towards me – distracted. "Let us fly, dear Alasi," she said. "Let us to horse instantly, and gain the desert, which is but at a few parasangs' distance; Zouloulou knows all its hiding-places, and will lead us to some spot where we may find shelter from the danger that threatens us."

"I fear nothing, beloved," I replied, "now that thou art found again; and will follow thee whithersoever thou listest."

At the point of day we entered a wood so thick that the sun's rays scarce penetrated into its dark recesses. "Let us stop here," said Firouzkah, "and I will tell you of the strange adventure that befell me last night. I was sleeping by your side when Zouloulou woke me cautiously, and whispered in my ear that Rondabah was only about a hundred paces away, that she had wandered some little distance from the army she was leading into Kharezme, and that she was at the moment resting in her pavilion, with no other following than a few of her guards and some of her women; and, moreover, that these were all sound asleep. At these words I was seized simultaneously with fear and fury. I remembered the prediction of the Mage, and, dressing myself in haste, I felt the edge of my sword. 'What do you mean to do?' asked the eunuch. 'Moderate yourself. Be warned. You can accomplish nothing against the life of Rondabah. The Mage ordered me to tell you so, if occasion required, and to tell you further that you would yourself perish in the attempt. A Power against whom nothing can prevail, protects the Princess of Ghilan. But if you will be calm, and listen to my advice, we can do much worse to her than cut off her head.' While he was thus speaking we had left your tent and reached our destination. Zouloulou, who saw that I kept perfect silence, said, 'You are quite right to rely on me. I will cause all Rondabah's people to inhale certain fumes, and sleep for a long time without waking. We shall easily make our way, undetected, as far as her pavilion, and can then, as our fancy dictates, daub the face of your enemy with this unguent, which possesses the power of making the most beautiful countenance ugly and repulsive.'

"So said, so done. But Rondabah, whose slumbers were natural and undrugged, nearly prevented me from accomplishing more than half my purpose: I rubbed her face so hard that she awoke with a cry of pain and terror. Hastily did I finish my work, and then, having detached a mirror that hung from the girdle of one of her women, I presented it to her, and said: 'Acknowledge, majestic princess, that that little monster of a Firouz is a model of courtesy; he flatters himself that this beautifying unguent, which he has just applied to your countenance, will cause you to remember him – always!' Whether the masculine courage of Rondabah was daunted by my presence, or whether she was filled with despair at finding herself the most loathsome object in the world, I know not; but she fainted away. We left her to come to herself again at her leisure.

"I was naturally pleased at having prevented my rival from reaping the triumph predicted by the Mage; but that feeling soon gave way to fear lest we should be pursued. Now, however, we are in a place of safety. Let us rest here. This breast, which is still all a-flutter with its late alarms, will serve you as a pillow. Alas! Firouzkah and Firouz may have been guilty of acts of cruelty, but only when others have attempted to dispute with her the empire of your heart!"

The seductive turn which Firouzkah thus gave to her story did not altogether blind me to the atrocity of the crime she had just committed; and I was surprised that, with a heart so tender and full of feeling where I was concerned, she could yet be capable of frenzied hate and the most horrible cruelty. What struck me most, however, in her story was the argument used by Zouloulou to prevent her from carrying her criminal designs on Ronda-bah to even greater lengths. "The Power that protects Rondabah," said I to myself, "must love the good, for she is good. That Power, which is pure and supreme, cannot then be the same Power which is about to receive into its palace beings such as Firouzkah and myself, for we are wicked. But if it reigns supreme over all other Powers, what is to become of us? O Mahomet! O Prophet beloved of the world's Creator, thou hast forsaken me utterly and without hope! What refuge have I, save with thine enemies?"

With this despairing thought came the last feelings of remorse I was destined to experience. Such feelings I always owed to the Princess of Ghilan; but, alas! they always came in vain!

I willingly allowed Firouzkah to lure me from such melancholy reflections – reflections that seemed to make her anxious. I could not recall the past – probably I should not have recalled it if I could. No course was open to me save to leap, with eyes self-bound, into the yawning abyss of the future.

The cloud passed away in a soft rain of tender kisses. But

Firouzkah, by intoxicating me with love, redoubled my fear of losing her by some such unexpected danger as we had just avoided. She, on her side, was assailed with doubts as to Rondabah's permanent disfigurement. She regretted the time we had lost on the journey – a journey which, as she believed, and as I strove to believe, was to end in the abode of an even greater felicity. Thus, with a common consent, and to the great joy of our twenty black eunuchs, we now used the utmost diligence to reach Istakhar.

It was already night when we came to the Terrace of the Beacon Lights; and, notwithstanding all that we could say to one another of endearment and encouragement, we were filled with a kind of horror as we walked it from end to end. There was no moon in the firmament to shed upon us its soft rays. The stars alone were shining there; but their trembling light only seemed to intensify the sombre grandeur of all that met our gaze. We regretted, indeed, none of the beauties, none of the riches of the world we were about to leave. We thought only of living in a world where we should be for ever inseparable; and yet invisible ties seemed still to draw us back and hold us to the earth.

We could not repress a shudder when we saw that the negroes had done piling up our enormous heap of human locks. With trembling hands we approached our torches to set it on fire; and we thought to die for very fear when the earth opened before our feet, the rock shattering into a thousand pieces. At the sight of the stairway that seemed so easy of descent, and the tapers illuminating it, we were somewhat reassured. We embraced in a transport, and, each taking the other's hand, began cautiously to descend – when the twenty negroes, whom we had forgotten, hurled themselves upon us so impetuously that we fell, headlong, against the ebony portal at the bottom.

I will not describe the dread impression produced upon us by the aspect of the place in which we now are – all who are here have had that fearful experience – but one object of terror peculiar to ourselves was the sight of the Mage. He was pacing to and fro amid the restless, miserable crowd, with his right hand on his breast. He saw us. The flames devouring his heart leapt out through his eyelids. He darted upon us a fearful glance, and hurried away. A moment after, a malevolent Dive accosted Firouzkah. "Rondabah," said he, "has recovered her beauty. She has just ascended the throne of Kharezme; the hour of her triumph is that of your undying despair!"

At last Eblis declared all the horror of our fate. What a god have we served! What a fearful doom has he pronounced upon us! What! we who had loved one another so well, must our love be turned to hate? We, who had come hither to enjoy an eternity of love, must we hate each other to all time! O dire, O accursed thought! O for instant annihilation!

Sobbing, sobbing, as they uttered these words, Alasi and Firouzkah threw themselves into each other's arms; and for a long space a mournful silence reigned in that unhappy company.

But at last this silence was broken by Vathek, who asked the third prince to relate his story. For Vathek's curiosity was still intact. He had yet to suffer the last punishment those criminal souls were destined to endure: the final extinction of every feeling save hatred and despair.

The Story of
Prince Barkiarokh

My crimes are even greater than those of the Calif Vathek. No rash and impious counsels hastened my ruin, as they have hastened his. If I am here, in this abode of horror, it is because I spurned the salutary advice, oft repeated, of the most real and loving friend.

I was born on the borders of the Caspian Sea, in Daghestan, not far from the city of Berdouka. My father was a fisherman, a worthy man, who lived quietly and in comfort by his toil; and I was his third son. We lost our mother while still too young to feel her loss; but we saw our father weeping, and we wept too. We were, my brothers and I, very industrious, very obedient, and not altogether ignorant. A dervise, my father's friend, had taught us how to read, and how to form various characters. He often came to spend the evening in our dwelling; and, while we were making wicker baskets, would pass the time in discourses of a pious nature, and explain to us the Koran. Alsalami, for such was the dervise's name, was really a man of peace, as his name suggested: he settled our little differences, or else prevented them, with a mildness and affection that endeared him to us all. When his maxims and apophthegms seemed over-serious and to incline to dullness, he would enliven them with stories, and thus the principles he wished to inculcate became the more acceptable.

A fairly large garden, which we had planted under the dervise's direction, supplied him with a new field for our occupation and amusement. He taught us the art of cultivating plants, and their virtues. We went with him to gather such flowers as are health-giving or agreeable, for distillation, and were transported with pleasure as we watched them undergoing transformation in our alembics. I was active and eager to learn, so that Alsalami treated me with a flattering distinction. His favour made me vain, but I affected great modesty while in his presence, only to indemnify myself by a greater arrogance when he was away; and, in the quarrels which ensued between my brothers and myself, I always had the art of putting them in the wrong. By the profits derived from our distilled waters, our wicker baskets, and our fishing we lived in relative affluence. Two black slaves kept our sylvan dwelling in a state of cleanliness that added much to its charm; the food they prepared for us was, if simple, always wholesome and pleasant to the taste; and finally, baths, conveniently disposed, helped to afford a degree of comfort which few persons, in our condition of life, were able to enjoy.

Surrounded by so much that was agreeable and calculated to make life pleasant, my evil nature yet asserted itself more strongly day by day. There was, in the wall of one of the upper chambers of the house, a cupboard, which my father never opened before us, often declaring that he would bestow the key upon the one of his three sons who showed himself most worthy of that distinction. This promise was so frequently repeated, and the dervise let fall so many vague hints implying that we were by birth superior to our present obscure position, that we imagined the cupboard contained some great treasure. My brothers coveted its possession, no doubt, but did not on that account refrain from indulging, among our friends and neighbours, in the amusements natural to their age. As for me, I languished, I withered, at home, and could think of nothing but the gold and precious stones which, as I supposed, were hidden in that fatal receptacle, and my one desire was to get them into my own hands. My seeming steadiness, my assiduity in all home duties, were greatly approved; my father and his friend never tired of praising my industry and wisdom: but, ah! how far were they from reading my heart!

One morning my father said to all three of us, in presence of the dervise; "You have now, my children, reached the age at which a man should select a companion to help him in bearing the ills and sorrows of life. But I in no wise wish to influence your choice. I was allowed to make mine in full freedom, and I was very happy with your mother. I think I may fairly hope that each of you will find a good wife. Go and look for her. I give you a month in which to prosecute your search, and here is money sufficient for your needs during that time. If, however, you should return this very day, you would give me a very agreeable surprise, for I am old, and desire very passionately to see my family increased before my decease."

My brothers bent their heads in token of submission. They went out with an alacrity from which I augured that they would have not the slightest trouble in satisfying my father's wishes.

I was outraged at thinking of the advantage they would thus obtain. I had nothing better to do, however, than to go out as they did. They went off to their friends in the neighbourhood, and I, who had made no friends, addressed my steps to the adjacent city. As I went through the streets I asked myself: "Where am I going? How can I find a wife? I know of none. Shall I accost the first woman I meet? She will laugh at me, and look upon me as a fool. No doubt that, in strict terms, I have a month before me; but my brothers seem quite ready to satisfy our father's wishes this very day. He will bestow his key upon the one or the other of them, and that dear, that sweet, that lovely treasure, the treasure that has cost me so many sighs, will be lost to me for ever. Wretch that I am! Better never to see the place again than not return home before nightfall! Shall I go and see the dervise? – this is the hour when he is usually in his oratory. He has always preferred me to my brothers, and will take pity on my trouble. Pity!" I repeated, "oh yes; the pity of contempt! 'This boy,' he will say – 'I thought him a lad of spirit, and here, at twenty years of age, he is incapable of finding a wife! He is nothing but a goose, and does not deserve the key of the cupboard.'"

A prey to these bitter reflections, I traced and retraced

my steps over the same ground; I wandered hither and thither, restlessly, aimlessly; the mere sight of a woman made my heart beat. I went two steps towards her and four steps backwards. Every one laughed at me; the passers-by thought me crazy. "Is that the son of Ormossouf, the fisherman?" said some. "How wild he looks! has anyone molested him?" "What a pity," said others, "that he has gone out of his mind; fortunately he seems quite harmless."

Outraged by these insults, worn out with fatigue, and seeing that night was coming on, I took my way at last towards a caravanseray, determined to leave Daghestan on the morrow, and so never suffer the mortification of seeing my brothers in the enjoyment of the treasure I had myself so greatly coveted.

It was already rather dark, and I was walking slowly, with my arms crossed over my breast and despair written large upon my countenance, when, at the corner of the street, I saw, coming from some distance towards me, a little woman, veiled, who appeared to be in great haste. She stopped suddenly, however, as we passed, and, after bestowing on me a gracious salutation, inquired: "What ails you, young man? At your age, and with a face so pleasing, grief ought to be a thing unknown, and yet you seem altogether borne down with trouble."

I took heart on hearing these words. I seized the woman by her hand – which she left in mine – and replied: "Auspicious star, that hidest thyself behind this thin cloud of lawn, is it not possible that Heaven intends thee to be my guiding star indeed? I am looking for a woman ready to espouse me this very night, and to accompany me instantly to the house of my father; and such a woman I have been unable to find."

"She is now found, if so be that you are yourself willing," she replied, in gentle and timid accents. "Take me. I am neither young nor old, neither beautiful nor ugly, but I am chaste, industrious, and prudent; and my name is Homaïouna, which is a name of happy augury."

"Oh, I take you right willingly!" cried I; "for, even if you are not all you say, yet there can be no question of your goodness, since you are thus ready to follow one who is quite unknown to you; and goodness was the one indispensable quality required by my father. Quick, quick; let us hasten to anticipate, or at least not to be behind, my two brothers."

Immediately we began to walk – or rather to run – as fast as we could towards our house. Poor Homaïouna was very soon out of breath, and I perceived that she limped slightly. I was myself very strong, and took her on my shoulders, not putting her to the ground till we reached the door. My brothers, and their two intended brides, had arrived long before me; but the dervise, who was ever my friend, had insisted on waiting till nightfall, so that the three marriages might, if possible, take place simultaneously. My future sisters-in-law were still veiled, but when I contrasted their entrancing figures with that of Homaïouna my face grew red with shame. And I felt even more perturbed when, after our vows had been reciprocally exchanged, the time came for raising my wife's veil: my hand trembled; I was tempted to turn my eyes away; I fully expected to disclose the features of a monster. But what a pleasant surprise awaited me! Homaïouna was not indeed of extraordinary beauty, like the wives of my two brothers, but her features were regular, her face expressive and intelligent, and she attracted by an air of indescribable candour. Alsalami, who perceived the ironical smiles of my brothers, whispered in my ear that he was quite sure I had made the best choice of the three, and would see reason to congratulate myself over the wife who had fallen to my lot.

The fatal cupboard was in our sleeping apartment; and, though I was not insensible to my wife's charms, I could not help sighing, as I always did, when looking at that mysterious article of furniture. "Have I the misfortune of not pleasing you?" said Homaïouna tenderly.

"By no means," said I, kissing her. "But, in order quite

to reassure you, let me explain that this cupboard contains a treasure of which my father has promised the key to the one of his three sons who proves most worthy. He is not in as great a hurry to make his choice as we are to obtain possession of the treasure!"

"Your father is wise," rejoined my wife; "he is afraid of choosing rashly. It remains for you, by your conduct, to solve his doubts. Nevertheless, bear in mind that I am called Homaïouna, and should bring you luck."

The gracious and affectionate air with which she pronounced these words made me entirely forget, for that night at least, the riches that filled my imagination; and, if I had not been the most foolish of men, I should have forgotten them altogether, since I already possessed the greatest, the most inestimable of treasures — a real friend. And indeed I soon perceived that chance had done more for me than foresight had done for my brothers. Their wives were idle, full of vanity, and constantly quarrelling with each other; and though they did not love Homaïouna, whose modesty and housewifely virtues constantly brought them to blush, yet they always referred to her in their differences because they could not help regarding her with respect. My father saw all this well enough, though he said not a word; but I read his thoughts in the looks he cast at the dervise, who, without making any bones about it, praised my wife highly.

One day, having drawn me apart, he said: "Barkiarokh, I have a question to ask, and you must answer it truthfully, for I ask it in your own interest: How did you come to know Homaïouna?"

I hesitated a moment; but, finally, the wish to know the reason of his curiosity prevailed, and I replied fully and without disguise.

"That is a very strange adventure," cried he, "and your story confirms me in an opinion I had already formed. Have you ever observed, my son, that when your wife is coming and going in the garden, the flowers, as she passes, assume livelier colours and a more delicious fragrance; that the plants and the shrubs, as she touches them, grow visibly; and that the water shed from the watering-pot by her hands rivals in its effects the bright and fertilising dews of the later spring? I have seen your wicker baskets take on an unwonted lustre and fineness as she arranged them for market upon the camel's back. Twice has she got ready your nets, and on both occasions the draught of fishes was miraculous in its abundance. Oh, she is assuredly protected by some powerful jinn! Cherish her, therefore, honour her as the destined source of all your happiness."

I assured Alsalami that I should have no difficulty in following his advice, seeing how well I knew my wife's inestimable qualities. And immediately I retired, being anxious to think over what I had just heard. "If it be true – and all appearances point that way" – said I to myself, "that Homaïouna enjoys the favour of some supernatural power, why does she not open the cupboard, or, at least, determine my father to give her the key? Probably she has never turned her thoughts that way. Shall I suggest it to her? Ah! but dare I? Her wise conversation, her heavenly looks, hold me in awe. Let me rather studiously hide my excessive covetousness in my own bosom. If she knew me as I really am she would despise me, and certainly not aid or abet my evil designs. To veil their vices from the sight of the good is the only resource of those who are not blind and know themselves to be vicious." Thus was I confirmed in habits of hypocrisy; and these, for a time, worked only too effectually to my advantage.

So all went well, and peaceably enough, in our little family; till one night, when we came home, my brothers and I, from selling our fish, we found our father suffering from a most acute attack of gout – a malady to which he had for some time been subject, though he had never before experienced an attack of such violence. Immediately we assumed an air of great consternation, and squatting down on our knees, at a little distance from him, remained there in mournful silence. The dervise and the two black slaves held him up, while my wife busied herself about such alleviations to his sufferings as were possible. As to my sisters-in-law, they had retired to their own rooms, under pretext that they were not strong enough to witness so harrowing a spectacle.

The acute paroxysms of Ormossouf's malady at last left him. Then, turning his eyes upon us, he said: "My dear sons, I know, and very well perceive, how much you love me; and I make no doubt that, however weary, you will hasten to satisfy a whim that has just entered into my head. I have eaten nothing all day, and I should greatly like to have for supper fishes of a rare kind, and pleasant to the taste. Take your nets, therefore, and see what you can do for me. But let each keep apart whatever he chances to catch, so that his wife may cook and prepare it separately. Nevertheless, do not cast your nets into the sea more than once: I give you this direction because it is late, and some accident might befall you. I am not in a condition to bear the anxiety that would ensue if your return were long delayed."

We rose immediately, and, taking our boat, which was moored to the shore close by, went some little way, to what we knew to be a likely spot. There we threw in our nets, each, as we did so, making vows for his own success and the failure of his two brothers. The night was dark. It would have been impossible to examine then and there what we had taken. We returned home, therefore, in ignorance; but, during our short walk from the boat, my brothers suffered all the pangs of envy, for they saw that I was nearly borne down by the weight of my nets, while they carried theirs without the slightest difficulty. Their anxiety, however, proved to be only transient. How did they triumph when it turned out that each had taken an enormous fish of a rare kind, and covered with magnificent scales, while mine was so small, and of a colour so brown and uniform, that it looked rather like a reptile than a denizen of the sea! It needed not the shouts of laughter of my sisters-in-law and their husbands to add to my confusion and mortification. I threw my seemingly worthless fish on to the ground, and was about to trample it under-foot, when my wife, having picked it up, said in my ear: "Take courage, my dear Barkiarokh; I am going to cook this little fish, which troubles you so much, and you shall see that it is the best of the three." I had such confidence in her that these words caused hope to revive in my breast, and I quite came to myself.

Ormossouf could not help smiling when he saw that atomy of a fish, which had been placed between the other two on the platter, and presented a most pitiful appearance. "Whose fish is this?" said he.

"It is my husband's," answered Homaïouna; "and a most exquisite delicacy, though it will make but two mouthfuls. Deign, therefore, to eat it entirely yourself, and pray eat it at once. May it do you as much good as I desire. May every best wish we could form for your health and welfare be accomplished as you partake of it!"

"Any article of food coming from thy hand must needs be delicious, seeing how graciously it is offered," replied the good old man; "therefore I will satisfy thee, my dear daughter." Saying these words, he put a piece of fish into his mouth.

Then my elder brother, jealous of this small act of favour, cried: "Ah! if good wishes only are wanted to win favour here, then who can go further than I, who would willingly exchange my age for that of my father, and give him my strength to take upon myself his weakness!"

"I say the same," interrupted my second brother, "and with all my heart!"

"Oh, I do not yield to either of you in filial tenderness!" cried I, in turn. "I would willingly take to myself the gout that torments my most cherished father, and so deliver him from it for ever, and that is much worse than merely assuming to oneself the wrinkles of his age."

Though I pronounced these words with every show of enthusiasm, yet I held my eyes down, and fixed on the table, for fear lest Homaïouna should see how far they were from expressing my real thoughts. But suddenly, at the sound of the piercing cries uttered by my sisters-in-law, I lifted up my head. Oh, marvel unspeakable! oh, miracle! – which still causes my heart to cease beating when I think of it! I saw my brothers bent half double, wrinkled, and showing all the signs of age, and my father irradiated with youth!

Terror took hold upon me. I had, as they had, uttered a rash wish! "Heavens!" I cried, "must I ..." I was able to say no more. Sharp pains shot through me, taking away all powers of speech. My limbs stiffened. My heart failed me. I fell to the ground in a sort of trance – from which, however, I was soon recalled by the noise and tumult in the room. My sisters-in-law were heaping a thousand reproaches on their unhappy husbands, and upbraiding them for the wishes they had uttered. They, on the other hand, were crying out that they had not meant what they said, and that what they had really said could not properly be described as wishes. On this Homaïouna, having told them that Heaven, to unmask knaves, often takes them at their word, they all fell upon her, calling her a witch and a wicked Dive, and began to beat her. Ormossouf and the dervise, who undertook to defend my wife, were not spared; but they returned the blows they received a hundredfold, the one having regained all his old vigour and strength, and the other having never lost them: thus they necessarily had the advantage of men broken and trembling with age, and of two women rendered incapable by a blind fury. At last my father, weary of such a disgraceful scene, and outraged by his wicked children's want of filial piety, took a scourge armed with a hundred knots, and drove them out of the house with the curses they deserved.

During this scene, in which I would otherwise willingly have taken part with my brothers, I did, notwithstanding my sufferings, remember the key of the cupboard, and prudently judged that, in order to get possession of it, I must put a curb on the rage by which I was possessed. To this end I stifled my involuntary cries by putting the end of my robe into my mouth, and remained as if senseless, stretched out upon the floor.

So soon as my brothers and their wives were out of the house, the dervise, Homaïouna, and my father ran to me, and tried to lift me up. Their care, and the pity I read in their looks, touched me but little. I was especially furious against my wife, whom I regarded as the cause of all that had taken place. In order to contain myself I had need of the self-control acquired during a long course of habitual hypocrisy. "Deign," said I, in a voice interrupted by many groans, "deign to have me carried to my bed, where I may, perhaps, obtain some relief to my most excruciating pains; but, whatever happens, I shall never repent having delivered my dear father from such an insupportable malady."

"Oh! it is thou, and thou alone, who by thy filial piety hast deserved to possess the key of the fatal cupboard," cried Ormossouf. "Here it is," continued he, presenting it to me. "In thee will be accomplished the promises made to my race. Ah! what joy will be mine when I see thee glorious and happy!"

"To contribute to thy happiness will ever be my only joy," said I, with a grateful look; "but I am in great suffering, and at the present moment nothing but sleep can afford me any pleasure."

Immediately I was carried into my room – the room that contained the cupboard – and where I was burning to find myself; and left alone with my wife.

"Here," she said, "is a healing balm which I will apply to the soles of your feet. It will ease your pain."

"Oh, I have not the slightest doubt that you know what you are about," said I, looking at her gloomily enough; "there does not seem much that you do not know."

Homaïouna made as though she did not notice my ill-humour. She applied the balm, and my sufferings ceased. This good office reconciled me to her somewhat. I kissed her as I passed, and ran to the cupboard. Then I turned the key, trembling with curiosity. I expected to be dazzled by the brightness of the gold and precious stones I should find there; but, in lieu of any such treasure, I found only a very small iron box, containing a leaden ring, and a piece of parchment well folded and sealed. At the sight of this I was utterly confounded. The idea of all it had cost me to obtain possession of what I regarded as pure rubbish stopped the beating of my heart and took away my breath.

"Do not be too soon discouraged," said my wife, "and especially do not begin to regret your act of filial piety: read."

I did as Homaïouna advised, but not without blushing because she had divined my thoughts, and I read these words, written in fine characters upon the parchment: "Take this ring. When placed on the little finger of thy left hand, it will make thee invisible. By this means thou shalt be enabled to regain the kingdom of thy ancestors, and to reign as either the best, or the vilest, of kings."

At these last words Homaïouna cried out, in a voice so loud and piercing that the very chamber shook withal: "O Allah, Allah! leave not the choice of this alternative to the husband thou has given me! Compel him to be good and let me remain for ever a simple mortal. I consent never to revisit my own happy home, and to pass all my days in this my present exile, provided only that my dear Barki-arokh becomes the good king mentioned in this parchment!"

At these words, and on seeing the rays of light that seemed to issue from Homaïouna's eyes, and her form as if transfigured, I fell at her feet with my face to the ground, and, after a few minutes' silence, cried in turn: "O you, whom I scarcely dare to look upon, deign to lead my steps in the way that is set before them, and may your generous wish on my behalf be accomplished!"

"The decrees of Heaven are supreme, and they only are sure of accomplishment," said she, raising me up softly and tenderly; "nevertheless, listen with all your ears, and may my words be engraved upon the tablets of your heart. I will hide nothing that relates to myself, and nothing that relates to your own future duties and responsibilities; and then I shall submit to my fate, whatever it may be." She

spoke, sighed deeply, and then began her story in the
following words:–

"I know, O son of Ormossouf, that you and Alsalami,
the dervise, have come to the conclusion that I am protected
by some celestial Intelligence; but how far, even so, were
you from guessing to what a glorious race I belong! I am
the daughter of the great Asfendarmod, the most renowned, the most puissant, and, alas! the most severe of all
the Peris! It was in the superb city of Gianhar, the capital
of the delightful country of Shaduka, that I came into the
world, together with a sister, who was called Ganigul. We
were brought up together, and loved one another tenderly,
notwithstanding the difference in our dispositions. My
sister was mild, languid, quiet – she only cultivated a
poetic restfulness – while I was alert, active, always busy
about something, and especially desirous of doing good
whenever I could find an opportunity.

"My father, into whose presence we never came without
trembling, and who had never seemed to trouble his head
much about us, caused us one day to be summoned to the
foot of his resplendent throne. 'Homaïouna, and you,
Ganigul,' said he, 'I have had you both under my observa-
tion. I have seen that the beauty, which is the common
inheritance of all the Peris, shows equally in the face and
form of both of you – but I have also seen that your
dispositions are different. Such diversities of character exist,
and must exist: they contribute to the general good. You
have come to an age when it is fitting that each should
consult her own heart, and choose in what manner she
prefers to pass her life. Speak! what can I do for you? I am
the sovereign of one of the most marvellous countries in
Ginnistan – a country in which, as its name implies, desire
and its fulfilment, so often separated, go nearly always
hand in hand – and you have but to ask in order to obtain.
Speak first, Homaïouna.

77

"'My father,' I replied, 'I am fond of action. I like to succour the afflicted, and make people happy. Command that there be built for me a tower, from whose top I can see the whole earth, and thus discover the places where my help would be of most avail.'

"'To do good, without ceasing, to mankind, a race at once flighty and ungrateful, is a more painful task than you imagine,' said Asfendarmod. 'And you, Ganigul,' continued he, addressing my sister, 'what do you desire?'

"'Nothing but sweet repose,' replied she. 'If I am placed in possession of a retreat where Nature unveils her most seductive charms – a retreat from which envy and all turbulent passions are banished, and where soft pleasure, and a delightful indolence for ever dwell – then I shall be content and happy, and shall, with every returning day, bless a father's indulgence.'

"'Your wishes are granted,' said Asfendarmod. 'You can, at this moment, betake yourselves to your respective habitations. At a glance from me the Intelligences, who do my bidding, have already made every preparation for your reception. Go! we shall meet again. You can sometimes come hither, if such is your wish, or visit one another. Nevertheless, bear in mind that a decision once taken in Shadukan is taken for ever. The celestial race, to which we belong, must never know the unstable desires, still less the feelings of envy, that afflict the feeble race of man.'

"After saying these words, my father motioned to us to retire; and immediately I found myself in a tower, built on the summit of Mount Caf – a tower whose outer walls were lined with numberless mirrors that reflected, though hazily and as in a kind of dream, a thousand varied scenes then being enacted on the earth. Asfendarmod's power had indeed annihilated space, and brought me not only within sight of all the beings thus reflected in the mirrors, but also within sound of their voices and of the very words they uttered.

"The first scene that chanced to attract my attention was such as to fill me with righteous anger. An impious mother-in-law was endeavouring, by feigned caresses and artful words, to induce her weak husband to give his daughter in marriage to a negro, hideously deformed, who, as she declared, had seduced the girl's innocence. The young virgin, like a lily already half severed from its stem, bent her lovely head, and awaited, pale and trembling, a fate she deserved so little; while the monster to whom she was destined asked pardon, with the eyes of a basilisk, and the sighs of a crocodile, for an offence he had not committed, and was careful to hide in his heart, which was as black as his countenance, the crimes he *had* committed with the mother-in-law. In the twinkling of an eye, I saw all this in their faces, and flew, quick as lightning, to the spot. With my invisible wand – in which lies concentrated a celestial power distinctive of the higher order of Peris – I touched the wicked woman and her vile paramour. Instantly they altered their tone, looked upon one another with fury, recriminated the one upon the other, and said so much that the husband, transported with rage, cut off both their heads. He then caused his trembling daughter to approach, wept over her tenderly, and afterwards, having sent for a youth as beautiful as herself, had them married on the spot.

"I retired to my tower, well satisfied with having performed an act of justice and equity, and made two amiable creatures happy. And thereupon I passed a delightful night.

"At the point of day I ran to my mirrors: the one before which I stopped reflected the harem of an Indian sultan. I saw there a superb garden, and in it a woman of great beauty, of majestic figure, and of proud and haughty bearing, who seemed to be in a state of great agitation. She was walking on a terrace, with large strides, and looking in every direction most anxiously; nor was her anxiety allayed till she saw a black eunuch coming towards her. He approached with every mark of assiduity and respect, and said, bowing almost to the ground: 'Queen of the world! your commands are obeyed. The imprudent Nourjehan is confined in the black grotto. The sultan will certainly not look for her there; and to-night the slave dealer, with whom I have conferred, will take her hence for ever.'

"'You have only done your duty,' said the lady; 'but I shall not fail to reward you liberally. Tell me, however, how you succeeded in overmastering my odious rival without disturbance, or clamour on her part.'

"'I accosted her as she came out of the apartment of our lord and master, whom she had left asleep,' replied the eunuch. 'She was about to retire to her own apartment, when, quicker than lightning, I seized hold of her, and wrapped her up in a rug, with which I had provided myself; I then carried her, running as fast as I could, to the black grotto. Then, in order somewhat to allay her fears, I told her she should depart this night with a slave merchant, who might, perhaps, sell her to some other king; nor could she hope for a better lot. Calm yourself, therefore, I conjure you, my dear mistress. As soon as the sultan awakes, he will wish to see you, for, notwithstanding his fits of inconstancy, you, and you alone, reign supreme in his heart.'

"'I would not share his love with the unworthy Nourjehan,' cried the lady; 'nevertheless, since I am avenged, I will smother my just anger.'

"I misliked this plot, and its instruments, the lady more especially, and resolved to protect the unfortunate object of her jealousy. So I flew to the black grotto, unclosed the secret door, and, having plunged Nourjehan into a deep slumber, enveloped her with a cloud that rendered her invisible, and in this state bore her to the side of the sultan, who was still asleep. Then I took my flight towards the immense city adjoining the imperial palace.

"I passed the rest of the day in floating over streets and houses, and observed several matters that seemed somewhat out of order, which I proposed to redress. Nevertheless, I felt a certain curiosity to see what was happening in the harem, and returned thither at nightfall. What was my surprise when, in an immense hall, illumined by a thousand lamps, I saw the dead body of the haughty lady whom I had left alive in the morning: it lay in a coffin of aloes wood, and was all covered with livid spots. The sultan, at one time plunged in speechless sorrow, shed torrents of tears, at another time foamed with rage, and swore he would discover the atrocious hand that had cut short the days of his favourite sultana. All the women, ranged in circles round the bier, sobbed in a heartrending manner, and, amid groans and sighs, uttered the most touching eulogies upon the departed. None manifested more sorrow than Nourjehan, nor was more prodigal of her praises. I looked at her fixedly. I read in her heart. I immeshed her in my occult influence. Immediately, rolling on the floor like one possessed, she accused herself of having slipped poison into a bowl of sherbet that was being prepared for her rival — and added that she had been led to commit an act of such atrocity by a dream: she had dreamt that the favourite had caused her to be confined in the black grotto, and meant to have her handed over to a slave merchant. The sultan, in a fit of fury, ordered the culprit to be taken from his presence, and immediately strangled. I let things take their course, and returned, pensive and in confusion, to my tower.

"'Ah!' said I to myself, 'Asfendarmod spoke only too truly when he warned me that the task of benefiting mankind is hard and ungrateful; but ought he not rather to have said that we cannot tell, when we think to do good, whether we may not be really doing harm! I prevented certain designs inspired by jealousy and revenge, but not involving the death of the victim, and have, on the other hand, been the cause of a horrible crime, committed by a furious woman acting under the influence of what she took to be a dream. How perverse are these creatures of clay to whom I have devoted my care! Would it not be better to let them prey upon one another, and to live as my sister does, in the enjoyment of the happiness inherent to natures as perfect as ours? But what am I saying? Am I still in a position to choose? Did not my father tell me that my choice once made was irrevocable? What shall I do? I shall not always be able to read people's hearts from the expression of their countenances. Their stronger emotions I may be able to follow from outward, involuntary signs; but premeditated malice will ever hide behind a mask. It is true that my mysterious influence excites remorse, and leads to the criminal's confession of his crime; but by that time the harm is done, the crime is committed. I cannot anticipate the intention of the wicked; and my intervention, however well meant, may be the cause of a thousand evils.'

"These thoughts tormented me night and day. I remained inactive in my tower. In vain did the objects that presented themselves to my gaze excite my compassion, and seem to call for intervention. I refrained from yielding to all such impulses. If I saw a grand vizier trying to ruin a rival by vile intrigue, and all the arts of flattery and calumny, I would be on tiptoe to contravene his designs – and then I would stop suddenly, at the thought that the rival might perchance be even more wicked than himself, and a worse oppressor of the people, and that I should thus possibly hear, at the great day of judgment, thousands of voices crying out against me, 'Allah, avenge us!' Events, as they passed before me in their daily pageant, almost always justified these previsions.

"One day, having cast my eyes on the flourishing city of Chiraz, I saw, in a very decent dwelling, a woman whose modest beauty and grace charmed me. She had but just entered a very pretty chamber in which there was a little oratory, when she first attracted my attention. Kneeling there, she began to pray with edifying fervour; but, as she was so occupied, her husband burst in the door, which she had closed from the inside, seized her by the hair, took a whip of knotted cords from underneath his tunic, and beat her unmercifully. At the sight of this piece of savagery, I could not contain myself, and hastened to the poor creature's help, arriving, however, just in time to hear the sound of a most sonorous sneeze that came from a cabinet hidden behind some Indian matting. The husband ran to the place from which the sound proceeded, and dragged, out of an obscure recess, a fakir hideous to behold. His hair was matted, frizzled and filthy, his beard red and disgusting, his complexion olive and oily, his body almost naked and covered with old scars. The exasperated Persian was no less confounded than I at the sight of such an object. He looked at it for some moments speechless, and then at last broke out: 'This, then, you infamous creature, is the fine lover you prefer to myself! I knew well enough that a man was shut up with you here, but I never expected to find a monster such as this! And you,' continued he, addressing the fakir, 'how did you have the impudence to come here?'

" 'I came,' replied the hypocrite, quite unabashed, 'to do what you yourself can evidently do far better than I. Flagellation is meritorious. It mortifies the body, and uplifts the soul. I came to apply the whip to your wife, who is in the habit of confiding to me her little spiritual troubles. For the purpose I had brought with me the penitential instrument which you see here, but you have forestalled me. Sufficient for the day – she has had enough, and so I withdraw.' Saying these words, he took from a kind of belt, which composed his only habiliment, a large scourge, thickly knotted, and stepped towards the door.

"The husband stopped him, half mechanically, for he remained quite confused and uncertain. His wife, seeing this, at once threw herself down at his feet. 'Ah, my beloved spouse,' cried she, 'finish your work, make me die beneath your blows, but do not imperil your soul by falling foul of this worthy man. He is the friend of our holy Prophet; beware, yes, beware of the curse that will surely light upon your own head if you molest him and do him wrong.'

" 'What does all this mean?' said the unhappy Persian, utterly bewildered and almost convinced of the innocence of his wife. 'I am not so easily frightened. Be more coherent, and explain how this pretended saint came to be here, and how long you have known him. I should be glad enough to believe that you are less guilty than you at first appeared, but I must have a full and reasonable account of what has taken place, and, above all, I must have the truth.'

"He had it only too completely, for at that moment I touched his perfidious spouse with my wand, and she rose from the ground like a wild thing, and cried in a loud voice, 'Yes, I love this vile seducer to distraction, and more than I have ever loved thee, thou tyrant of my life! A hundred times have I kissed his bleared eyes, and his livid, discoloured mouth; in a word, I have made him master not only of thy means, but of my person. On his side he has taught me to laugh at Allah and his Prophet, to utter the most infamous blasphemies, and to deride the most sacred things. I knew that thou wert spying upon me, and had knelt down in prayer, so as to deceive thee – not anticipating the trivial accident that revealed my paramour's presence. Such are my crimes. I hold them in abhorrence. Something, I know not what, compels me to disclose them. Let my accomplice refuse to reveal *his* if he dares.'

"The fakir, though utterly confounded, opened his lips to reply. I don't know what he might have said for himself – I had not taken the trouble to subject him to my influence – but the enraged Persian did not give him time to utter one syllable. He took him by the middle, and hurled him from the top of the balcony, and then sent the wife the same way. They fell from a very great height, into a courtyard paved with sharp stones, and were dashed to pieces.

"I was returning, very pensively, to my tower, when lamentable shrieks, coming from a thick wood, assailed my ears. I ran forward, and saw a young man, more beautiful than the angels in the seventh heaven, defending himself against three negroes, whose shining scimitars had already wounded him in several places, and who cried to him without ceasing: 'Where is your brother? What have you done with your brother?'

"'Barbarous wretches,' he replied, 'he is, alas! where you wish to send me. You have murdered him, and it is now my turn.'

"These words touched me. The air of the youth, scared as he was, seemed so interesting, that I thought I might venture to intervene. I was about to snatch him out of the hands of his enemies, by whom he had at last been disarmed, when another youth, covered with blood, appeared upon the scene, painfully dragging his wounded body from behind some bushes. 'My friends,' said he, in a feeble voice, to the negroes, who ran forward to meet him, 'carry me instantly to the palace of my beloved Adna. Let my last looks be fixed on her, and may Heaven grant me enough of life to give her my troth. You could find no better means of avenging me of my brother, who has only murdered me in order to prevent our union, and possess my goods. I see that you became aware, but too late, of his atrocious designs, and have begun to punish him. Go no further. Let us leave him to bleed in this remote spot. That will be punishment enough. We are not bound to help him further.'

"The negroes obeyed. They bore away their master. The criminal remained, stretched upon the ground, pale and haggard as a spectre come from hell; nor was I in any wise tempted to give him any help of mine.

"These two adventures convinced me, finally, that acts of benevolence, on my part, might often be much misplaced. I resolved to make appeal to the justice of Asfendarmod with regard to the change which such events had naturally operated in my sentiments.

"Nevertheless, as I well knew how stern and strict he was, I thought it would be to my advantage to obtain my sister's countenance and help. So I left my tower, and took flight for her habitation.

"The habitation Ganigul had obtained from my father was in every respect conformable to her tastes and wishes. It was situated on a little island, which a river, translucent and bordered with flowering thorns, encircled seven times. In the interspaces between these circles the grass was so moist and fresh that the fishes would often leave the silvery waters of the river and disport themselves there. Various kinds of grass-eating animals browsed in these moist meads, which were starred with flowers; and all enjoyed such happiness in the regions assigned to them that they never thought to stray. The island itself was at once a flower garden and an orchard. It seemed as if the sweet-smelling shrubs had joined in friendship with the fruit-trees, so closely were their branches interlaced. The daintier flowers grew on the more immediate borders of the stream, and the shores of the stream itself were of the finest golden sand. A bower of orange-trees and myrtle, surrounded by a palisade of gigantic roses, formed my sister's palace, and was the spot to which she retired at night, together with six Peris who had attached themselves to her company. This delightful retreat was situated in the centre of the island; a brook ran through it, formed by a thousand rivulets of water, that joined on entering its confines, and separated again at their exit. As these running streamlets ran over a stony, uneven bed they made a constant melodious murmur, that harmonised perfectly with the voice of the nightingales. On both sides of the brook were ranged beds, made of the shed petals of flowers, and of feathers of divers colours which the night birds had shaken from their tiny wings; – and on these beds one slept voluptuously. Thither Ganigul often retired in the daytime to read in quiet the marvellous annals of the Jinns, the chronicles of ancient worlds, and the prophecies relating to the worlds that are yet to be born.

"After the days of agitation I had spent in my tower, I seemed to pass into a new life on entering into this abode of peace. My sister received me with a thousand caresses, and her friends were no less eager to provide for my entertainment. Sometimes they challenged the creatures of lightest foot to run races with them; sometimes they joined their heavenly voices to the voices of the birds; or they sported with the goats, which, like, the ewes and cows, would gladly present to them udders full of milk; or else they matched themselves in feats of agility against the sprightly gazelles. Amid all the creatures thus daily ministering to their pleasure, the dog, faithful and caressing, the lithe and supple cat, were not forgotten. But none were more amiable and delightful than a little Leiki which never quitted the happy Ganigul. The divine warbling of this lovely bird, the brilliant colours of its plumage, were even less to be admired than the extreme sensibility of its heart, and the supernatural instinct with which it had been endowed by some superior power. Whether at rest in the bosom of its mistress, or whether, fluttering among the shadeful myrtles, it gave voice to song of an endless variety, it never ceased to be attentive to all her movements; and it seemed ever on the watch to forestall and obey her slightest wish. By the beating of its wings it expressed its joy when anything was found for it to do: it would dart like lightning to fetch the flowers, the fruits, that Ganigul desired; it would bring them in its vermeil beak, which it would lovingly insinuate between her lips as asking to be rewarded for its service. I occasionally had a share in its caresses, and returned them willingly; but as I did so I sighed to think I had no such companion in my solitude.

"My sister had wisely reminded me that this was the time of the great assemblage of the Peris, over which Asfendarmod presided in person, and that it would be better, therefore, to defer our proposed visit to a more convenient season. 'My dear Homaïouna,' said she to me one day, 'you know how tenderly I love you, and you know also that I desire nothing better than to have your company. Would to Heaven that you had, like myself, made choice of the peace and tranquillity of this abode! May my father allow you to share in its delights! Nevertheless, I advise you to make further trial, for a little while, of the kind of life you yourself selected. Either you will find therein unexpected satisfaction, or you will have new reasons to allege in urging the stern Asfendarmod to relieve you from further trials. As to the time of your departure, let us postpone it as much as possible. Rejoice here in my friendship, and in all the delights by which I am surrounded. Art is excluded from my domain; but Nature is here prodigal of her gifts. I possess everything I had desired, and even more; for I had no conception of such a gift as a happy chance has bestowed upon me.'

"'You mean, doubtless, your beloved bird,' said I, much moved. 'How did you obtain possession of it?'

"'Oh, I am quite ready to tell you the story,' answered she. 'I always think of it with renewed pleasure. I was seated in the shade of that great lilac-tree, whose flowers diffuse such a pleasant odour, when, suddenly, the sky put on the liveliest colours, rosier than the most brilliant sunrise. A light, intense beyond description, spread over all, diffusing everywhere a feeling of unspeakable joy and content. It was a light that seemed to pour down direct from some sanctuary, or, if I may dare to say so, from the very throne of the Supreme Power. At the same time strains of a divine harmony floated in the air – strains ravishing, indefinite, that appeared to lose themselves in the vague infinity of space. A cloud of almost indistinguishable birds went sailing across the firmament. The murmur of their innumerable wings, mingling with the far flutings of their song, threw me into an ecstasy. While I was lost in the enjoyment of these marvels, one bird detached itself from the rest, and fell, as if exhausted, at my feet. I lifted it up tenderly. I warmed it in my breast. I encouraged it to resume its flight; but it refused to leave me. It came back and back, and seemed desirous of becoming altogether mine. Its shape, as you see, is that of a Leiki, but its gifts of mind and soul equal those of the most favoured creatures. A heavenly inspiration seems to breathe through its songs; its language is that of the empyrean; and the sublime poems it recites are like those which the ever-happy Intelligences declaim in the abodes of glory and immortality. Supremely marvellous, even in a country where everything is a marvel, it follows me, it serves me like the most willing of slaves. I am the object of its tenderest gratitude – it is the object of my admiration, and of my care. Ah! how rightly is it called the Bird of Love!'

"These last words troubled me so that I had some

difficulty in hiding my perturbation. Envy took possession of my soul: no doubt I had contracted that degrading passion in my intercourse with mankind, for, so far, it had not been known among us. Everything about me turned to gall and wormwood. I longed to be alone, and, when alone, could not bear my own company. I issued at night from my sister's bower of perennial blossoms, to stray, as chance dictated, through the surrounding wilderness of leaves, and, when there, the brilliant light shed by thousands of glow-worms only served to exasperate me. I would fain have trampled on these little creatures, whose amazing numbers and marvellous brilliance had before excited my admiration. Darkness was what I sought as a fit cloak for my shameful thoughts. 'Oh, Ganigul!' I said, 'how happy are you, and how wretched am I! What comparison is there between your isle of peace and my tower of discordant sights, between your delightful leisure and my continual agitation, between the smiling natural beauties, the innocent and faithful creatures that surround you, and the rude world, the wicked and ungrateful race of man, that I have ever before my eyes? Ah! your sweet bird is more necessary to me than to you! You have friends ever assiduous to please you, an infinite number of creatures at beck and call for your amusement – why, why should I not have at least this one thing which would stand to me in lieu of all the rest? Yes, I will have it. I will take it from you, for you would doubtless refuse to give it me. I will take it away with me, and you will certainly not remain uncomforted for its loss in this delightful sojourn.'

"Though at first I put away with horror the thought of such a crime, yet, insensibly, I grew accustomed to it, and all too soon there occurred a sad opportunity for the perpetration of the theft. One day I was alone in a little grove of jasmine and pomegranates, when the Leiki came thither seeking for flowers. I called him. He flew to me. Immediately, binding his feet and wings with a slight piece of fibre, I hid him in my bosom. As I was about to fly with the stolen bird, I heard my sister's voice calling me. I trembled in all my limbs. I was unable to move a step. 'What do you want with me?' cried I, in a peevish tone.

"'Ah! why,' asked Ganigul tenderly, as she hastened up, 'why do you thus seek to be alone? In the name of all our love for one another, let me at least have a share in your troubles.'

"'No,' cried I, in great agitation, and pressing to my heart the bird, which was trembling pitifully, and which I wished to keep from uttering any sound. 'No, I will no longer burden you with my presence. Adieu, I am going hence.'

"Scarcely had I pronounced these words, when a thick, black cloud cast its veil over the firmament, and dimmed the brilliancy about us; and the hiss of rain and growling of a storm filled the air. At last my father appeared, borne on a meteor whose terrible effulgence flashed fire upon the world. 'Stay, wretched creature,' said he, 'and behold the innocent victim that hath fallen a sacrifice to thy barbarous envy!'

"I looked, and, oh, horror! I had smothered the marvellous, the greatly loved bird.

"At this moment all grew dark before my eyes. I tottered, I fell to the ground lifeless.

"When the great voice of Asfendarmod brought me back to my senses, I saw neither my sister, nor her friends, nor her fatal Leiki. I was alone with my inexorable judge.

"'Daughter of crime,' said he, 'go and crawl upon that earth where Allah alone is the dispenser of events, and whence thou hast carried away nothing save its vices. Study mankind at leisure before pretending to afford them help and protection. Thou shalt still retain some of the privileges inherent in thy nature, but thou shalt at the same time be liable to some of the most cruel sufferings to which men are liable. And you, O winds, mysterious invisible powers, who do my bidding, bear her to the obscure sojourn of men! May she there, by patience and wisdom, regain her title to come back once more to our regions of light!'

"On hearing this fulminating sentence, I threw myself, utterly distracted, on my knees, and, unable to speak, lifted up to my father suppliant hands. Then, all of a sudden, a whirlwind, palpable, overmastering, surrounded me, and having lifted me from the place where I knelt bore me downward, circling ever, during seven days and seven nights. At the end of that time, I was deposited on the dome of a palace overlooking an immense city, and knew that I had reached my destination. I acquiesced very humbly in the fate I had so well deserved.

"When I began to examine my surroundings, I was at once struck by the signs of utter gloom that reigned throughout the city. Men, women, children, all had put ashes on their heads, and were running hither and thither in great perturbation. Little by little they trooped together in a large place before the palace, and seemed to be in expectation of some extraordinary event. As I was not sure of having retained the power of moving at will from place to place, I formed a wish, trembling as I did so, to mingle with the crowd: and, at the same moment, found myself side by side with a great black eunuch, who was trying to keep order with his cane, striking out to right and left. Notwithstanding his truculent air, I thought he looked really good natured, and tried to attract his notice. At last he turned his eyes upon me.

"'What are you doing here, girl?' said he, in tones half of reproof, and half friendly. 'Here, and without your veil, like a wanton! Yet you seem to be a modest girl too, unless your looks belie you. Follow me into the palace. You would certainly be insulted in this crowd; and, besides, I like to hear tell of adventures, and you can tell me yours.'

"I bent my head in submission, and taking hold of the eunuch by his robe, made it my business to follow him. He forced a way through the press with his cane. By his orders the guard at the palace gate allowed me to pass, and he led me into his apartment, which was cleanliness itself. 'Sit down,' said he, 'you must be tired. I have no time, at the present moment, to listen to a long story. Tell me only, and in few words, who you are, and how you came to be outside, in the midst of the populace, half dressed, and, as it seemed to me, quite alone.'

"'I am,' I replied, 'the unfortunate daughter of a mighty prince, who dwells very far from hence. I have been carried away from his palace – by whom I know not. My captors compelled me for several days to travel so rapidly that I was quite unable to distinguish the road by which I was being taken. At last I was left by them in the place where you found me, and in the same apparel, the apparel I wore when they tore me from my home; and,' I added, 'I shall be less unhappy than I thought myself if I succeed in obtaining your distinguished protection.'

"'Yes,' said Gehanguz, for that was the eunuch's name, 'such apparel as you have on you is fine; and, moreover, there is an air of distinction about you conforming fairly well with what you tell me concerning your birth. But be quite frank with me, and tell me truly whether your captors committed any outrage against your person during the journey.'

"'Oh, by no means,' I replied. 'Revenge was their motive, and revenge closes the heart against the ingress of all other passions.'

"'Enough for the present,' said Gehanguz, 'you do not seem wanting in intelligence, and may be as useful to me as I to you. Rest here a while, and take some refreshment; dress yourself as befits. I will see you again in a few hours.'

"Having spoken these words, he clapped his hands, gave various orders to several young girls who instantly appeared, and departed.

"The young girls drew near to me with great respect, put me in a bath, rubbed me all over with precious essences, clothed me in a very beautiful dress, and served me with an excellent collation. Nevertheless, being plunged in the deepest sadness, I maintained the while an absolute silence. 'What shall I do?' said I to myself. 'Shall I stay here under the charge of Gehanguz? He seems to be kindly and humane, but I have learnt to distrust appearances. I feel that it is within my power to take flight to any habitable corner of the earth; but wherever I go, I shall find men, and wherever there are men I shall have to face the same troubles and anxieties. Will it not be better, seeing I deserve my punishment, to undergo that punishment in its entirety, and submit altogether to my fate, only using my supernatural powers in circumstances of absolute necessity? Besides, the dread executors of Asfendarmod's decree brought me hither. That is a further reason for remaining where I am, and striving, by an unbounded submission, to re-enter those happy regions from which I am not to be for ever excluded.'

"Sleep at last closed my eyelids. A happy dream took me back to Shadukan: I stood beside Ganigul in the bower of orange-trees and myrtle. She looked at me with sad eyes full of pity. Her Leiki flew about her uttering plaintive cries. As she strove to quiet it, I threw myself at her feet. Then she took me in her arms and held me tenderly pressed to her bosom.

"But at this point, while still in this ecstasy of happiness, I was awakened by the voice of the eunuch. 'Come,' said he in his harsh voice, harsh yet not altogether unsympathetic, 'come, let us for a while discuss your affairs; and begin by telling me your name.'

"'I am called Homaïouna,' said I, uttering a deep sigh. 'It was, without doubt, a mistake to bestow that name upon me.'

"'Not at all!' cried Gehanguz; 'there is no life, however fortunate, in which at least one reverse does not occur. That reverse you have just experienced. Henceforward we shall have nothing but uninterrupted prosperity. Now, listen, and I will explain matters. You are now in the famous city of Choucan, the capital of the greatest and richest country in the Indian peninsula. The king who reigned here a few days ago, had twenty other kings as vassals, elephants without number, treasures that could not be counted, and an untold host of subjects both industrious and obedient; but, with all this, he has had to fall asleep, like any ordinary man. He was placed this morning on the bed of everlasting rest; and that is why you saw all the people in mourning.'

"'That means,' I interrupted, 'that this great king is dead, and that he has just been buried.'

"'Fie! fie!' cried the eunuch, with a sour look. "'How dare you utter words so offensive to self-respecting ears. Such expressions are banished from Choucan. Keep a strict watch over your tongue, or you would at once give the lie to all I mean to say concerning your birth, and the superior education it should imply.'

"'Fear nothing,' I rejoined, with a smile. 'I shall know how to conform to so delicate a custom.'

"'Very well,' he pursued in a milder tone, 'you must know then that our good king never had any children save two daughters, twins, and equally beautiful and amiable. Whether he found it difficult to make a choice between the two, or whether he had some other reason for leaving the question open, I know not; but he never, during his lifetime, gave people to understand which of the two was to inherit his crown. Nevertheless, a little time before he entered into his last sleep, he summoned four old men, whose profound wisdom had never once been found wanting during the fifty years they had served him as viziers – and to those old men he entrusted the sacred parchment containing his last instructions, and signed with the twenty-one seals of the Empire. This parchment was opened a few moments ago, and it decides nothing.'

"'How,' said I, 'he has not named any successor?'

"'No,' replied Gehanguz; 'all he has left to his daughters is a problem for their solution – a problem which, as I am assured, is full of difficulty, – with the order that the one who best solves it, according to his own views, as communicated to the four viziers, shall be proclaimed queen absolute of Choucan, and its dependencies. I had received some inkling of his intentions from one of the favourite sultanas, who has extended to me her protection, even more because of my zeal in my office than because I am chief of the eunuchs. But, as she did not herself know the question to be propounded, she was unable to impart it to me. If one may judge by the countenances of the princesses, to whom alone it has been communicated by the four viziers, it must indeed be thorny. They seemed to be plunged in deep thought on leaving the divan. They were even overheard whispering to each other that they would require every one of the forty allotted days in order to ponder out a solution. This is the present state of things,' continued Gehanguz, 'and here is my project: I will assign you as companion to the two princesses, who live together, to all appearances, in perfect harmony. They will receive you gladly, for they like novelty, and are tired of all their girl slaves. You will insinuate yourself into their good graces, and so divide your attention as to retain the confidence of the one who ultimately becomes queen. You will speak to them often about me, and dissipate, as far as may be, the effect of anything that the little crazy-pated slave girls may have said to my disadvantage. If you see that one of the two is better disposed in my favour than the other, you will help her with your advice, and with mine, in case she confides to you the question of questions. In any case you will do your best to keep me in favour with both. The few words I have heard you speak, show that you possess intelligence; your eyes give promise of even more. You will have no difficulty, therefore, in obtaining over the princesses that ascendancy which people of intelligence naturally acquire over those who are not so gifted. Moreover, in acting as I propose, you will cause me to retain my office, and be yourself the favourite of a great queen – a position not to be despised. And I may say that it is not ambition, and still less self-interest, that prompts me in all this. It is the desire to see the harem maintained in the admirable order I have established there. I should be in absolute despair if any wrong-headed person were to come and destroy the work I have accomplished with such unimaginable pains. You will see for yourself the results of my efforts, and, I make no doubt, will from a feeling of justice consent to serve me. But that will in no way dispense me from acknowledging my indebtedness.'

"I had listened attentively to what Gehanguz was saying. I had carefully watched his eyes to see if I could detect in them the little cloud of embarrassment almost certain to appear when a speaker is animated by some sinister design; but I had been able to discover nothing save zeal, kindliness and sincerity. Nevertheless, I determined to be circumspect and careful in the observations which, by his means, I should be in a position to pursue, and only to serve his interests in so far as he might be worthy of assistance.

"On the same day he presented me to the Princesses Gulzara and Rezie, indulging in such eulogies and encomiums on my merits as would not have been excessive even if he had known my real condition. At everything he invented concerning my ability and accomplishments, I could not help smiling, and looking at him in a way that disconcerted him somewhat. But I took pity on him, and reassured his mind by another look, intended to signify that I should perform everything he promised.

"There was I, then, late a sovereign in Shadukan, now a slave in Choucan – my heavenly beauty a thing of the past, my face and form quite ordinary, my youth gone too, and an indeterminate and unattractive age assigned to me instead; and condemned to remain under this altered shape, an exile for a limitless period, and to be subject to evils both unknown and unforeseeable. My fall was indeed terrible; but I had brought it on myself, and I did not repine.

"Both my new mistresses conceived for me, from the first, a very lively affection. I told them interesting and amusing stories. They were transported with pleasure when I sang, accompanying my voice, which was melodious, upon the lute. If I devised for them some new adornment, it seemed to add to their beauty; the refreshments prepared by my hands were always agreeable to the taste, and diversified in flavour. At all my successes poor Gehanguz opened great eyes, and went into ecstasies of surprise and pleasure.

"Gulzara I liked much better than her sister. But I had the best of reasons for mistrusting first impressions – those instinctive attractions that are, for the most part, deceptive. I was not sorry, therefore, when the two princesses took to quarrelling as to which should have most of my company in private. This would give me an opportunity of better studying their characters. I took advantage of it, and soon became convinced that, in this particular instance, my first inclination had not played me false. Rezie, under the outward seeming of a seductive affability, hid an evil heart; she might have imposed, if her violent passions had not sometimes caused her to reveal her real self. When her vanity had made her believe that I preferred her to Gulzara, she opened her mind to me freely, and acquainted me, not only with the question propounded by the king her father, but also with her proposed reply. I saw with pleasure that she had no chance of becoming queen; she deserved to be a queen so little! all her intentions were unjust as concerned the people, and malicious as concerned her sister. Gulzara, more reserved, did not give me her confidence so easily. I had to merit it by devotion, and kindly care, which, indeed, cost me nothing, because I really loved her, and wished to do her service. At last she confessed, in tones that were persuasive, because simple and unaffected, that she had no ambition, and only wished to be queen for the sake of the good she might do; but that in this respect she was fully prepared to trust her sister, and had not even troubled her head to think about her father's question. All she said made me deem her so worthy to rule that I thought it only right to tell her it was her duty, in conformity with the king's last wishes, to aspire to the throne. She hesitated, however; but was at last persuaded – especially after I had thrown light on the perplexing problem propounded by the late king, and had furnished a reply with which she appeared to be more than satisfied.

"On the day when this great matter was to be settled, the city resounded with the noisy instruments of music in use in that country. The people again trooped together with the murmur and rustle of swarms of angry bees. And Gehanguz, drawing me aside, asked if I had any idea of what was likely to be the issue.

"'Set your mind at rest,' said I. 'All will be well. You will be retained in your office, because I am convinced that you only desire to remain chief eunuch from good motives.'

"At these words he began to caper like a roebuck, and ran to open the door of the divan for the princesses, whom I was following.

"The assembly was already complete, and the spectacle most striking. At the end of an immense mysterious hall stood a throne of blue enamel, all dotted over with unnumbered phosphorescent lights like stars, brilliant and terrible. This symbolic throne was raised on four columns – two of jasper, blood-red, and two of the purest alabaster – and I knew at once that the Jinns had fashioned it. I understood that the red columns stood for justice, and the white for mercy, and that the stars symbolised the rays that emanate from a good king, and serve as light to lighten his people. The four old viziers entrusted with the commands of the late monarch, now asleep, stood within a latticed grating of steel, surmounted with spikes, that surrounded the throne. A few paces from it carpets were set, similar to those used for prayer in the Mosques, and on those carpets knelt the ambassadors of twenty kings, vassals of the king of Choucan. The grandees of the State knelt at a greater distance, all profoundly inclined, and holding a finger to their lips.

"The princesses advanced up to the steel grating, with their eyes lowered and hands crossed over their breasts. Then one of the viziers, having shown to the assembly the seal of the king, inscribed in large characters on the parchment, read these words, in a loud voice:

"'Rezie and you, Gulzara, I have not thought it well to decide which of you two shall pass beyond the sharp spikes of steel that guard the royal seat. I make you the arbiters of your own fate. Reply: which is the more worthy of reigning – a virgin princess who marries, loves her husband, and provides heirs to the throne, or a virgin princess who, not marrying, has yet a whole multitude of sons and daughters whom she cherishes like the apple of her eye?'

"'Wise and reverend sires,' said Rezie, 'it must be clear to you that the king, when he propounded this strange question, wished to pass a jest upon us; and that it is only a woman chaste, and solely attached to her husband, who can be worthy to fill his throne. My sister doubtless thinks as I do, and we will reign together, if such be your good pleasure.'

"The viziers answered not a word. They turned towards Gulzara, who, with a modest mien, spoke thus: 'I think the king, our father, wished to intimate that a princess whose sole desire is to be the mother of her subjects, who thinks rather of making them happy during her lifetime than of providing them with masters after her death, and who has no other care save the public good, that such a princess is most worthy of being queen. I promise never to marry, and to have no children save my people.'

"Scarcely had she uttered these words than the four viziers, having impetuously opened the door of the steel grating, threw themselves at her feet, crying, with all the strength of their lungs: 'Honour and glory to Gulzara, Queen of Choucan! Happy for ever be Gulzara our Queen!'

"The ambassadors and grandees repeated these acclamations in even louder tones, so that their shouts reached the people assembled before the palace. These latter made the air resound with their cries, at the same time beating one another without mercy. Blows, cuffs, even dagger thrusts, passed freely on all sides. The hubbub was so horrible that I should have been frightened if I had been susceptible to fear. 'What does this mean?' said I, in a low voice, to Gehanguz. 'Have all these people gone mad?'

"'No, no,' he replied; 'they are only doing what they ought to do. Here it is customary, when any great and happy event takes place, to engraven it on the popular memory after this manner. Recollection is thereby greatly quickened. Fortunate are those who, on such occasions, have lost an eye, or a limb! Their family is then regarded as really zealous for the public good; and children, seeing upon their fathers such honourable scars, glory in them from generation to generation. Indeed, the custom is sound and salutary, for the people are ever fickle and forgetful, and would keep nothing in mind unless some special means were taken to jog their memory.'

"Meanwhile the four viziers had displayed to the whole divan the writing of the king, showing that Gulzara had answered according to his intentions, and ought to be made queen. She was accordingly installed formally upon the throne, at the foot of which Rezie came to do homage, with a smile that seemed to the assembly generally a smile of congratulation, but that to my eyes showed only as a mask for spite and disappointment. The new queen assured her sister of her love – then raising her own right hand three times above her head to command attention, she said: 'Venerable councillors of my father, I shall never undertake anything of importance without your advice; but who will serve as an intermediary in our communications, and inform you of my decisions? Who will enter with me into such details as are necessary for the good of the State? I am a virgin, and I have promised to remain so, always. Daily intercourse with a man would in no way be convenient. I declare, therefore, that Homaïouna, whose ability and competence are well known to me, shall be my grand vizier; and I ordain that she shall be invested with all the powers appertaining to that office.'

"The four old councillors, the twenty ambassadors, and the grandees of the kingdom, all acquiesced unanimously. Gehanguz came, trembling with joy, and led me to the first step of the royal dais. All spoke my praises in a loud voice – not one of them having the least knowledge of me. Then Rezie, no longer able to contain herself, asked permission to retire, and whispered in my ear as she passed: 'This is another new trick of yours, vile slave; you shall pay dearly for your presumption and insolence!' I pretended not to hear the threat or the insult, deciding to hide them from Gulzara, whom they would only have grieved and alarmed. Indeed, I was filled with admiration for that amiable princess, having received no previous intimation of the generous engagement into which she had entered for the good of her people.

"'Why, my queen,' said I, when we were alone, 'why have you promised not to marry? It would surely have sufficed if you had merely replied according to the views of the king, your father.'

"'The sacrifice was not so great as you imagine, my dear Homaïouna. But more I cannot tell you. To go into details would but envenom the wound still bleeding in my heart; and we must devote our attention to other matters. I feel that in you there is something above nature; and it is on you that all the weight of kingship must devolve. Rule in my empire; and, if I am at all dear to you, so rule that my reign shall be famous to all time for justice and good government. The hope of living with glory in the memory of men will comfort me for having lived my life among them unhappily.'

"I respected Gulzara's secret, and succeeded, even beyond her hopes, in fulfilling the wishes she had formed for her people's good. All India resounded with her name. The prosperity of her Empire was the admiration and envy of all kings. The twenty princes, her vassals, insisted on paying a double tribute, and mostly brought their tribute to the capital in person. Bands of musicians were constantly posted on the beautiful terraced roofs of the palaces of the great in Choucan, and there they sang the praises of the queen, or played loud and lively music, to which the people danced. All this contributed to Gulzara's gaiety. As to Gehanguz, he could not contain himself for joy, and blessed the day when he had come across me.

"For five years my efforts had been thus successful, and I was congratulating myself on having, at last, made so many people happy, when, one day, the zealous eunuch entered my apartment looking utterly terrified and bewildered. 'Homaïouna,' said he, 'come quickly to the queen. She has quite lost her wits. She laughs and cries at the same time, passes from a transport of joy to the extremity of despair, and shows every symptom of complete mental derangement. Ah! we are lost! Rezie will wish to govern. The great fabric of happiness which you have erected in Choucan, and my own little masterpiece of good government in the harem, will alike fall to pieces. Oh, unhappy day! Oh, day for ever marked with a black sign! Why did I not die before seeing its baleful light?'

"I did not trouble to answer Gehanguz; I made haste to follow him. Gulzara ran to meet me with wild eyes. Seizing my hand, she cried: 'He is come! He is not dead! His lovely eyebrows alone were burned, and his hair singed! But eyebrows and hair have grown again, magnificent as ever, and he asks to see me! What unforeseen happiness! Ah no! what an overwhelming misfortune,' continued she, throwing herself on a sofa and shedding a torrent of tears. 'I have renounced him for ever! Alas, I did not do so for want of love, but because I loved him too well! What is to become of me? Advise me, Homaïouna! Perhaps I shall follow your advice – perhaps you will lose my favour by giving it me!'

"'Calm yourself, my queen,' said I, 'and explain. I don't understand what you mean, nor do I know of whom you are speaking.'

"'True,' she rejoined, 'I have never told you about Prince Tograi, my mother's nephew – Prince Tograi whom I have cherished from my earliest infancy; who responded to my love with all his heart; who was said to have perished in a great fire; and who now returns, now when, faithful to his memory, I have promised never to marry. What will he say?'

"'He will,' I replied, 'be overwhelmed doubtless with grateful feelings when he knows that the sacrifice – vaunted everywhere as an act of unspeakable generosity – was really made for his sake; and, if worthy of you, he will applaud you greatly.'

"'You speak coldly and calmly, wise Homaïouna,' rejoined the queen. 'You are as unendurable snow to the fire burning in my heart! Retire, and do you, Gehanguz, at once introduce the Prince Tograi.'

"I obeyed, condemning myself, even more than Gulzara did, for having tried to make head against the assault of a passion so violent and overwhelming, instead of allowing somewhat for its first fury.

"During three hours – the saddest hours passed since my exile from Shadukan – I did nothing but sorrow over my amiable princess, and deplore the instability of the happiness I had thought to build on secure foundations. It was she herself who broke in upon my sad forebodings. She came to me open-armed, and began by flooding me with tears. At last, growing somewhat calmer, she said: 'I have come back to my senses, dear Homaïouna, but my deep grief will not pass away as easily as my fit of unreason. Listen, tremble, and pity me! The Prince Tograi appeared before my eyes looking as though he had just bathed in the Prophet Kedder's Spring of Immortality. He was radiant with beauty, youth and, as it seemed to me, with love. He threw himself on his knees to kiss the hem of my garment. I held out my hand, and would, I think, have kissed him, if the presence of Gehanguz, whom I had ordered to stand near by, had not restrained me. He read in my eyes the feelings of my heart; but instead of showing the loving gratitude of which you spoke a while ago, he began to upbraid me angrily. I forgave his first outburst. I tried to pacify him. I went so far as to offer to resign the crown of Choucan so that we might be united. I told him I must certainly renounce the throne if I infringed the solemn engagement into which I entered when I accepted it, but I protested truly that, with him, I should never regret my abdication. "And, indeed," I added, "how could I cherish my people like a tender and loving mother, when my husband was the sole object of my affection, and occupied all my thoughts? The fame I had earned," I told him, "was but a small alleviation to the grief caused by your loss.

Now that I possess you once more, I can well do without it." I feel,' continued the queen, addressing me, 'all the shame attaching to such a confession. But will you believe it, Homaïouna, the ungrateful Tograi dared to take advantage of my weakness. He was not afraid to unveil to my eyes a heart as black as the face of an Ethiopian. "What talk is this about abdicating the throne of the Empire of Choucan?" cried the arrogant prince. "Is it Gulzara, the queen, who holds such language – nay, who utters a rhapsody worthy of the hermits of the desert of Hejaz? Let us put all this rubbish aside, and talk seriously. If you have really sighed over my exile, if you love me as you say you do – place me at once on the blue throne with the phosphorescent stars. All your father's nonsense can in no way affect your right to the throne – the more so that you are in assured possession. That right I will maintain, and that possession I will confirm by my valour. Rivers of blood shall be made to flow before a word of reproach reaches your ears. All those who come near you will respect you, as they respect me. Whosoever occupies a throne is bound by no promises. Meanwhile, begin by getting rid of a wretched creature whom you have ridiculously appointed to be your Grand Vizier. She is suspected of being a witch, and is, perhaps, only artful and malicious – but that is quite reason enough for putting her into a sack, and throwing her into the river. Go, my well-beloved, and settle this at once; don't look so startled. Have you not waited all too long for the happiness you are to enjoy in my arms?" Tograi was quite right in saying I was startled and troubled. I felt as if I should die. But my horror at such impiety and insolence reanimated me. Instead of replying, I clapped my hands; Gehanguz whistled; and immediately fifty eunuchs appeared with their swords drawn. Yet, such is the marvellous power of a passion which shame itself cannot utterly destroy, that I took pity upon him, and said, rather firmly than angrily: "My mother's nephew, I give thee thy life in consideration of the ties of blood by which we are united. Go from my presence, and let me never see thee more, unless thou art prepared to undergo the punishment thou hast justly deserved, and be cut into a thousand pieces by these glittering swords." Having uttered these words, I made signs to the eunuchs to remove the unhappy prince. But they had to carry him out; so terrified was he that he could scarcely stand. For a whole hour I remained as if turned to stone on my divan. Then a crowd of quick and agonising thoughts coursed through my brain, and threw me into a kind of delirium. I thought I saw before me Tograi, amiable and compliant, as, when banished by my father, he came to say good-bye to me, seven years ago – and then that old Tograi vanished, and, behold, the new Tograi, overbearing and perfidious, took his place, and gave me advice, or rather commands, unrighteous and dishonourable. Never, never, Homaïouna, will these two images cease to haunt me. Death alone can deliver me from them; but I shall die worthy of your regrets. Nevertheless, listen, and observe these my orders; come every day, after the hour when the Divan has been held, and be a witness to my tears, and, if you will, mingle with those tears your own. See that Gehanguz makes the interior of my palace as sad and sombre as is my heart. I direct that my musicians sing and play doleful and dirge-like airs, and such airs only. I shall not cause all public rejoicings to cease; but whoever appears before me with a smile upon his lips will add to my pain.'

"I assured Gulzara that it would be to me a solace to mingle my tears with hers, and that she would be strictly obeyed; for I had resolved rather to cheat than openly combat her sorrow. The duties of her position furnished opportunities and means of distraction, which I did not neglect to utilise, and, without a fatal occurrence, I should perhaps have succeeded in restoring peace to that generous spirit.

"Rezie had retired to a palace she possessed on the top of a neighbouring mountain. She appeared rarely in the presence of her sister, and then only to play such parts of feigned affection as she had studied in solitude; while

Gulzara, who had not yet unmasked her real character, repaid her false attachment with genuine affection. It was long since the perfidious princess had made her appearance at Choucan, when, one day, her chief eunuch came, on her part, to ask for an audience. I wished to retire, but the queen kept me back. The messenger was introduced, and spoke thus: 'The Princess Rezie, whose seal of credence I here present, prostrates herself at your august feet, and recognises that your Highness has, by her superior lights, justly earned the throne to which she had herself aspired. Nevertheless, she ventures to ask, as some compensation, that you will suffer her to espouse the Prince Tograi, who now basks only in her presence, and who, moreover, stands in need of some consolation for the misfortune into which he has fallen – the misfortune namely of losing the good graces of his glorious sovereign. The uncertainty in which my princess stands with regard to the nature of your reply keeps her in a state of cruel anxiety, and the prince himself does not dare to appear in your presence. Without these obstacles, they would both have come to ask you, on their knees, to graciously accomplish the common desire of their hearts.'

"On seeing the pallor that had overspread the countenance of Gulzara, and the heaving of her breast, I saw she was about to faint. I told the fatal eunuch to leave us, and wait in the neighbouring gallery for a reply to his message. Gehanguz, who, like myself, had taken immediate alarm, at once put him out, and was just in time to help me in holding up the queen, as she fell into my arms. We had no wish to cause her enemies to triumph, and so did what was necessary without calling for help. She remained senseless for some time. At last she opened her eyes, turned them sadly on me, and said, after some moments of silence, and with a fairly tranquil air: 'What shall I do, Homaïouna?'

"'What the generosity of your heart dictates,' I replied.

"'But my sister,' she rejoined, 'could not be happy with a man so depraved, and my people would most certainly, at a day which cannot be far distant, be most miserable.

106

Should I not save them all, while I am yet able, by causing Tograi's head to be immediately cut off? I tremble at being reduced to such an extremity; but here, as it seems to me, cruelty is a necessary evil. What do you say, Homaïouna?'

"'It belongs to Allah alone,' I answered, 'to rule the present in view of the future, for he only sees the future unclouded.'

"'You would have me then give my consent to this odious union,' said she, in a voice choked by emotion. 'Very well, let me do this further violence to my heart. But the blow will be mortal. Go, Gehanguz, go, and carry a favourable reply to my sister's request, and to her...' She did not conclude, but uttered a sad and piercing cry, and fell back senseless on her divan.

"We were now no longer able to hide her condition. The twelve leeches in attendance were summoned. They all felt the pulse of the unconscious Gulzara at the places where the pulse is most marked. I was plunged in the most agonised uncertainty, till these birds of evil omen croaked the cruel words: 'She sleeps, she sleeps for ever!' They spoke but too truly, Gulzara had just expired.

"It is impossible to depict the sorrow I felt at this terrible catastrophe; and my grief was all the greater in that I thought I had myself to blame for the premature demise of the amiable Gulzara. 'Fool that I was,' said I to myself, 'I spurred this too generous princess to an effort beyond her powers, and thereby hastened to its end her useful life. I do not yet understand the violence of human passion, or the infirmity of human reason; and yet I wish to govern men! O bitter experience, which has cost me a friend almost as dear as Ganigul herself and her fatal bird! But should I have allowed her to soil her conscience with the blood of a prince whose only fault was ambition, and whose designs Allah could have made to be as dust blown before the wind! Should I have suffered her so to act that her sister could accuse her of mean jealousy, and that she herself would be humiliated in the eyes of her subjects? O fair and radiant soul, now receiving the reward of virtue in the company of heavenly Intelligences, forgive the excess of my zeal! Thou shalt live, as thou didst desire to live, in the memories of men, and never to the end of time shall thy sweet and lovely image fade from my heart.'

"Absorbed in these thoughts, I was kneeling beside the royal bed, which I was watering with my tears, when Rezie's eunuch, having rudely struck me on the shoulder, said: 'What are you doing here, too brazen Homaïouna? Why have you not, like your companions, retired to your own apartment? It is the rule here that the slaves of the sleeping queen should be confined to their rooms till she is borne to the place of her long rest. Come, follow me; you have ceased to be Grand Vizier. You are no more than a vile and dangerous slave.'

"I rose at once, and followed the eunuch without answering a word. He caused food for three days to be brought to me, said a few more rude things, and took great care to see that my door was secured. I could easily have braved him, and escaped out of his hands, but I was curious to see what Rezie would do with me. I wished also to take public part in the funeral of Gulzara. Moreover, the sounds of lamentation, which I heard on all sides, were as a balm to my own grief.

"'She is sleeping, our good queen is sleeping,' cried unnumbered voices, 'and she will never wake again. She who was our mother is asleep, and perhaps Homaïouna, who did us so much good, will slumber likewise!' These sad words, ceaselessly repeated round and about the palace, echoed in my ears during three days. On the morning of the fourth day, the same eunuch who had shut me up in my apartment came, bringing with him a long robe of red silk, striped with black, and a thick veil of the same colours, and, having himself dressed me in them, said: 'This is the mourning worn by the personal slaves of Gulzara. You will lead the women – that is the place of honour assigned to you. Similarly Gehanguz will lead the eunuchs. The two bands will be placed, one to the right, and the other on the left of the equipage which is to convey the sleeping queen to the plain of tranquillity. Follow me!'

"We proceeded to the great court of the palace, in the centre of which stood a litter of sandalwood, drawn by four black unicorns. Amid the strident strains of a thousand lugubrious instruments of music, and the cries, even yet more piercing, of the inhabitants of Choucan, the body of Gulzara was placed on this litter, and over her was spread a pall of cloth of silver, while the gracious countenance of the lovely princess – who indeed appeared to be only sleeping – was left uncovered.

"Several persons on horseback, singularly accoutred, and bearing in their hands what looked like sceptres of white agate, ordered the procession. At once we began to move forward; but the flowers strewn upon our way in ever-increasing quantities – for the people never ceased to throw them in large basketfuls – made our progress extremely slow. At last we reached a silent and solitary plain, where, by order of succession, were ranged the tombs of the kings and queens of Choucan since unnumbered ages. The aspect of the place was strange and striking. Only the domes of the tombs were visible, and these domes were of black marble, highly polished, and from each protruded a large number of golden pipes. All save the domes was under-ground, and we descended by an easy declivity to a vault of seemingly limitless extent. As an infinite number of perfumed wax tapers made this gloomy place as light as day, I looked on all sides for the doors of the tombs whose domes I had admired outside. But I could see none. I perceived at last that each tomb was walled in, and marked with a great slab of gold, on which these words were graven: 'Here lies such and such a king. He reigned so many years. Let no one dare to touch this wall, or trouble his repose. His memory alone is at the mercy of the people.'

"We had to go a very long way before reaching the tomb assigned to Gulzara; and we entered it, without disturbing the order of our procession, through a very large door, which had just been removed. The internal walls were covered with the same black marble that we had seen outside; but a quantity of little golden lamps, suspended from the dome, shed a pure bright light, and diffused a delightful perfume.

"The litter was placed in the midst of this vast sepulchre. The viziers, the twenty ambassadors, and the grandees of the State came, one after the other, and prostrated themselves before the sleeping queen, wishing her a pleasant repose. Tograi himself, the iniquitous Tograi, dared to fulfil this pious duty, but he presented himself last, and stammered his complimentary words with a haggard and troubled look. I shuddered as I looked upon him, and felt greatly tempted to punish his temerity, when an old man, pale, fleshless, and sinister of aspect, cried out with a shrill, harsh voice: 'Homaïouna, and you, Gehanguz, be it known to you that the wise viziers who govern Choucan during this short interregnum have decreed that, as you were the two favourite slaves of Gulzara, you must keep her company. Be duly grateful for the honour shown to you, and fail not in respect for your queen.'

"Having said these words, and produced some most lamentable sounds out of a brazen trumpet, he resumed, in tones even more dismal and lugubrious: 'The queen Gulzara is in the bosom of eternal rest. Suffer her to sleep, and let all due honour be paid to her.'

"I scarcely heard these last words, so utterly confounded was I by the dread sentence that had preceded them! All the assistants had retired, and the door had almost been bricked up, and still I had not cast one glance at poor Gehanguz, whereas his faithful and loving heart was only afflicted on my behalf. He was the first to break the silence, crying: 'Oh, Gulzara! oh, my beloved mistress, here is your dearly loved Homaïouna, the divine damsel who has made your subjects so happy – here is she immured for ever! You wished to save her: I was to have taken her out of your kingdom. Alas! you never anticipated falling so suddenly asleep!'

"'Is it then,' said I very quietly to Gehanguz, 'an established custom in Choucan to bury people alive?'

"'Yes, yes,' he replied. 'It is one of those absurd and cruel customs which the people of Choucan have taken it into their heads for ages to call sacred and venerable: it is a compliment they pay to the most faithful servants of their kings and queens, a distinction, be it said, with which those upon whom the so-called honour happens to fall would very willingly dispense. I have always thought the custom barbarous, and unworthy of an intelligent people; but the lamps of love and gratitude, to which we owe the lovely light now shining here – that at least is a fine conception!'

"'Explain yourself,' cried I.

"'You have seen,' said he, 'all the golden pipes that bristle on the dome of each tomb. Well, they answer to the lamps suspended within, and, by a curious contrivance, are used to feed those lamps with oil, and supply them with wicks. The cost of these is not defrayed by the State. It is defrayed by the people in their gratitude. When they have lost a good king or a good queen, men and women, old and young, are eager to maintain in his or her tomb such an illumination as you see here. Their zeal, in this respect, is more or less lively according to the benefits received, and is maintained from father to son. There is, you must know, an aperture at the top of each dome, and in that aperture a mirror of polished metal. Looking into this one may see, in some of the tombs, the lamps still burning, though the king has been asleep for several centuries, while in the greater number of tombs the lamps have long gone out. There are even some unjust sovereigns who have found themselves in total darkness at the end of two or three days, for their favourites, wicked as themselves, were necessarily ungrateful, and never thought of supplying the wicks and oil they might owe to their benefactors. It is with reason, therefore, that these lamps are called the Lamps of Love and Gratitude, and the brilliant mirror of polished metal, the Eye of Justice. Oh! we are never likely to find ourselves in darkness here. The tomb of Gulzara, thanks to all your cares, will shine resplendent till the day of judgment!'

"I was so touched with the sentiments of Gehanguz, and with the holy calm that reigned over his countenance in a moment so terrible, and when all human help seemed altogether hopeless, that, wrapping myself up in pious thoughts, I addressed this prayer to Asfendarmod from the very bottom of my heart: 'Sovereign of Shadukan the blessed, you who, as a reward for your zeal in the cause of the holy Prophet, are able to hear the voice of your subjects in whatsoever part of the world they may happen to be, vouchsafe to grant to your unhappy daughter the power of saving this honest and generous creature. I know by experience that I have lost the faculty of affording any active help to others save the help of counsel and care, but oh! grant me your aid, at this time, so that Gehanguz may not die in this place a lingering and cruel death.'

"Suddenly, in a moment, I was filled with that feeling of confidence which, in beings of our nature, is always a presage of success. I went up to the eunuch, and said, taking him by the hand: 'Your pious resignation and serenity are about to be rewarded. Take firm hold of me, and have no fear.'

"Scarcely had I said these words, when, the dome opening above our heads, I sprang upward, and, in accordance with my wish, found myself, together with the eunuch, at the gates of Ormuz. 'Here you are in safety,' said I to him. 'Remember the Peri Homaïouna, and ever continue to be beneficent and just.'

"The surprise and astonishment of Gehanguz prevented him from replying, and I must have been far away indeed before he would sufficiently recover to open his lips. As for me, I took flight back to Choucan. I wished to know what had become of Rezie and Tograi. I wished – but the night is already far spent," said my wife, interrupting herself. "I will finish my story at greater leisure. We will now discuss your own affairs, and then take some rest. Suffice it to say that Rezie and Tograi were never united:

on the contrary, they came to hate one another cordially, and were mutually destructive. I had left them a long time, and wandered through various countries, and been the witness of a thousand calamities – in which, however, I took no part – when, after visiting the mountains of Daghestan, I met you in the streets of Berdouka. You pleased me, notwithstanding the wildness of your looks: a feeling to which I had so far been a stranger took possession of my heart. You know the rest, and whether I have kept the promises I then made. I had often, while in Shadukan, read the annals of the Jinns, and, as soon as you spoke of the fatal cupboard, I knew what it contained. But I could think of no just means of inclining your father to give his decision in your favour, till the little fish, which you caught, provided an expedient. A Jinn was hidden in that vile shape, a Jinn who, for his crimes, had been thus transformed by Asfendarmod. His restoration to his own form offered great difficulties. It was first necessary that the fish should be caught, and this was not easy, owing to the smallness of its size, and its great weight, so that it always either slipped through the meshes of the nets, or else broke them. It was then necessary that the indwelling spirit should be squeezed out of the fish, while still alive, and without injury. Being aware of all this I effectually liberated the Jinn; and, as he had sworn to fulfil any wish uttered in favour of whomsoever should eat the little fish from whose body he had been happily delivered, I urged Ormossouf to eat the fish, and afterwards induced you all three to make vows in Ormossouf's favour – vows which you alone did not afterwards seek to revoke. Thus you have deserved to ascend the throne which one of your ancestors lost through not following the advice of a Peri who protected him, and who, as some consolation, gave him the wonderful ring contained in the leaden box – at the same time telling him that one of his descendants would open the box, and regain possession of the throne of Daghestan. The tradition of this promise passed from father to son for several generations, but every effort to open the box had proved ineffectual. At last your father, who had vainly made the attempt himself, resolved, on the advice of Alsalami, to give it to the one of his sons who should display the most filial piety.

"Those are the facts, with which it is right you should be made acquainted; and now this is what you ought to do. So soon as Ormossouf and the dervise are up, you will apprise them of your intentions, and ask them to give you their blessings, and then make your way to Berdouka, with the ring on your left finger. You will thus enter, without being seen by anyone, into the king's garden. At the bottom of the garden you will find the trunk of a large tree, which no one has ever been able to destroy. Touch the tree with your ring. It will at once fly open, and you will find therein a bag made of a serpent's skin – of which you will take possession. The bag contains an assortment of gems more brilliant than any in Shadukan; bring these gems to me, and I will go and sell them wheresoever I am most likely to find the best market.

"With the money so obtained, we shall have no difficulty in enlisting the services of the hillmen in Daghestan, who indeed are attached to your family, and hate the usurper. Thus will you be able, as becomes a prince, to take possession of your kingdom at the head of an army."

END OF THE STORY OF THE PERI HOMAÏOUNA

Here Homaïouna ceased speaking; and I, utterly confounded, and indeed terrified, by the marvels she had related, knelt down again at her feet, assuring her of my unbounded respect, and limitless obedience. This seemed not to please her at all. She asked, with tears in her eyes, whether what I now knew about her had in any way altered my affection. Then I kissed her. We retired to bed; and I made believe to sleep, so that I might, without interruption, consider my position; a position, no doubt, infinitely superior to any for which I could have dared to hope; and yet I was in despair. "What," said I to myself, "shall I gain by being king? It is this most redoubtable Peri, and not I, who will really bear rule in my kingdom. She will want to treat me as she treated the Queen of Choucan, and insist on my doing all her behests, even though I should die for it! What do I care about the public good, regarding which she prates so much? My own private good is the one thing I have at heart, and *that* I shall never secure with her. Well enough if she confined herself to advice and reproaches – mere words I could treat with contempt – but, though she speaks modestly enough of what remains of her former supernatural powers, she may be deceiving me, even as I am deceiving her. She may still have in reserve her terrible wand. She made no mention of it in her story about Gulzara, but then that story is not yet finished. I must hear her tale to the end, so as to lay this most cruel doubt. Ah! better a hundred times to remain a poor fisherman than to be a slave upon a throne!"

The storm had not ceased raging in my evil heart when day appeared. I was about to curse its light, and might indeed have done so with very good reason, for it was by that day's light that I took the first steps leading to the abyss in which we now are.

I used all my powers of hypocrisy so as to hide my perturbation of spirit from my wife, my father, and the dervise, and left them offering up, on my behalf, prayers, which I have always taken good care to render vain.

On my way to Berdouka, I met several persons whom I knew very well, and as not one of them seemed to see me, I began to feel in my ring a confidence which had so far been wanting. I entered with some assurance into the king's garden, and ran to the tree Homaïouna had described. I touched it. It opened, and I took out the bag of serpent-skin. I was so impatient to behold the incomparable Shadukan gems that I could not wait till I was out of the garden. I took them from the bag one after the other, and, though half blinded by their brilliancy, examined them again and again. They were sixteen in number: four diamonds, four carbuncles, four emeralds and four rubies, each of the size of a Khoten orange.

To contemplate them at greater leisure, I placed them on the grass in an unfrequented alley to which I had retired, and was in an ecstasy of joy and admiration when a dwarf, who was perched on a tree, and whom I had not observed, leapt toward me. I had only just time to return my treasures to the bag, and hurry away, the dwarf, meanwhile, in great agitation, peering about under the grass, and scratching the earth with his nails. He cried at last: "Alas! the resplendent vision has disappeared! But it may return. I will go and fetch my beautiful princess – if some Jinn be about, playing his pranks, he will not refuse to gratify her with such a lovely sight." Speaking thus he sped towards the palace, so light of foot that the grass and flowers scarce bent beneath his tread.

Clearly I had rendered the gems visible by suffering them to leave my hand, and I was frightened at the possible consequences of this act of imprudence. I thought the best thing I could do was to get out of the garden as soon as possible; but, as I was a long way from the gate by which I had entered, I had time to think – though I sped along quickly enough: "Where am I going? Shall I venture to place these inestimable gems in a woman's hand? Even supposing that my wife is above her sex's passion for jewellery, supposing she faithfully brings back to me the price she obtains for them, what good shall I derive from the purchase of a throne on which I shall sit loaded with her chains? No! Far better sell them myself and indulge freely in all pleasures and delights – better far to live forgotten but happy, in some obscure corner of the earth! It is to be hoped that Homaïouna may not discover my place of retreat. She does not know everything; still less does she know all she would like to know. I will go down to the port. I will enter, invisible, into the first ship that sails hence. I can be quite happily without bidding good-bye to the Peri, Ormossouf and Alsalami. Enough that the one should have inflicted upon me her exhortations, and the other his gout – while as to the third, he is of no account. I shall not regret one of them.

116

While indulging in these reflections, I perceived that I had lost my way among the garden walks, which formed a kind of labyrinth. What was my surprise at finding myself once more close to the place where I had discovered the precious gems; and I now heard the accursed dwarf screaming to a whole crowd of eunuchs who were following him: "Yes – this is the spot where I saw those marvels, I saw them with my two eyes, I swear it by my own tiny soul, and by the great heart of the Princess Gazahidé, my dear mistress."

On this I was going to fly, when a young beauty, more dazzling than my diamonds, my rubies, my emeralds and my carbuncles, pressed forward through the throng, and with an air of wilfulness that became her well, and was not without dignity, cried: "Silence, all! and listen to the commands of the daughter of your king, the Princess Gazahidé! Be it known to you that I firmly believe all that the little Calili has just told us: cease, therefore, to treat him as a mere visionary. I insist on seeing the precious stones which the Jinn had spread out upon the grass, and I shall compel the Jinn to show them me by all such persistent means as my curiosity may dictate. Come, erect a pavilion for me on this very spot – I shall not leave it till I have obtained sight of the gems. If any of you says a single word of objection, I will give him cause for repentance. If the objection comes from my father, I will take vengeance upon him by refusing to wear in my hair the aigrette of blue flowers he likes so well!"

While Gazahidé spoke, my eyes were fixed on hers, my soul seemed ready to take to itself wings to fly to her. Nor did I regain my presence of mind – so was I intoxicated with love – till I saw that her attendants were preparing to satisfy her caprice. Then did all the tremors of an anticipated delight go coursing through my frame. I leant against a tree at a little distance, fully determined, at all hazards, to personate the imaginary Jinn.

Standing thus, I grew impatient at the dilatoriness with which the eunuchs prepared the pavilion, and would, most willingly, have torn in pieces all the ornaments with which they slowly decorated it. She had said she wished to be left alone, and by the orders of the king, who had done nothing but laugh at her whims, every wish of hers was to be satisfied. It was about the middle of a fine summer day; but the heat was tempered by the thick umbrage of the trees, and by gauze curtains that interrupted such of the sun's rays as would have done more than diffuse a soft and voluptuous light.

I had again to keep my soul in patience while jars of excellent sherbet, and basins of comfits and ginger, were presented to Gazahidé, with a lengthy ceremonial. She partook of these dainties very quickly, so as the sooner to be quit of her eunuchs, and slave girls. They retired at last; and to such a distance that they could only have come to the help of their young mistress if summoned in very loud tones.

I went forward on tiptoe, I warily raised the curtains and entered into this paradise of delights. Gazahidé lay at full length on the too happy divan, and my greedy eyes feasted their full on her fair proportions and delicate limbs. My emotion was such that I could scarcely stand. I had thrown myself on the ground not far from the princess, when, raising herself suddenly, she put her little white hands together, and cried: "Oh, Jinn, mighty Jinn, who has shown thy precious gems to my dwarf, refuse not, I pray, to grant the same favour unto me."

Scarcely had she uttered these words, when I placed on the ground a carbuncle whose rays would have put to shame the rays of the sun. Gazahidé's surprise was so great that, fearing lest she should cry aloud, I whispered: "Admire in silence what is less beautiful than yourself."

She smiled, and, emboldened by my flattering words, advanced, precipitately, to take hold of the carbuncle, which I, as rapidly, withdrew.

"Oh, heavens!" cried she, "I did not mean to steal it; I only wanted to hold it in my hands for an instant. You speak passionate words to me, but ah! you are cruel!"

"No, Queen of Beauty," I replied, "I am far from desiring to give you pain; but you can only touch these precious stones on one condition – and that I will tell you after I have placed them all, and all together, before your eyes. Lie down again, therefore, on your divan, and have patience for a few moments."

Gazahidé obeyed me with an air of respect, and even of fear. Then I arranged the jewels in a square, placing them in such juxtaposition that each should add to each a new lustre; and this I did, hiding them the while with the skirt of my robe, so that all might be uncovered at once.

I had every reason to repent of the effect of the spectacle thus presented to the amiable Gazahidé. She was so dazzled and bewildered that she fell backward on her divan, and looked as if life itself had flown. Frightened in turn, I ran towards her, first taking the precaution to replace my treasures in the serpent-skin bag, which I attached to my belt. I found her pale, with her eyes closed, and deprived of all power of motion. But how lovely she was in that state! I opened her dress to give her air. . . . I was quite beside myself, when, reviving from her trance, she cried: "Who has dared to touch me?"

"It is the Jinn Farukrouz, who has come to your help," I replied.

"Ah!" she rejoined, in softer accents, "your name is not so fair as your jewels! But where are they? Tell me what I must do to obtain leave to hold them in my hands, one after the other; and, above all, do not show them to me all at once, for fear of accidents."

"For each one you must give me a kiss," I replied, in a voice trembling with fear and hope.

"What! no more than that!" she said. "Oh! most willingly. The kiss of a spirit will be as the breath of the wind blown from the evening star; it will cool my lips and rejoice my heart."

I did not ask her to repeat a permission so delicious. My kiss was a long one. She accepted it with a kind of agreeable impatience, and was about to complain of an ardour which she had so little expected, when I placed in her hand a ruby, whose brilliant hue harmonised with the charming blush my kiss had raised upon her cheeks. She turned the stone over and over, with an abstracted air, and then, giving it back to me, said: "Let me now have an emerald of the same value."

As I gave her the second kiss, I pressed her in my arms so closely that she gave a start, and said, with some emotion in her voice: "Farukrouz, as you are palpable, you can doubtless make yourself visible. Ah! I would rather see you yourself than your precious stones!"

I had too high an opinion of my own face and figure to be bashful about showing them, and, moreover, I had that day donned my best attire. I therefore removed the ring from the little finger of my left hand; and, as I saw that the first glance Gazahidé cast upon me was favourable, I immediately took her back into my arms. At first she returned my caresses with a very good grace; suddenly she violently shook herself free, and cried out in great wrath: "Go! you are a rough and a wicked Jinn; go away! I won't listen to another word about your precious stones; if you are so bold as to come near me again, I shall call out with all my might."

This threat made me tremble. My invisibility was not like that of the Peri, whose body became not only invisible but impalpable, so that no obstacle could arrest its movements. I could be imprisoned, and in various ways made to perish. During a few moments I remained thoughtful and silent; but the danger in which I stood, and the love still burning within me, sharpened my wits, and I cried: "O daughter of the king, O fairest of earthly women! I see it is now time to reveal the glory and happiness to which you are destined. Be reassured, and listen to me. You will then do me justice, and become more kindly and sweet than the Leiki, whose grace and sensibility you possess."

"Speak," said she eagerly; "I will give you all my attention. But seat yourself at the other end of the divan, and, above all, don't touch me."

Then, with Homaïouna's marvellous story still fresh in my memory, I began the following recital of my own imaginary adventures:-

"You have doubtless heard tell of the great Asfendarmod, monarch of Shadukan, and sovereign over all the Peris, Jinns and Dives who have existed either before, or after, the Preadamite kings. Well, I am his son, his favourite son, in whom he had placed his full confidence. He gave into my charge two of my sisters who are as flighty as the bulbul, and unruly as the zebra, and directed me never to lose sight of them. In order to facilitate my task, he had removed their wings, and shut them up in a tower – of which I safely held the key. A friendly Jinn took it into his head to deliver them, and set to work for that purpose with considerable cunning. We had been, he and I, on terms of great friendship for a long time, and were accustomed to spend whole days together. For half-a-moon he kept away from me, and when I reproached him, on the occasion of our first meeting, he only answered my reproaches with a deep sigh. My friendship took alarm; I pressed him to open his heart.

"'Ah!' cried he, at last, 'only a Peri, nay, only the son of Asfendarmod himself, is worthy of her. I am mad to have lost so much time in contemplating her charms! Yes, dear Farukrouz,' continued he, 'the Princess Gazahidé, only daughter to the King of Daghestan, ought to belong to you and to none other. I saw her emerging from her bath like the sun rising from the bosom of the sea; a portion of her hair, pure gold and like to rays of blinding light, still floated in the transparent waters, while the remaining locks enriched her ivory forehead; her eyes of a tint more lively and brilliant than the azure of the firmament, were agreeably shaded by the tiny threads of black silk that went to form her delicate eyebrows and long eyelashes; her nose suited well the little portals of supple coral that neighboured it – little portals that enclosed the loveliest pearls of the Sea of Golconda. As to the remainder of her charms, do not expect me to describe them: I saw naught because I saw too much. I only know that that perfect shape seemed to have come straight from the studio of the celebrated Mani, who had not forgotten to add the lovely hues of life to a form whiter than snow.'

"This portrait, which, as I have since discovered, was in no wise flattering, inflamed me to such a point that I cried: 'Ah! cease to torment me, my cruel friend! you know that I cannot abandon the care of my sisters, who at every moment ask me for some new thing. Wherefore, then, inflame me thus? Yes, I burn to see Gazahidé, but alas! how can I?'

"'Go, my dear Farukrouz,' said the Jinn, in tones of affection; 'go and satisfy a desire that is so natural. *I* will remain in the tower, and do the behests of the daughters of Asfendarmod, who will never know that you have left them under my care. Give me the keys, and go.'

"Madcap that I was, I accepted the offer of the false and malicious Jinn. I took my flight hither. What he had told me of your charms was so true that I never entertained a suspicion of his treachery, and thus he had full leisure to escape with my sisters before I thought of returning to Shadukan. I was looking at you; I was following your steps; I was altogether forgetting my own existence; when, suddenly, the whirlwinds that execute my father's commands seized upon me, bore me hence, and placed me at the foot of his throne. Asfendarmod heaped upon me the reproaches I deserved, and, in the first fury of his indignation, condemned me to remain a hundred years among men in the shape you now behold – but without depriving me of my invisibility. More afflicted because I had offended him than because of the punishment to which I was condemned, I embraced his knees, and watered them with my tears. He read in my heart, and was touched by my filial affection: 'Unhappy Farukrouz,' he said, 'I cannot revoke my sentence, but I will make thy lot more endurable. As Gazahidé is the cause of thy disgrace, so shall she be its consolation. Go, go to her once more; gain her love; marry her; and tell her that, for wedding gift, I allow her to retain, unimpaired, her beauty and her youth, during the hundred years she will live with thee!'

"After speaking these words, he gave me the jewels you have seen, promised me his help on due occasion, and caused me to be borne hither. The fear of alarming you by a too sudden apparition suggested the thought of first awaking your dwarf's curiosity, and so exciting your own. I succeeded, and should now be altogether satisfied, if only you had loved me enough to take me as your husband before learning my history."

Gazahidé had listened to this rhapsody of mine with such marks of credulity and admiration as afforded me the liveliest pleasure. She came nearer when I finished speaking, and, taking my two hands in hers, said: "My dear Lord, do not doubt of my love. The first look you cast upon me gave you the possession of my heart; but I have a good father, to whom respect is due, and in that respect I must not be found wanting. He alone can dispose of me. Let me direct Calili to go for him at once. He will be transported with joy when he hears of the honour you propose to do me. All will be settled according to your wishes, and in a manner conformable to the position of the son of Asfendarmod."

I had gone too far to turn back. Besides, I imagined that the King of Daghestan, like most of his fellows, would not be over-gifted with sense, and I hoped to impose upon him as easily as I had imposed on his daughter. She, therefore, with my consent, left the tent, and called loudly for Calili.

The dwarf ran up out of breath. "Well, my Princess," said he, "what have you seen? The jewels doubtless?"

"Go," she replied. "I have seen something much better than jewels; run and tell my father that happiness and wonders transcending all he can imagine await him here."

"What?" cried the dwarf, "have you seen anything more beautiful than what I saw myself? Oh! tell me what it is, dear mistress; tell me what it is, I conjure you, I cannot walk a step unless you satisfy my curiosity."

As he was repeating these words with a quite childish importunity, Gazahidé boxed his ears twice soundly, which caused him to run off so quickly that she could not help laughing with all her heart. She then called me – for I had made myself invisible before Calili – and, having asked me to entrust her with one of the carbuncles, told me to listen to the conversation she was about to hold with her father, and only show myself at the right moment.

At the sight of the king, and at the first words he uttered, I perceived that he could be easily gulled. He listened to my story, and considered my carbuncle with large astonished eyes and a mouth widely opened. Then he cried: "Oh, son of Asfendarmod! generous Farukrouz, appear! appear! Suffer me to pay you such honours and give you such thanks as are justly due. This very day you shall be the husband of Gazahidé, and to-morrow I will abdicate in your favour. I ask for no greater boon than to see my daughter always fair, young and happy – unless, indeed, you should be willing to add to your favours by prolonging my days so that I may behold the lovely children to be born of your union."

The sight of me did not in any way diminish the good monarch's predilection in my favour. My attire was not indeed magnificent, but the precious gems made up for any deficiency in that respect, I offered them as a wedding gift for his daughter; but he refused, saying that the carbuncle – which he would keep for the love of me – was of greater value than all the women in the world – a statement that caused Gazahidé to pout her lips very prettily.

We all returned to the palace. The eunuchs, on seeing me issue from the tent, were filled with fear and grimaced hideously; the slave girls, too, were somewhat scared, but soon reassured. As to Calili, whether from aversion, or some presentiment of evil, he always looked at me askance.

After having been bathed, perfumed, and clad in garments of great magnificence, I was married to Gazahidé, putting the while a veil upon the extravagance of my joy so as to maintain an air of dignity conformable to the splendour of my supposed origin. The remainder of the day was spent in regales, dances, and concerts, which amused me not at all, and in which my princess seemed to take but little pleasure. It was otherwise with the king. His satisfaction was huge. He played like a child with the pages and slave girls, and made the vaults of the chamber re-echo to the shouts of his laughter.

When he bade us good-night, he again told me that, on the morrow, he would resign to me his crown; but I asked him to defer the honour, and to suffer that I should spend three days in the harem, altogether devoted to my dear Gazahidé, and enjoying the pleasures of his royal company; and this he conceded, very graciously, and even with thanks. I had my reason for preferring the request. I was madly in love, and wished to enjoy my happiness, without interruption, during the three days in question, not doubting that Homaïouna would come and disturb it so soon as she knew of my adventures — adventures so contrary to what she had herself intended. But who can be quite happy while haunted with the fear of what he has only too richly deserved? I was seized with terrors in the very midst of my delights. At the slightest noise I was on the point of snatching myself from the arms of Gazahidé — fearing to be surprised by the incensed Peri. In short, those three days — which are yet the only days in my whole life that remain dear to my memory — passed in alternate transports of love and paroxysms of terror.

The fourth morning had scarce begun to show on the horizon when whole files of eunuchs came to conduct me to the divan. My heart beat. I was filled with the most dire presentiment, but could find no plausible excuse for futher delay. Nor would the king have brooked it. He had, with infinite trouble, composed and learned by heart a harangue in which my story was set out, and greatly amplified, and would have been afraid to trust his memory further. He delivered his address accordingly, to the amazement of his hearers, who never ceased looking at me all the time he was speaking. He was at last about to affix the royal plume to my turban, when an aged emir, whom I knew very well, approached, and spoke some words in his ear. The good monarch changed colour, said that he did not feel well, and broke up the assembly; and I was escorted back to the harem.

A few minutes afterwards Gazahidé was summoned to her father's apartment. She came back all in tears. "Ah! my beloved husband," said she, "a strange accusation is being made against you! The Emir Mohabed says that you are the son of the fisherman Ormossouf, that you used to come and sell your fish at his house, and that he has spoken to you a hundred times as you passed along the streets. He declares that your story is but a fable, and that your precious stones are all false, and only seem to be genuine by magic art – and, in a word, that you are an imposter, and upheld by some wicked Dive. My father is not altogether convinced, but he doubts; and he trembles, moreover, at the mere mention of Ormossouf, whom he knows to have a better right than himself to the throne of Daghestan – and whom, for that reason, he holds in execration. He was about to send to the good fisherman and have him arrested, together with all his family, and to subject them to a most rigorous examination, but I besought him to delay this order until to-morrow. I represented that, if you really were Farukrouz, you would never forgive such an outrage, that he would draw upon himself the vengeance of Asfendarmod, and make me miserable for the remainder of my days. I ended by assuring him that you loved me well enough to give me your entire confidence, and that whatever confession you might make to me would be fully imparted to him. Tell me, then, the whole truth, without hesitation, and place entire reliance both on my heart and my troth. If you really are Barkiarokh, the son of Ormossouf, I love you none the less, and I do not despair of so arranging matters that we may yet be happy."

I was myself too false to have faith in anyone; and I was very far from wishing to place myself at the mercy of my second wife – the power which my first wife exercised over me was too terrible for *that*. I was for the moment embarrassed, and Gazahidé renewed her entreaties in the tenderest manner – when, suddenly, an atrocious thought occurred to me, and seemed, in my utter perversion, to afford a means of escape. I affected confidence and security, and said to the princess, smiling: "I admire your prudence; you know that pleasures in the hand are worth more than pleasures in anticipation, and have been unwilling to resign those of to-day. I am far, indeed, from being of a contrary opinion, and it will not be my fault if we do not pass this day as pleasantly as the three which preceded it. Besides, if all the circumstances I relate to you – circumstances which you can, in turn, relate to your father to-morrow – fail to content him, he may, if he likes, consult every fisherman in Berdouka. In the end he will beg my pardon, and I shall forgive him for the love of you."

Like a rose well-nigh faded in the noonday heat, and into which a light cloud distils new freshness, so did Gazahidé breathe life from my words. Her cheeks resumed the sweet rose tints of their full beauty; her eyes sparkled with love and joy; I became more inflamed with love for her than ever. I returned, transported, all the caresses she lavished upon me, striving thus to make her forget the indignity to which, as she thought, I had been subjected; and every moment confirmed me in the resolution of doing my utmost not to lose the happiness I was then enjoying. The hours passed only too quickly. Towards evening the king, who, doubtless, did not dare to appear before me, sent the chief of his eunuchs to inquire how his daughter fared. She caused him to be informed, in reply, that she had never been better in her life, and that he might sleep in peace.

I had not forgotten my promise to give the princess a more circumstantial account of my history, but had deferred doing so till a time when I could frame it in such a manner as to further my designs. Shortly after we were in bed I began my story, but made it so absurd, so long, and so tiresome, that, as my intention was, I sent her to sleep, and should have gone to sleep myself – but dark plots are ever wakeful.

The night was far advanced when, after placing the ring

on my left hand, I took my way to the king's apartment, which I knew, as he had before conducted me thither. Calili the dwarf, and Gazahidé's other eunuchs, slept in her antechamber. Those who guarded the king himself watched in rows on either side of the entrance to his sleeping-room, which was closed by a curtain only. I passed noiselessly between the eunuchs, and found the venerable monarch plunged in the deepest slumber. By the light of the tapers illuminating the room, I applied a cushion to his counte-nance, and stifled him so adroitly that he never even exhaled a single sigh. I then arranged the body with the head drooping over the side of the bed, in such a way that any clots of blood found upon him might seem due to some natural accident, and retraced my steps, trembling. I was so distracted that, losing my way, I traversed two or three unknown corridors. At last, however, I succeeded in discovering where I was, and had come to Gazahidé's door, when, making a false step, I fell at full length upon the floor. Aghast at my fall, to which I attributed a supernatural cause, I whispered in low and fearful tones, "Oh! cruel Homaïouna, do not so soon subject me to your too terrible influence; let me at least, for a little while, enjoy the fruits of my crime!" I suffered, however, on that occasion, from nothing worse than fright. I picked myself up quickly, and went to lie down again by the princess, only keeping as far from her as possible, for fear lest she should wake, and perceive that I myself was not asleep.

I had had some fear that I might be troubled by remorse; but such was so far from being the case that I began to find excuses for my horrible deed – was it not right to defend my own life? And then I congratulated myself on possessing the love of the heiress to the throne, and so being sure of the throne itself.

Amid these reflections, I saw the day dawn without anxiety, and was in no wise alarmed by the cries that soon resounded through the harem. Gazahidé woke with a start, half rose, and then fell back upon the bed, senseless, on hearing of the sudden death of the king her father. Her slave girls, her eunuchs, utterly distraught, ran hither and thither in the palace. Calili alone remained near her, and helped me to try to bring her back to consciousness. For a long time our efforts proved vain; at last she opened upon me her beautiful eyes, as if to ask for my pity! I stretched out to her my perfidious arms; but, before I could clasp her to my breast, I received on my left side, which was uncovered, a terrible blow from the fatal wand. It struck me prostrate, and, rolling on the ground, I cried like a mad creature: "Cursed be thy existence, O infamous Barkiarokh! Cursed be thy perversity, thy hypocrisy, thy ingratitude to Homaïouna, and thy wicked perfidy towards the innocent Gazahidé! Cursed above all be thy ring, which, by making thee invisible, has favoured the perpetration of this thy last crime! May the earth open to swallow up the murderer of his sleeping sovereign, of the venerable old man who had adopted thee as his son! Ah! let me, at least, with my teeth, tear in pieces these horrible hands by which he was done to death, and thus avenge outraged Nature!"

Shrieking out these furious imprecations, I bit my arms, I beat my head upon the floor, and my blood flowed freely, while Gazahidé, as if turned to stone, looked upon me, not hindering.

After about half-an-hour thus spent in agony, the terrible overmastering influence ceased to operate, and my evil nature reasserted itself. I saw I was lost unless I had recourse to some new stratagem, and with a deep-drawn sigh I said: "Heaven be thanked! this fit of madness is over; be assured, my dear wife, it will not recur for a long while. This is only the second fit I have had in my life."

Saying these words, I tried to drag myself towards her bed, when the dwarf, his eyes ablaze with anger, threw himself between us, crying: "Don't come near my princess, detestable monster! Vainly wouldst thou attribute to a momentary aberration the confession of the monstrous act of which thou art really guilty. I heard thee myself, this very night, return from the king's apartment. Thou didst fall down at four paces' distance from my couch, and didst there entreat that very Homaïouna, whom thou has just named once more, to suffer thee to enjoy the fruits of thy crime. I thought I had only dreamt some evil dream, but I had heard the truth only too well! If thou darest to come forward one single step I will, with these nails of mine, tear off the remains of flesh which this supernatural fit of remorse has left upon thy bones!"

Though my recent attack had left me in a state of extreme weakness, rage at being thus convicted of what I sought to deny, supplied me with sufficient strength to rise, to seize Calili, and to hurl him into the sea, which, on that side, bathed the walls of the palace. Unfortunately for me, instead of drowning, he swam off with a surprising agility.

I then stood confounded, and Gazahidé fell back into a swoon, when, suddenly, an infinite number of voices rang through the palace: "Vengeance! Vengeance! Let all doors be closed, let every sword be drawn! Barkiarokh has killed our king, let us not suffer the wretch to escape!"

At this fearful tumult, I trembled for my life, like a coward; I abandoned the princess, and, having rendered myself invisible, I made all haste to get out of the palace. But every avenue was closed; swords swept glittering in all directions. In this extreme peril I seized hold of a sycamore, some fifty cubits high, that grew in the middle of the great court, climbed up quickly, and perched myself as well as I was able, on the top. Thence I looked down, with unspeakable terror, upon the multitude of people who swarmed below seeking my life. They increased in number with every moment, while the furious dwarf never wearied in urging them on. This scene, of which I was at once the wretched spectator and the horrible cause, lasted without intermission during the whole day and the following night; and, to add to my miseries, the uncomfortable posture I had to adopt, and my agitation, brought on an attack of the accursed gout from which I had relieved my father. I could have screamed so as to make the welkin ring, but fear restrained me. And, as I felt that I was growing weaker from hour to hour, I unwound my turban, and bound myself firmly to the tree so as not to fall on the pikes and spears of my enemies.

In this condition, with unuttered curses on my lips, and despair in my heart, I spent yet another day in contemplating the frightful confusion that reigned below. At last I began to see things dimly, as through a cloud, and to hear nothing distinctly, and almost to lose consciousness of my own existence, when a great noise of axes, applied from the outside to the gates of the palace, caused me to start and tremble and lose all consciousness.

What was my surprise, on coming to my senses, to find myself softly lying on silk mattresses bedewed with the most delightful odours! I opened my eyes, and perceived, by the light of a great crystal lamp, that I was in a long chamber, at the other end of which was an oratory. In this oratory a dervise was muttering prayers with great fervour, and repeating my name over and over again in his orisons. I knew not what to make of such a vision. I looked on in silence for a long time, and at last thought I must be in the regions of the dead. Much surprised at my favourable treatment there, I could not help exclaiming: "Ah! little have I deserved to receive such mercies!" These words caused the dervise to turn round. He made haste to come to me, and I recognised Alsalami. "My son," said he, "I like to hear these first ejaculations of a contrite heart. Heaven be praised! You will not die in a state of impenitence!"

"Am I still in the land of the living?" I inquired.

"Yes," he replied; "thanks to the benevolence of Homaïouna."

"If my life had depended on that cruel Peri," I rejoined, "I should long since have ceased to breathe – she has done everything for my destruction!"

"No, no!" returned Alsalami; "she has only done what she ought to have done. It would not have become a pure Intelligence, such as she is, to suffer you to touch Gazahidé with hands still reeking of the breath of which you had just deprived her father. She made you feel her formidable power, not in order to divulge your crime, but so that you might not add to that crime an element of such atrocity. Nevertheless, when she saw you suspended from the sycamore – for you could not make yourself invisible to her eyes – she took pity upon you. 'He must be saved,' said she, 'and have time given him for repentance.' Immediately she took flight, sought out the brave men who live among the mountains, and induced them to take arms for your release. Under her leadership, they vanquished your enemies, broke open the gates of the palace, and, after she had made you visible by removing the fatal ring to another finger, took you down from the tree. Then she gave you such care as your condition demanded; and now, leaving me here to watch the effect of her restoratives, is gone to complete the work of assuring the throne to your family. You might easily have ascended that throne without a crime, O Barkiarokh! But now the steps thereto must be fashioned out of your repentance. Daoud was a murderer even like yourself, but he became the best of kings."

This consolatory and pious discourse, which I deemed to be in the last degree dull and commonplace, made me feel that if ever hypocrisy could be of use to me, it was now. I began, therefore, to beat my breast, with no great violence indeed, but with an air of well-feigned compunction. I accused myself, I condemned what I had done in no measured terms, and besought the dervise to intercede for me. At last, after seeing the holy man bathed in tears, I said: "Alas! what has become of the innocent princess whom I have caused to be an orphan?"

"She is in this palace," he replied, "and very ill, in the bed where you left her. But Homaïouna is taking care of her, and will, I have no doubt, restore her to life and health. The Peri has also appeased the friends of the dead king. Though she has been strictly careful to tell no lies they are beginning to doubt whether you are really guilty of the crime Calili alone imputes to you; for Gazahidé herself has never opened her lips on the subject; she has never even uttered your name."

"What have they done with that accursed dwarf?" cried I passionately.

"Peace, peace, my son," said the dervise. "You must yourself forgive, if you wish Allah to forgive you. The dwarf has fled, and has not been pursued."

"May heaven be his guide!" said I, with an air of compunction. "Who indeed can be as wicked as I? But may I see my father, and testify my gratitude to Homaïouna?"

"Ormossouf," he replied, "governs the kingdom, though he has not yet assumed the title of king. He is too busy, at the present moment, to see you, and, to tell you the truth, he does not seem to have any great wish to do so. As to the Peri, you will no doubt see her, as such is your desire. But now keep quiet. Too much excitement might be hurtful." Saying these words, he returned to the oratory.

I asked for nothing better than to be left to my own reflections. I had to think out some plan for obtaining possession of the crown, which I should mainly value as a means of pacifying Gazahidé, or at least of subduing her to my ends: for that too charming princess was ever present to my thoughts. But my fate for the present depended on Homaïouna, and it was not so easy to cajole her as the dervise. Exaggerated protestations, all untoward grimacing and show, would have been lost upon her. I indulged in neither. I left it to my looks and actions to convince her, not only of my repentance, but also of a return of tenderness towards herself. Notwithstanding her previous experiences Homaïouna was not suspicious; and she loved me. Alsalami spoke strongly in my favour, and Ormossouf himself wanted to return to obscurity and quiet. So they decided among them that I should be proclaimed King of Daghestan. Nor did I think it wise to feign reluctance. I merely said to the Peri: "I can only repeat the words which the Queen of Choucan spoke to you on a similar occasion, 'All the burden of kingship will fall on you, my dear Homaïouna.'"

This utterance afforded great satisfaction to my active

spouse; and in my own interests, I thoroughly acted up to it during the first days of my reign. I allowed her to make all the arrangements she liked; and even to appoint Alsalami as my Grand Vizier, though, to myself, in truth, such a choice seemed somewhat ridiculous. What I wanted was to gain the love and respect of my people, and I neglected no steps to that end. I was constant at my attendance at the Mosques, where I distributed great alms to the poor, and gave excessive gifts to the Imans. I administered justice almost every day in person, and only allowed Alsalami to take my place occasionally, and to gratify Homaïouna.

One day, when they were both particularly well pleased with me, and I stood high in their good graces, I caused the conversation to turn on the subject of destiny, and allowed them to embark, according to their custom, in a long disquisition upon that subject. After listening to them for some time, with apparent interest, I said: "Alas! who more than myself can believe that we are the slaves of fate! My love for Gazahidé caused me to commit a crime which I shall never cease to deplore, and yet, notwithstanding, I burn to see once again that unfortunate princess; the thought of her follows me everywhere; it troubles me in my devotions; and if I do not satisfy this unconquerable desire I shall never be myself again. Do not be angry at my saying this, dear Homaïouna," I continued, "my tenderness towards you is founded on admiration and gratitude, and will be eternal. My blind passion for your rival can only last so long as it is thwarted."

"I am not jealous," replied the Peri, with an air of majesty, calm and unruffled, "but I fear the violence of your character, and foresee, with great pain, the evils you are drawing down upon yourself. Gazahidé holds you in such abhorrence that she would rather see the Degial than yourself. Your presence might kill her."

"Oh! people do not die so easily," said I. "I shall succeed in pacifying her if you do not set yourself to counteract my efforts; and, as to that, your energies might be more profitably employed in other directions."

"As you please," said she. "I must submit. But I have the most dread presentiments."

I pretended not to hear these last words, and still less the deep sighs with which Alsalami accompanied them; and instantly made my way towards Gazahidé's apartment.

The eunuchs and the princess's slave girls were transfixed with terror at my approach, and at the intimation of my desire to see their mistress; but I ordered them on pain of death to keep silence, and forbade them to follow me. I entered noiselessly, but, for fear of alarming Gazahidé, without making myself invisible, and looked at her for some time unperceived. Seated on a pile of cushions, her back was nearly turned to the door. Her flowing hair looked like golden embroidery on the simar in which she was clothed. With her head bent over her knees, she bedewed with tears the carbuncle which I had presented to her father – and which he had given her to keep. I went round behind her on tiptoe, and, throwing myself at her feet, clasped my arms round her, and held her tight, for fear she should endeavour to escape.

As, notwithstanding all my hardihood, I could not, without strong emotion, see and touch a woman for whom I entertained such a violent passion, and whom I had so deeply wronged, I was scarcely able to stammer a few words of excuse; but she at once interrupted them by a heartrending cry, and fell back in a fainting fit that seemed to be accompanied by every symptom of death.

So dire an accident ought to have been as a curb to my passion; on the contrary, it acted as a spur. . . . Ashamed and despairing, I issued from the apartment, hiding my head with the skirt of my robe, and ordering the eunuchs and the girl slaves to go to the help of their mistress.

I stood at that moment in no need of strokes from the fatal wand; my heart was already sufficiently tortured, but rather with despite and rage than remorse. This first visit was followed by several others of a similar kind. The woman I sought to embrace was as always inert and seemingly dead, and I always quitted her with horror. Often, after issuing from Gazahidé's apartment, I rushed away to the Mosque, and there beat my breast with such violence that the spectators were lost in admiration at seeing a king as zealous, as much a martyr in the cause of penitence, as the most enthusiastic of fakirs.

All this time Homaïouna, who could not have been ignorant of my fatal visits to Gazahidé, never spoke of them to me; and she acted wisely, for I regarded her as the first cause of the unspeakable misfortune that had befallen me, and should have lost all patience with her. Alsalami did indeed venture to utter a halting word of remonstrance, but I reduced him to silence in tones that froze the very blood in his veins. He took to his bed and remained there till he died. It was the Peri who came to tell me of his death, and to propose another vizier in his stead. I was too embittered against her to comply. I reproached her with having utterly overburdened a poor recluse who, from his youth up, had been accustomed to live a quiet life, and had naturally succumbed beneath the weight of the duties she had absurdly imposed upon him; and I gave her to thoroughly understand that henceforward I should choose my own Grand Vizier.

"I understand," cried she, and her air was rather sad and pitiful than angry; "you will only give your confidence to one who flatters the inordinate and unruly passion by which you are now tormented – a passion that makes you the byword of your harem. Ah! unless Heaven intervenes, you are about to become the wicked king with whose advent the fatal parchment threatens mankind."

She retired after saying these words, and I was tempted to make her repent having uttered them, by beating her to the ground; for I knew by what she had told me of her history that, though it was not possible to kill her, it was possible to inflict upon her the most cruel and excruciating torments. Only fear lest she should find means of depriving me altogether of my princess restrained me; but alas! I soon lost this reason for remaining with her on decent terms.

I was scarcely awake on the following morning, when I

heard terrible sounds of lamentation coming from Gaza-hidé's apartments. I got up in alarm, I ran thither; her eunuchs, her slave girls, prostrated themselves to the ground before me, vociferating hideously. Altogether beside myself, I stepped over them, I entered into the princess' chamber. There, on her divan, I found my carbuncle, and a paper containing these terrible words: "Take back thy accursed carbuncle, detestable Barkiarokh! The sea is about to receive this miserable body of mine, and will never give it up again into thine arms. Would to heaven that the waters had engulfed it ere that first fatal hour when it was profaned by thee!"

Like a sick man, who, though consumed by present evils, thinks of a long life, and feels the sudden dart of the Angel of Death, so was I smitten to the heart by the loss of her who was my daily torment. I threw myself down on the divan, and remained there, heedless of outward things, for half the day. At last I regained the power of consecutive thought, and my first use of it was to accuse the Peri. "She it is," said I to myself, "who, with that wretched little fish of hers, caused me to acquire the fatal ring, and with it to take upon myself my father's gout. She it is who, in her spite and jealousy, compelled me to confess my crime before Gazahidé, and placed me in extreme peril. She it is, doubtless, who threw the princess into those deathlike swoons which prevented her from listening to me; for, had the princess been in a condition to hear my excuses, she was far too gentle, and loved me far too much, not to have forgiven me; nor certainly was it of her own motion that she preferred death to myself. But is she really dead? Has she thrown herself into the sea? Should I attach implicit faith to a piece of writing placed here perhaps only to deceive? It is true that Gazahidé could not otherwise escape, save by supernatural means. The height of these walls, and the incorruptibility of her guards, make this certain. But can I be equally certain that the Peri has not spirited her away, and removed her to other lands? Did she not obtain that power and make use of it, when she succoured the eunuch Gehanguz? Did she not, in some sort, warn me yesterday that she might exercise it again? Ah! I would rather Gazahidé were really drowned than in another man's arms! In any case I must be revenged on Homaïouna, and to be revenged I must dissemble."

After these reflections I concocted a plot quite worthy of my own turpitude, and left that fatal chamber, with a countenance sad indeed but composed, and retired to my own apartments. Far from refusing to admit Homaïouna, who came to me almost at once, I received her with a grateful air. "You had told me," said I, "that Heaven would put an end to my criminal excesses, you are a true prophet. Unfortunately, I always believe your warnings after the event, and too late. I am now myself again, and though I cannot help deploring the loss I have experienced, I shall bear it with resignation. Help me with your counsels; continue to rule over my kingdom; while I devote myself to those pious exercises so necessary to my soul's welfare."

"Now Allah and his Prophet be praised for this return of your better self!" cried the Peri. "But, alas! was it necessary, in order to bring you to your right mind, that that poor princess should be sacrificed and forfeit her life? I loved her, and would at least have wished to pay due honour to her mortal remains. Vain hope! Nothing of her has been recovered save this veil found floating on the surface of the waters. She must have sought to rest for ever buried beneath the waves."

"You think, then," said I, looking fixedly at Homaïouna, "that the amiable Gazahidé has perished irretrievably?"

"Do I believe it?" replied she. "I believe it only too assuredly. And you yourself, can you still have any doubts? Ah! dear Barkiarokh, cease to entertain visionary hopes that would neutralise your good intentions. Seek a refuge from your sorrow rather in such pleasures as are lawful. If you are happy without shame, and without crime, my utmost desires will be accomplished!"

This affectionate speech, instead of touching me, only served to further exasperate me against the Peri. I knew her to be incapable of falsehood; and was assured, therefore, that she had not actually removed Gazahidé; but still I regarded her as the prime cause of Gazahidé's loss. I became more than ever determined to execute my cruel designs for her punishment, and carried out those designs to the full, after giving her, for three days, so as to allay her suspicions, every mark of affection and confidence.

The wicked easily recognise wickedness in others. I had discovered that Ologou, chief of my eunuchs, was a thorough scoundrel, and just such an instrument as I required. I ordered him to find among his fellows two or three cut-throats fit for any act of violence. He brought me two, and said he could answer for them. "My friends," said I, "by a fatal mischance I am married to a magician, who first presented herself to me as a simple and innocent creature. Shortly after our wedding, she did indeed perform, at my expense, two or three of the tricks of her trade; but, as these were of no great malignity, I passed them over in silence. Afterwards she passed to deeds of atrocity. In order that I might reign, or rather in order that she might herself exercise sovereign power, she stifled the late king, and, in her jealousy, has just thrown the princess into the sea. I am bound to punish crimes so execrable; the trouble is to find the means. She can disappear at pleasure, and at pleasure move about from place to place. It would be useless, therefore, to give her up to public justice. Only by surprising her asleep can she be punished as she deserves."

"Sire," interrupted Ologou, "I have long been aware of the wickedness and hypocrisy of Homaïouna; if you so order, we will, this very night, enter, fully armed, into her chamber, and run her through and through before she can wake to consciousness."

"I am perfectly agreeable," I replied; "the act will be an act of justice, and not go unrewarded."

This new crime of mine was executed to my entire satisfaction. The Peri would have died a thousand deaths if she could have died at all. Her body was one great wound, when, by the exercise of her supernatural powers, it disappeared from before the eyes of her cruel assailants, who, by my orders, published the crimes of which I accused her, and the magician's trick by which she had eluded the full punishment I meditated.

The veneration in which I was held, and the number of my witnesses, caused these lies to be generally believed. Men pitied me, the partisans of the murdered king, and of the drowned princess thanked me for the justice I had wished to execute, and suggested that I should forbid any of my subjects, on pain of death, to afford help, or shelter, to Homaïouna. Ormossouf alone could have thrown light on this mystery of iniquity; but he was naturally indolent, and no longer supported by his friend the dervise, so that he caused me but little anxiety; as a matter of fact, he gave me no trouble whatever.

Nothing could equal my joy at the thought that the Peri would now be fully occupied in getting healed of her wounds, and must perforce leave me alone for some time. I resolved to take advantage of these moments of respite, and to drown in debauchery my too poignant memories of Gazahidé. The tranquil pleasures of the harem were too insipid for such a purpose. My ring could procure me delights of a more pungent nature, and without the loss of my reputation for sanctity. I imparted my design to Ologou, and he brought me a list of the most beautiful women of Berdouka. Among these was the favourite of Mohabed, the Emir who had so unseasonably recognised me as Barkiarokh at the very moment when I was about to be made king under the name of Farukrouz.

It was with genuine delight that I began my adventures with this lady. In order to effect my purpose, I sent Ologou, at the dawn of day, to the Emir, summoning him at once to attend the Divan. I entered her apartment invisibly, at the same time as my messenger, and squatted down in a corner. There I listened to the good old man's comic complaints. "Must I leave thee, Light of my Eyes?" he said to his wife. "That fool of a Barkiarokh, who is much more fit to be a fisherman than a king, wants to make men move about by starlight as he used to propel his boat hither and thither in the old days. Moreover, he has lost two wives, and does not want to take to himself any more, and is restless at nights. He does not bear in mind that husbands more fortunate than himself do not like to rise so early in the morning."

"Ah! speak no evil of that pious monarch," cried a soft and silvery voice, "he is so good and so beneficent that all the world should love him. Go – don't keep him waiting, I shall remain patiently in bed till you return."

The Emir murmured a few words more – made his adieus, and departed.

His back was no sooner turned than the lady cried out in indignant tones: "Go, odious old bag of bones! and may you never come back! Alas! why do I not belong to that amiable Barkiarokh, who is more beautiful than the sun at noonday!"

With a woman already so favourably disposed, any great precautions on my part were unnecessary. At first she was somewhat alarmed by my sudden appearance, but not long; I soon reassured her, and we spent together the whole time that the Grand Vizier – who for that day presided over the Divan in my stead – occupied in idle discussion – and in the art of idle speech he was a past master.

I several times renewed my visits to this lady, and witnessed various scenes, to which she gave occasion for my amusement, between herself and her husband. Then I became inconstant, and the wife of the Iman of the Great Mosque took my fancy. Her husband had in no way offended me. On the contrary, we were the best of friends. But what did that matter? I had the same success here as in my first adventure, and indeed never failed in any of the similar adventures in which I subsequently embarked. Ologou, who frequented all the harems where he thought I might find advantage, would adroitly prepossess the ladies in my favour, and they, in their own interests, kept my doings secret.

But oh! my unhappy companions, how ill do these frivolities consort with our horrible situation here! I shall dwell on them no more, but pass at once to events more fitted for recital in this our present abode.

Though I regarded my adulteries as little more than a multiplicity of jokes, yet I could not but be surprised that the Peri paid so little attention to them. She must, by this time, have been long healed of her wounds, and nevertheless I received no strokes from the fatal wand. At last I came to the conclusion that the daggers of my eunuchs had brought her to a more reasonable frame of mind, and that she had elected some other field for her energies.

Pleasures so facile at last brought satiety. After some years my fits of gout became more frequent, and the hypocrisy, which I continued to practise, became insupportable. Ologou, who had made himself master of all my secrets, often journeyed to divers parts of the world to find for me young beauties, whom he had afterwards the mortification of seeing me despise. I did nothing but talk to him about Gazahidé, whose charms, now that I was more than satiated with chance amours, assumed in my memory even brighter hues than before. At last the wretched slave was at his wit's end, and knew not what to do, when an accident occurred, very unexpectedly, that woke me from my lethargy.

One day, when I was giving audience to the people, two women, veiled, presented themselves at the foot of the throne, and, with timid and suppliant voices, besought me to hear them in private. Without knowing why, I felt moved by their accents, and had them conducted into my harem, whither I shortly followed. What was my surprise on seeing my two sisters-in-law, as pretty and as fresh as in the days when they had first excited my admiration. "Wives of my brothers," I said, "be assured of my goodwill, but let us postpone to some future time whatever communication you may desire to make to me. In my harem pleasure is the first business of all, and to that business every other is postponed."

I devoted, therefore, some days assiduously to their entertainment. Afterwards I reminded them that they had something to say to me.

"Oh! we had forgotten our old husbands," cried the younger, "and no wonder, seeing what wretched creatures they are, and how utterly incapable of work, or of doing anything for us! We have wandered from city to city, living by the alms of the faithful, ever since the day when Ormossouf drove us from his door. The faithful gave us bread, but no comfort. The Afrite of the Miry Desert alone seemed to enter into our troubles; but your brothers were afraid to avail themselves of the remedy he proposed."

My sister-in-law blushed as she uttered these words, and was silent.

"Conclude," said I sharply. "You have excited my curiosity. I desire to know the whole of this adventure."

STORY OF BARKIAROKH'S YOUNGER SISTER-IN-LAW

"Well, you shall know it," she rejoined; "but you will be even more frightened than your brothers. This it is: a good woman, to whom we had told the story of the little fish, and of the misfortunes it had brought upon us, came one day, in great haste, to the hovel into which we retired at night-time. 'My children,' she said, 'I have just been told something that may be of use to you, and I have lost no time in coming to impart it. It is confidently asserted that at thirty mountains' distance from here is to be found the Miry Desert, inhabited by an Afrite, who is very obliging, and never refuses advice, or help, provided only that the applicant does not go counter to any of his singular fancies; and as you are good folk, easy and obliging because you are poor, you will doubtless be welcome. True, the distance is somewhat great, but, as you are always on the move, begging hither and thither, distance in your case must be a slight matter. I think it will be to your advantage to undertake the journey; and if you gain nothing, why, you will lose nothing, seeing that you have nothing to lose.' This conclusion was unassailable. We thanked the good old woman, and instantly set out.

"We travelled no great distance day by day, our husbands being feeble and unable to walk long at a time. As to my sister and myself, we were buoyed up by the hope that the poor old things might recover their youth and strength, and were as light of foot as two does pursued by a hunter. Nor should we fail to acknowledge what we owe to the good Mussulmans who inhabit that great stretch of country, and allowed us to want for nothing. True, we never told them the end and object of our pilgrimage, for fear of scandalising them – the Afrites being no friends to the Holy Prophet in whose name the alms were bestowed upon us.

"At last we reached the Miry Desert. But there our hearts failed us, so evil and horrible was the place. Picture to yourself an immense tract of land covered with thick black mud – neither pathways, nor trees, nor any beasts save certain swine that wallowed in the filth, and added to its horror. We perceived, afar off, the caverned rock, the dwelling of the Afrite; but we were fearful of being swallowed up in the slime, or torn to pieces by the porkers, before we could reach it. As to the odious brutes, we had no means of attacking or repelling them, and from their numbers it was evident their master greatly liked their company.

" 'Let us retrace our steps,' cried your two brothers. 'Nothing can be more unendurable than this!' At these words my sister and I lost all patience. We upbraided them so hotly, both for their wretchedness and our own, that, after much weeping, they suffered us to drag them into the slough. Here we upheld them as best we could, notwithstanding the difficulty we experienced in extricating ourselves. The sun darted upon us its fiercest rays, and this seemed greatly to enliven the pigs, which, without appearing to notice us, indulged at our sides in a thousand gambols, and tumblings, splashing us in such a manner as to make us frightful and filthy to behold. Nevertheless, what with swimming, and wading, and falling, and getting up again, we at last succeeded in reaching the foot of the rock, which was situated in the midst of the Miry Desert, and surrounded by dry moss – the latter very comforting.

"We found the Afrite seated at the entrance of a spacious cavern, and enveloped in a robe of tiger skins, so long and so ample that it stretched round him for several cubits. His head was out of proportion with his gigantic stature, for it was of ordinary size, and his face was strange to a degree. His complexion was of fine yellow; his hair, his eyebrows, his eyelids and his beard, purple; his eyes black as night; his lips pale red; his teeth narrow, white and sharp like fish bones, and the general effect rather extraordinary than pleasing. He received us graciously. 'Poor people,' said he; 'I am so filled with pity for all you have suffered in coming here, that you may be sure I shall do my utmost to help you. Speak boldly therefore; in what can I serve you?'

"Encouraged by these words we related to him our woes in greatest detail, and then asked if he knew of any remedy.

"'Yes, yes,' he replied; 'I know of a remedy sure enough, and a very easy one; but we will speak of it by-and-by; go now to the bottom of my cave, and you will find there a spring of pure water; cleanse yourselves thoroughly; then, turning to the right, you will see clothing of all sorts; take the garments you most fancy, and, after donning them, come back and rejoin me here.'

"The offer came opportunely and we accepted it with joy and gratitude. We bathed deliciously, and were no less glad to change our old rags. We afterwards found the Afrite at the same place where we had left him, and arranging fruit of all kinds in baskets. 'Sit here near me,' said he, 'and eat, for you must be hungry.'

"And so indeed we were. The Afrite laughed with all his heart when he saw how we devoured our food. At last he observed: 'You don't at all look like over-scrupulous Mussulmans, and, I take it, would drink wine with pleasure if it were offered. Come,' he continued, seeing from our looks that we wished for nothing better, 'you shall have it in abundance.'

"Saying these words he stretched out his hand over the dirty waters surrounding us, and these changed immediately into a stream flowing with red wine, whose smell was a delight, and along the stream grew fruit trees. The swine had disappeared. In their stead an immense number of gracious and graceful little children played about the stream, and presented to us great vases of crystal full of the sparkling wine, which we relished with transports of delight. For a whole hour we had only opened our lips to drink, when your elder brother, quite hilarious, cried: 'Ah! how happy you are, my Lord Afrite, and how happy should we be in turn if you would consent to keep us with you here!'

"'Poor fool,' replied the Afrite; 'poor fool who, like the rest of mankind, dost judge of happiness by outward appearances! See if I am happy.' Speaking thus he lifted up his robe, and we saw that his two legs were fixed into the ground as far as the knees. At this strange spectacle, terror and compassion were depicted upon our countenances. He saw it, and resumed, with a more tranquil air: 'Do not be too sorry for me, my friends. Though the Power who holds me half buried here, may cheat the eyes of those who come to visit me, by making that appear a filthy slough which is indeed a delightful watercourse, yet he cannot prevent my ultimate deliverance – which is perhaps not far distant. However that may be, I cannot retain you here. Go, leave me with those fair children whom you mistook for swine, and of whom, very happily, I have not been deprived; but before we separate, let me tell you this: the imprudent wish by which you brought upon yourselves age and its infirmities can only cease to have effect with the death of your father. It is for you to consider how far you are prepared to wait for that event – which, in the ordinary course of nature, may still be far distant – or to hasten its approach. As for me, I know very well that if I had a hundred fathers, I should not spare a single one of them in order to put an end to misery such as yours and that of your amiable consorts.'

"By our consternation, by our silence, the Afrite perceived that his suggestion failed to meet with our approval. This appeared to disconcert him; and suddenly changing his manner he said rudely: 'Go, and pursue your reflections elsewhere. I am mistaken in you. I thought we might meet again to our common advantage; but you are no better than cowards. Go this minute. I dispense with all ceremony and farewells.'

"We were too frightened to wait for a repetition of this command. We rose without saying a word; but, O heavens! the beautiful stream, which it would have been a joy to traverse, had become once again a slough, foul and infamous. And now our husbands, who were even more indignant against the Afrite than ourselves, showed us the way. They threw themselves, without hesitation, into the muck heaps, and we followed dolefully. The horrible passage proved far more difficult than before. We were up to our necks in filth, and the swine molested us in a thousand ways. Vainly did we say one to another that we were wading in clear wine, and surrounded by pretty children. The lie was too palpable.

"Weary to death, we emerged at last from the Miry Desert, and reached dry land. Immediately your elder brother cried: 'Cursed for ever be that child of Eblis who dared advise us to commit parricide.'

"'Cursed,' said your second brother, 'be the infamous breath that uttered the impious words; cursed, I say, be he who spoke them, cursed from his purple locks to the soles of his feet – if, indeed, he has any feet, as he pretended.'

"'Cursed,' added my sister, 'be everything that belongs, or has belonged, to that monster, save only his clear wine, and the good clothes we are carrying away with us.'

"After these just imprecations, we sat down under a big tree to rest for the night, which was approaching with great strides. Our feeble husbands, thoroughly worn out, slept profoundly, while my sister and I kept awake consulting as to what was to be done. In the morning I made the two old men acquainted with the conclusions at which we had arrived. 'Believe me,' said I, 'banish all false shame, and the fears that have hitherto prevented you from appealing to the King, your brother. Barkiarokh is too good, too full of piety, to blush at our poverty, or to bear in mind our ancient quarrels. Let us go and throw ourselves at his feet, and tell him all that has befallen us. He will help us if only to spite the Afrite, for he has sufficiently proved, by the banishment of Homaïouna, that he has no love for such malign spirits.' This advice was approved of by your brothers. We set forth once more, and, after a long and tiring journey, at last reached Berdouka – where our husbands are awaiting your reply."

END OF THE STORY OF BARKIAROKH'S YOUNGER SISTER-
IN-LAW

I had trembled with joy on learning, in the course of this narrative, that I might hope one day to be delivered from my fatal gout. The means by which the happy hour could be hastened had at first somewhat startled me, but my heart, in its utter depravity, soon grew reconciled to the horrible thought. The only question was how to commit such an odious crime without exciting suspicion; and to this point I had addressed my thoughts during the latter portion of my sister-in-law's story.

She had told it in such a way as to make me understand, even if I had not known it already, what kind of woman I was dealing with. So, when she had done speaking, I said to her, in a tone of contempt: 'Hence, leave my palace, you women who have neither spirit, sense nor courage! You are unworthy of what I intended to do for you. What! you did not persuade your husbands to recover their youth and vigour by taking the life of a monster, devoid of all right feelings, who showed indeed that he was no father of theirs, by hounding them out of his house in their infirm condition – a condition they had assumed out of love for himself, – and who afterwards had such fearful inhumanity as to see them perishing with want! Had you not sufficient influence over your husbands to compel them, if need were, to enter secretly, by night, into a house of which every nook and corner was well known to them, and to cut off the wretch's head? Conduct so just and energetic, far from exciting my anger, would have deserved my praise. Hence, hence, I say! and let me never hear speak of you again!"

More was not wanted. My sisters-in-law were altogether beside themselves. They had been hoping to see their husbands no more, and to go on living with me. So they threw themselves distracted at my feet, and began to embrace my knees, crying out, both together: "Forgive us, dear lord, forgive us; it is not our fault if your brothers are so irresolute and spiritless. We were not as base as they. But what could we say or do? They would have killed *us* if we had insisted on their following the counsels of the Afrite. Now, however, since you tell us Ormossouf is not really their father, we know perfectly what to say to them. Promise to take us back into your good graces – which we value far more than the restoration of our husbands to youth and vigour – and we will show that we have more spirit and sense than you think."

And here, O my companions! I must draw a veil over an act too abominable to be spoken of without horror, even in these subterranean halls of Eblis. My sisters-in-law succeeded only too well; and, in concert with them, I caused their wretched husbands to be surprised at the very moment when they had consummated their abhorred murder. Ologou, to whom I had given orders to that effect, had their heads cut off on the spot, and brought their wives to my harem. I was alone with the two wretches, and coldly listening to the recital of their accursed crime, when the Peri's wand struck me with such force that I fell down as if killed. A moment after I rose from the ground in an inconceivable fury, and having seized my two accomplices, I pierced them through and through again and again with my dagger, and cast their bodies into the sea. To this involuntary act of justice succeeded new transports of despair. I yelled imprecations against myself, till my voice failed, and I fell into a swoon.

Ologou had seen everything through the door curtains, but had taken good care not to come near during my frenzy. He entered when he saw the paroxysm was over, and, taking me in his arms, without calling for assistance, dressed the wounds I had inflicted on myself, and brought me back to my senses. I asked him, with a feeble voice, if there had been any dangerous witnesses to the scene just enacted. He reassured me on this point, but was as terrified as myself by this evidence that the Peri had not forgotten me. We grew calmer by degrees, and determined, by a conduct above reproach, to keep clear of the fatal wand for the future.

A fish might more easily live on the apex of a rock than a man accustomed to crime live a life of virtue. Vainly did the eunuch invent day by day new and innocent amusements – I was dying of rage and ennui. "Ah! I would brave Homaïouna," I used to say, "if only I were sure she would not punish me in public. The convulsions of remorse that she persists in inflicting upon me would only take the place of the attacks of gout, from which I am now delivered – but I risk all if ever she exposes me publicly in the eyes of my subjects."

The strictness I was compelled to impose upon my own conduct, made me so hard and harsh in my dealings with others that I was on the point of being hated by my people as much as I had formerly been beloved, when, one day, Ologou came to tell me, with an air of triumph, that he had found a sovereign remedy for my woes. "You have doubtless heard," he continued, "of Babek Horremi, surnamed the Impious, because he believed in no religion at all, and preached a universal subservience to enjoyment, and to every conceivable kind of pleasure. You know also with what ease he perverted all Persia and the adjacent provinces, and how, being followed by a prodigious

150

number of his adherents, he made head against the troops sent for his destruction by the Califs Mamoun and Motassem; and how, finally, he was captured by the latter through the treachery of a dog, the son of a dog. Well, this great man has not altogether perished. Naoud, his confidant and minister, survives him. He escaped from the prisons of Samarah, and, after wandering from land to land during several years, has, at last, come hither. I met him this morning in the neighbourhood of Berdouka, and greeted him as he deserves. He had been my master in old days, so I knew him well, and ventured to acquaint him with your sorrows. He pitied you, and offers you his services. Take him as your Grand Vizier; he is the man you want. The present holder of the office is but a fool, who carries out to the letter such orders as you may deign to give him. The ingenious Naoud will do much more – he will know how to preserve you from Homaïouna's wand, which he in no wise fears so far as he himself is concerned. Meanwhile, and little by little, he will establish the Horremitic sect in Daghestan, so that if you should throw off the mask of piety, which you have so far assumed, your subjects will be rather rejoiced than scandalised."

I eagerly seized upon this hope. I saw Naoud, and had no doubt that, with his gifts of seduction, he would soon relieve me from all anxiety. We conferred together several times. At last we settled the day on which I should, in full divan, declare him my Grand Vizier. I was thus hurrying to my ruin, without a thought that to establish impiety in my states would be the most unpardonable of my crimes. In a very few moments I was to perceive my error, but too late. Naoud, clothed in magnificent attire, was at my right; I pointed him out with my hand to the emirs, and grandees of the kingdom, who waited respectfully to hear my commands. "Here," said I, "is the man of whom I choose to help me in governing you, and making you happy. . . ." I was about to enlarge on the scoundrel's imaginary good qualities, when the fatal wand, without striking me to the earth, or troubling me in its accustomed manner, compelled me to change my tone: "He is," I continued, "with the exception of myself, the most infamous of men, he is the impious friend and disciple of the impure Babek Horremi; he has undertaken to corrupt you all, to make you abandon the religion of Mahomet, and to adopt instead the worship of unbridled enjoyment and illicit pleasure; he is well worthy to be the vizier of a monster, who has murdered your king, so outraged your princess that she was forced to throw herself into the deep, caused the Peri who protected him to be pierced with a thousand wounds, taken advantage of all your wives, and finally impelled his brothers to assassinate his and their father. Here is the ring that has favoured my crimes. It is this ring that made me invisible when you, the Iman of the Great Mosque, said dotingly to your wife that she was a little mouse whom the Angel Gabriel had let fall into the room of the prophet; it is this ring that enabled me to listen while you, Mohabed, on being summoned to the Divan, said I was more fit to be a fisherman than a king; but I forgave you, because I instantly took your place in your harem. A power, supernatural, irresistible, which often before has made me utterly beside myself, is this day constraining me, after a different fashion. It leaves me just enough of reason to convince you, circumstantially, that I am the most atrocious, the most detestable monster that the earth ever bore upon its surface. Glut your vengeance. Tear in pieces Ologou, my accomplice, and the perfidious Naoud; but beware lest you come near me. I feel that I am reserved for a yet more terrible fate."

After speaking thus, I was silent, looking round me with haggard eyes and a ferocious mien. I seemed to defy the general fury, which, as I looked, took the place of what had at first been consternation. But, when every sword was uplifted against me, I quickly put the ring on the little finger of my left hand, and, crawling like a reptile, escaped through the furious crowd. As I passed the court of the palace I heard the cries of Ologou, and of Naoud; but these were less fearful to me than the sight of the sycamore from which, in fancy, I saw myself a second time suspended – and the terror of it still held me long after I had left Berdouka.

During all the remainder of the day, I walked, or rather ran, mechanically, and not knowing whither I went. But at nightfall I stopped short, gazing fearfully at a forest that stretched out before me. The feeble and confused glow of twilight made everything loom large, and the dark green of the trees was so gloomy and lugubrious that I hesitated before penetrating into that black abode of solitude. At last, impelled by an evil fate, I entered the woods, groping. Scarce had I taken a couple of steps, when I was thrown down amid the thorns and briars by the great branches, that seemed to my fancy, so strong and irresistible were they, like great arms intent on repelling and keeping me out.

"Wretch that thou art," cried I, "even inanimate things have thee in horror! For thee there is no mercy in the heavens, or on the earth. Remain where thou art, a prey for the evil beasts of the forest, if even *they* do not disdain to devour thee! Oh, Homaïouna, well art thou avenged; triumph in my miseries; I am not worthy to excite thy pity!"

I had just done uttering these words when thousands of ravens and crows began croaking from the tops of the trees, and what they croaked was: "Repent, repent."

"Ah!" cried I, "is there still room for repentance? Yes, I may dare to hope so, and will do penance resignedly. I shall wait for the return of daylight in the place where I now am, and then, setting forth once more, will make haste to leave Daghestan. Fortunately the precious stones are still in my possession. I will sell them, and distribute the money as alms among the poor. Then I will retire into some desert, and browse on the grass of the field, and drink the water of heaven. I have been the abominable king foretold in the parchment, but I may yet become a holy hermit."

Amid these good resolutions, which somewhat quieted

my spirit – and being, moreover, overwhelmed with fatigue – I fell asleep on my couch of briars and thorns, and slept as profoundly as if I had lain on a divan with velvet cushions. The sun was already up when lamentations, proceeding from no great distance, awoke me with a start. A soft and childish voice was crying: "Oh, Leilah, unhappy Leilah, shalt thou leave thy mother's body to the vultures, or shalt thou still continue to drive them away, notwithstanding the hunger pinching thee so sore? Alas! my death is sure if I remain here. These ravenous birds will devour us all, and my mother will never be buried, according to her passionate wish, in the same earth as her father, who was murdered so inhumanly. Oh! why is Calili dead also? He would have helped me to honour the last wishes of his dear princess. Barkiarokh, cruel Barkiarokh! I will not curse thee, for thou art my father, and Gazahidé forbade it, but I curse the day that I owe to thee."

Surprised and utterly bewildered by such an amazing adventure, I was on the point of uttering a piercing cry in answer to my daugther's complaints; but I refrained, so as not to frighten her, perhaps to death; and, remembering that I was invisible, I advanced, without noise, to the place where she still sobbed out her heart. A palisade, bristling with spikes as sharp as javelins, barred my way. I looked through, and saw the innocent Leilah lying on the grass before a little house made of palm branches intertwined in reeds. Her lovely eyes were turned towards the gate of the palisade; though those eyes were tear-bedimmed, they seemed to shoot at me their full rays, and those rays pierced my heart – a heart which they reached indeed through accustomed ways, for their light was the same as Gazahidé's eyes had so often darted upon me. I was carried back to the fatal moment when my princess caused her tent to be set up over the spot where the dwarf first saw my precious stones. Leilah was of about the same age as her mother at that time – her features, her hair, her figure, her entrancing beauty, all were alike. Startled, beside myself, I did not know what to do. Clearly it was imperative that I should hide my name; but supposing anyone had given my daughter a faithful description of my person, how would it then be possible to escape recognition? Still something had to be done. I could not leave the lovely child without help. I removed the ring, therefore, from my little finger, and knocking at the gate of the palisade said, with a lamentable voice: "Whosoever you may be that inhabit this dwelling of canes and palm leaves, I pray you to afford your hospitality to a poor wretch whom the impious Barkiarokh has reduced to utter misery."

"Now Allah and his prophet be praised for the help they have sent me," cried Leilah, rising hastily, and leaping at one bound to the gate of the palisade, which she opened. "Come," continued she, "dear stranger, whom Barkiarokh persecutes; you will here behold other victims of his cruelty, and help me to bury my mother and her dwarf, so that the vultures may not devour them."

As she said these words she invited me to enter.

Considering how contrite I had been only a few hours before, who would not have thought that the sight of Gazahidé's body, even more effective than the Peri's wand, would overwhelm me with remorse? But, ah! the horrible effect of habitual indulgence in crime! I experienced, at that terrible moment, nothing but wild, ungovernable passion, and vowed that my daughter, my own daughter, should ere long become my prey! I called on Eblis to give me success in this my sinister design; and immediately set to work to carry out Leilah's filial wish with regard to the interment of her mother's body, so as thus to gain her confidence, and ultimately bring her into my arms!

I dug a large pit in which we deposited the corpse of Gazahidé, and that of the dwarf – on whom, in my inmost heart, I showered a thousand curses. Then, taking Leilah by the hand, I said: "Dry your tears. Let me lead you to some place where we can obtain the assistance of which you stand so greatly in need. Barkiarokh's wickedness has driven me out into this forest. I fancied I saw, a long way off, some peasants' cottages; let us go in that direction. You have done your duty to your mother. It is now time to think of yourself."

"I will follow you anywhere," she replied; "for surely Heaven has sent you to be my protector. Be a father to me, since my own father is a monster, whom both you and I have every reason to detest."

Leilah had more courage than strength. She could scarcely stand. I took her in my arms, and bore the lovely burden through the forest – not without trembling lest I should meet someone who knew me, for I dared not use my ring, except in case of absolute necessity, since its history must be well known to my daughter, and its use, therefore, would have involved instant recognition. I pressed the innocent creature to my bosom; and the impure fire within me was increasing in violence, when a sudden thought put an end to my infamous transports. "Fool that I am," said I to myself, "of what am I thinking? Homaïouna is hovering about me. It is she who, yesterday, caused the ravens and crows of the forest to utter their warnings. As she has no supernatural means of reading in men's hearts, she may believe it is only paternal love that makes me take care of Leilah; but if I yielded to my present mad desires, she would not spare me the worst effects of her fatal power. Then, by confessing my crimes, I should make myself known to my daughter, and the horrible scenes that I had erstwhile with Gazahidé would be renewed. Oh! is there no spot in all this wide world to which the terrible Peri cannot follow me? And if there is, cannot the Afrite of the Miry Desert point it out? His advice to my brothers shows well enough that all things are known to him, and that he hesitates at nothing. I will go and consult him; and, till then, I will hold myself well in hand with Leilah, and not even kiss her as a friend."

The honest peasants to whom we addressed ourselves, not only supplied our immediate and urgent needs, but also sold us a good horse. So I took Leilah up behind me, and made haste to leave Daghestan.

When I had nothing more to fear, I stopped in a large

city; and there, having disposed of one of my emeralds to the best advantage, I caused fine clothes to be made for Leilah, and gave her two woman slaves. She did not know how to thank me enough. The name of "father" which she bestowed upon me, her real affection, her innocent caresses, all excited me beyond measure; but I still had perforce to hold myself firmly, if reluctantly, in hand.

The necessary preparations for our journey to the Miry Desert required time. I had no desire to remain whole months on the way, like my brothers and my sisters-in-law. One quiet evening, after a very stormy day, I asked Leilah to tell me her mother's story; which she immediately did, with ready submission. That story I already knew only too well up to the time when I thought Gazahidé had thrown herself into the sea, and I paid little heed to what Leilah was saying, till she reached this point:

THE STORY OF LEILAH, BARKIAROKH'S DAUGHTER

"My mother only recovered from the swoons of which the unworthy Barkiarokh took such infamous advantage, to abandon herself to the most terrible despair. Neither her slaves, nor even the good Homaïouna, could comfort her. She pined away visibly, and must, ere long, have died; but, one night, when she had risen from her couch, and was, as usual, weeping over the accursed carbuncle, she heard, through the window, the voice of Calili saying: 'Open to me, dear mistress, open to me! I have risked all to save you.'

"And indeed the faithful dwarf had, at the peril of his life, climbed a gigantic fig-tree, which, rising from the border of the sea, covered with its branches the walls of Gazahidé's chamber. By the help of a silken ladder, which he attached to this tree, my mother escaped, with great courage, after leaving on the dais some words intended to throw Barkiarokh off the scent. The dwarf, after detaching the ladder, slid down, and made the princess enter into a little boat – by which he himself had come to the place –

157

and then, for he rowed quite as well as he swam, he hugged the shore, and ultimately reached the forest, and the dwelling in which you found me. That dwelling belonged to a holy woman called Kaioun, who had retired thither to pray and meditate. She had given shelter to Calili, and, hearing from him of Barkiarokh's crimes, and the sorrows of Gazahidé, had not hesitated to second that zealous servant in his enterprise. The poor princess was received with much respect and kindness by this pious recluse, so that she never ceased to thank heaven for the refuge she had found; and when Calili wished afterwards to persuade her to quit Daghestan, she refused to listen to his advice, protesting that she would end her days with Kaioun, and be buried in the earth of the same land that held the bones of her father. As Barkiarokh made no attempt to find the fugitive, the dwarf became more easy in his mind; and my mother was beginning to find comfort and peace, when a new misfortune befell her: she found she was with child. 'Oh, heavens!' said she, 'must I bear a child to that detestable monster! Ah! may it not be like him.'

"It was then with tears, and anguish, in the most mortal anxiety, that, at last, she brought me into the world. I did not want either for care, or good instruction, during my infancy – my mother, Kaioun, Calili, all had no thought but for me. I was grateful and submissive, and, I may say, happier than I shall ever be again. I sometimes went to the neighbouring town with the charitable Kaioun. She had bought a supply of sandalwood, with which we made little boxes, very neat, that we sold at considerable profit. It was not necessary to enjoin silence upon me with regard to the place of our retreat; for my mother had told me her story, and I feared even more than she did to fall into the hands of Barkiarokh, whom I hated with all my soul.

"So the years passed pleasantly and peacefully. We regarded the savage spot in which Heaven had placed us, as a real paradise; when, suddenly, the hand of providence, that so far had been our stay, ceased to give us its support. My mother fell sick of a slow fever, and we were greatly alarmed. Calili and I never left her for a single moment. Kaioun alone went to the town to purchase such necessaries as we required. She always remained away as short a time as possible, but at last a day came when she went and never returned. We passed the next two days in an indescribable torment of anxiety. At last Calili, seeing that his dear mistress was getting worse for want of the necessary food and comforts, resolved to brave all chance of discovery. He repeated, without ceasing: 'I am the cause of all that has happened, it is all due to my idiotic admiration for the accursed jewels of the thrice-accursed Barkiarokh; it is for me to do whatever can be done to remedy the irremediable.'

"My mother suffered him to depart out of pity for me. But, seeing that he did not return, any more than Kaioun, and fearing that he had been recognised and delivered over to Barkiarokh, she lost all hope, and had not the courage to suggest any remedy to our desperate circumstances. Indeed we had nothing left for our support save the water of the cistern, and she herself was far too weak to go outside our retreat, even had I dared to let her do so. I already felt the pangs of hunger most poignantly, and though I took great pains to hide this from Gazahidé, she perceived my agonies all too soon, and they added terribly to her own distress. She was dying like a lamp in which the oil is exhausted. I saw it. I mourned by her side in silence. She lost consciousness, to my inexpressible anguish, and then, coming to herself again, took me in her arms, and said: 'Daughter, most beloved, and most unfortunate, I recommend thy innocence to the protection of Allah. May he keep thee from falling into the hands of Barkiarokh, nay, take thy life with mine, if such be his will. Never curse thy father; but flee from him as thou wouldst flee from the fiery mouth of a dragon! If thou dost survive me, if Calili does not return, depart hence; seek out some charitable person who will help thee in thy distress, and see to my burial. I refused to leave Daghestan so that my bones might rest in the same mould as the bones of my father, and I should not like the vultures to carry them to some other land. O Allah! O Prophet! forgive me for having been the cause of the death of so good a father, and take pity upon my daughter.'

"She never spoke again, and I lay upon her breast almost as lifeless as she. I know not how long I so remained. I only came to myself when I felt, trickling down my throat, some liquor, which Calili was pouring out with a trembling hand. I opened my eyes. Oh, horror! It was blood, his own blood, he was making me swallow!

"'Unhappy Leilah,' said he, 'this beverage, odious as it is, will sustain you somewhat. I have been pursued by a tiger. I was quick enough to prevent him from seizing me altogether, but once, once he managed to catch hold of me, and tore my side with his claws. My blood has nearly all run out through this great wound. I am about to follow my dear mistress. I go to Allah's judgment seat, there to ask for justice on Barkiarokh, and help for yourself.'

"Having said these words, the good, the generous Calili, laid himself down at my mother's feet, and expired.

"I had slightly recovered my strength, but would only, in my despair, have used it to put an end to my own life, if it had not been for the fear lest vultures should eat the body of Gazahidé, and her last wishes thus remain unfulfilled. The same fear prevented me from leaving the spot. I contented myself, therefore, with uttering loud complaints outside the house, so that any chance passers-by might hear them. Often, however, did I go in again to shed hot tears over my mother's body. And I did the same over that of Calili! Alas! it was to his blood that I owed my small remnant of life. At last you came to save me. You helped me to bury my dear mother and her faithful dwarf. What a debt of gratitude is mine! But gratitude is not the only feeling I entertain for you. You inspire in me an affection akin to that I felt for Gazahidé. I should be happy with you anywhere, provided you were safe from the pursuit of Barkiarokh, who, as you tell me, is ever on the watch to take your life. Let us make haste, therefore, to go to the friend of whom you have spoken, and who, as you hope, will be able to show us the way to some place of retreat where the name of that cruel prince is detested. No fatigues daunt me, I am far more afraid for you than for myself. And be assured that I shall be guilty of no indiscretion. I was not myself when, in the forest, I uttered those complaints which might have caused me to fall into the hands of Barkiarokh. Fortunately they were poured into the ears of his enemy – his enemy who is for ever to be the friend of the unhappy Leilah!''

END OF LEILAH'S STORY

A narrative so touching should have cut me to the heart; a confidence so misplaced should have brought a blush to my cheeks. But borne away as I was by an unbridled passion, nothing gave me pause. I had been much more attentive to the simplicity and grace with which Leilah expressed herself, than to the harrowing scenes she had placed before my eyes. In her innocence she misunderstood the cause of my agitation. She thanked me for the interest I had shown in her mother's misfortunes, and in her own, and returned to her apartment, calling down blessings upon my head. But it was not Barkiarokh that she meant to bless, nor did any blessing come to him. On the contrary, the moment was imminent which would see him for ever accursed.

At last we started for the Miry Desert – my daughter and I in a palanquin, the two women slaves on a camel, and twelve eunuchs on horseback, as an escort. Our journey lasted only three weeks; but these seemed as long as three centuries, because of the war I had to wage continually between my criminal desires, and my fear of the fatal wand. I left Leilah, with the two women and the twelve eunuchs, in a caravanserai at a little distance from the Miry Desert – which I was in a hurry to reach. The slough, the swine, nothing stopped me. I came in a few moments to the Afrite, whom I found, as I had been told, seated at the entrance of his cave. He inclined his head, with civility, and asked me what I wanted. So I told him my story, without the least disguise, and finally besought him to show me the way to some place whither the Peri would be unable to follow me.

The Afrite, instead of replying, clapped his hands, with great glee, and cried, in a voice that made the very rocks tremble: "Now Eblis be praised! Here is a man who is more vile and wicked than I!"

The compliment was scarcely flattering. Nevertheless, I smiled, and asked the Afrite to explain himself.

"Be it known to you," said he, "that your redoubtable father-in-law, Asfendarmod, who is as full of storms as the winter month to which he has given his name, condemned me, about forty years ago, to remain here, with my legs buried and fixed in the ground, saying, 'He alone whose crimes surpass thine own shall have power to deliver thee.' I have waited long; I have been prodigal of evil and pernicious advice to all who came to consult me; but in vain, I was speaking to little men, to men altogether devoid of resolution. The glory of being my liberator was reserved to thee, O unconquerable Barkiarokh! and thou shalt have thy reward; I will convey thee, and thy daughter, to the Palace of Subterranean Fire, where are gathered together all the riches of Soleiman and the Preadamite Kings – and into that place Homaïouna can never enter. Rely upon my word, and lean both thy hands upon my knees."

No less pleased than the Afrite himself, I made haste to do as he wished, and immediately his long legs became disengaged from the earth. He rose, and walked thrice round the rock, crying with all his might: "Let all here return to its accustomed order!" At these words a palace, adorned with a hundred shining cupolas, took the place of the rock; the quagmire became a clear and rapid stream; and the surrounding desert, a garden stretching to the horizon. The children emerged from the swine, and resumed their native beauty and grace. They all flocked round me, and, after caressing me in a thousand ways, led me to the bath. There I was rubbed and perfumed by powerful eunuchs, who afterwards clothed me in rich garments, and led me back to the Afrite.

He was waiting for me in a pavilion, where, under a dais ornamented with priceless pearls, a splendid banquet awaited us. "I am no longer reduced to clear, thin wine, and fruit, for my sole sustenance," said he; "I am going to feed thee right well. But," continued he, "thou dost not seem happy. Ha! Ha! I had forgotten. Nothing pleases unless thy daughter is near. Go and fetch her. Indeed it is necessary that she should grow accustomed to the sight of me, otherwise she might not consent to travel in my arms to the subterranean palace – and that palace none enters save voluntarily. She will play with my children while we are at table; and, when night comes, we will start for Istakhar."

I made short work of returning to the caravanserai through alleys now strewn with flowers, and soon came back again with Leilah, who opened large and astonished eyes at the sight of all that surrounded her.

"Where are we?" said she at last. "Is this the dwelling your friend has chosen for us?"

"No, no," I replied. "It is not here; here we should have no peace, for the place is known to Barkiarokh. This is the dwelling of the giant who loves me, and will bear us this very night to a place of even greater wealth and beauty."

"Is your friend then a giant?" she asked.

"Yes," I replied. "Does that alarm you?"

"I fear nothing, except Barkiarokh, when I am with you," said she, with an innocent affection that somewhat disconcerted me. Happily we were interrupted at this point by the attractive little girls and the pretty pages, who came to meet us, skipping and gambolling. Leilah was so pleased with these graceful creatures that, following the dictates of her age, she began to play with them and caress them, and run after them in the gardens, and manifested neither surprise nor terror when the Afrite appeared.

"She is very pretty," said that wicked Giaour to me. "Ere dawn to-morrow thou shalt be beyond the reach of the wand that would disturb thy pleasures."

He kept his word only too well. We left Leilah, with the children, in charge of the eunuchs, and remained alone, feasting on exquisite viands, and excellent wines. Our talk was free and gay. We laughed at all restraints, holding that they had not been invented for people of our condition. The Afrite related to me his atrocious adventures; but, notwithstanding the charm of listening to the details of a thousand crimes, each one blacker and more abominable than its predecessor, I felt eaten up with impatience: I yearned for the society of Leilah. I therefore thanked my redoubtable host, and reminded him that the hour of our departure was approaching.

Immediately he called Leilah. "Come hither, entrancing little one," said he, "will you let me take you to the subterranean palace of Istakhar?"

"I am willing to go anywhere with my generous protector," she replied.

"That is clear enough," he rejoined. "Come, get up, both of you, on my shoulders. Hold tight, and the journey, far as is the distance, will soon be accomplished."

We obeyed. Leilah trembled somewhat; but I upheld and reassured her, putting one of my arms round her slender waist.

The night was so dark that we could distinguish nothing in the vast spaces through which we flew. I was all the more struck by the vivid light emanating from the subterranean vault on whose brink the Afrite deposited us, crying: "Oh, oh! the vault has opened of itself! Doubtless they expected you down below, and knew whom they are about to receive."

Scarcely did I give any heed to this exclamation, which ought to have made me hesitate, for I was too occupied in examining the magnificent flight of stairs that swept downwards before my eyes. It was very easy of descent, but there was a long space between the plane on which we stood and the first of the steps. To help Leilah, I sprang down to this first step, and held out my arms, into which she was about to spring, when the wicked Afrite called out, laughing: "Good-bye, Barkiarokh. I shall come shortly to inquire how you fare in your new abode, with your too credulous daughter!"

At these malicious words, Leilah uttered a great cry, and threw herself backward so suddenly that it was impossible for me to catch hold of her. I tried to leap up again, but an invisible hand held me down, paralysed and motionless. At the same moment I heard myself called by a voice from the upper air, a voice I knew only too well. I raised my head and saw Homaïouna, glorious, transfigured, and seated on a luminous cloud.

"Wretched Barkiarokh," she said; "thou hast nothing more to fear from the Wand of Remorse. Instead of profiting by its strokes, thou has sought to evade them. Henceforward the rod that will beat upon thy heart is the rod of Despair, and thy heart, hardened as it is, will be broken and crushed throughout every moment of a frightful eternity. I have done all that was possible to save thee from the abyss into which thou has now fallen. Thy crimes have merited their punishment only too fully; but Heaven would not suffer thy innocent child to follow thee in thy fall. Even if the Afrite had not treated thee as the wicked always treat one another, the same Power that now holds thee back, paralysed, would have prevented Leilah from following thy downward path. I bear away with me that dear child, so worthy of a different father. I shall place her on the throne of Daghestan, where, with the aid and counsels of the pious Kaioun, she will cause the horrors of thy reign to be forgotten. Then I shall myself return to my own happy land. I am recalled thither by my father, who considers that by the ills suffered at thy hand I have fulfilled the measure of my own punishment. He allows me henceforward to dwell with my sister Ganigul. I am about, in that loved companionship, to forget the interest I took in the human race, and to leave all to the care of

Allah, who suffers indeed the ephemeral prosperity of the wicked, but chastises those whom He regards as worthy of his ultimate forgiveness."

Having spoken these words, the Peri came down to the earth, gathered up Leilah in her arms, and disappeared.

I uttered a fearful yell when I saw my prey thus snatched away from me; and words of horrible blasphemy were still upon my lips when I was hurled down into the crowd of the damned – with whom I am destined, like yourselves, O my wretched companions, to be whirled about for ever, bearing in my heart the fearful furnace of flame which I have myself prepared and ignited.

The Story of the
Princess Zulkaïs and the
Prince Kalilah

My father, lord, can scarcely be unknown to you, inasmuch as the Calif Motassem had entrusted to his care the fertile province of Masre. Nor would he have been unworthy of his exalted position if, in view of man's ignorance and weakness, an inordinate desire to control the future were not to be accounted an unpardonable error.

The Emir Abou Taher Achmed, however – for such was my father's name – was very far from recognising this truth. Only too often did he seek to forestall Providence, and to direct the course of events in despite of the decrees of Heaven. Ah! terrible indeed are those decrees! Sooner or later their accomplishment is sure! Vainly do we seek to oppose them!

During a long course of years, everything flourished under my father's rule, and among the Emirs who have successfully administered that beautiful province, Abou Taher Achmed will not be forgotten. Following his specula-tive bent, he enlisted the services of certain experienced Nubians, born near the sources of the Nile, who had studied the stream throughout its course, and knew all its characteristics, and the properties of its waters; and, with their aid, he carried out his impious design of regulating the overflow of the river. Thus he covered the country with a too luxuriant vegetation which left it afterwards exhausted. The people, always slaves to outward appear-ances, applauded his enterprises, worked indefatigably at the unnumbered canals with which he intersected the land, and, blinded by his successes, passed lightly over any unfortunate circumstances accompanying them. If, out of every ten ships that he sent forth to traffic, according to his fancy, a single ship came back richly freighted, after a successful voyage, the wreck of the other nine was counted for nothing. Moreover, as, owing to his care and vigilance, commerce prospered under his rule, he was himself deceived as to his losses, and took to himself all the glory of his gains.

Soon Abou Taher Achmed came to be convinced that if he could recover the arts and sciences of the ancient Egyptians, his power would be unbounded. He believed that, in the remote ages of antiquity, men had appropriated to their own use some rays of the divine wisdom, and thus been enabled to work marvels, and he did not despair of bringing back once again that glorious time. For this purpose he caused search to be made, among the ruins abounding in the country, for the mysterious tablets which, according to the report of the Sages who swarmed in his court, would show how the arts and sciences in question were to be acquired, and also indicate the means of discovering hidden treasures, and subduing the Intelligences by which those treasures are guarded. Never before his time had any Mussulman puzzled his brains over hieroglyphics. Now, however, search was made, on his behalf, for hieroglyphics of every kind, in all quarters, in the remotest provinces, the strange symbols being faithfully copied on linen cloths. I have seen these cloths a thousand times, stretched out on the roofs of our palace. Nor could bees be more busy and assiduous about a bed of flowers than were the Sages about these painted sheets. But, as each Sage entertained a different opinion as to the meaning of what was there depicted, arguments were frequent, and quarrels ensued. Not only did the Sages spend the hours of daylight in prosecuting their researches, but the moon often shed its beams upon them while so occupied. They did not dare to light torches upon the terraced roofs, for fear of alarming the faithful Mussulmans, who were beginning to blame my father's veneration for an idolatrous antiquity, and regarded all these painted symbols, these figures, with a pious horror.

Meanwhile, the Emir, who would never have thought of neglecting any real matter of business, however unimportant, for the pursuit of his strange studies, was by no means so particular with regard to his religious observances, and often forgot to perform the ablutions ordained by the law. The women of his harem did not fail to perceive this, but were afraid to speak, as, for one reason and another, their influence had considerably waned. But, on a certain day, Shaban, the chief of the eunuchs, who was old and very pious, presented himself before his master, holding a ewer and golden basin, and said: "The waters of the Nile have been given for the cleansing of all our impurities; their source is in the clouds of heaven, not in the temples of idols; take and use those waters, for you stand in need of them!"

The Emir, duly impressed by the action and speech of Shaban, yielded to his just remonstrances, and, instead of unpacking a large bale of painted cloths, which had just arrived from a far distance, ordered the eunuch to serve the day's collation in the Hall of the Golden Trellises, and to assemble there all his slaves, and all his birds – of which he kept a very large number in aviaries of sandalwood.

Immediately the palace rang to the sound of instruments of music, and groups of slaves appeared, all dressed in their most attractive garments, and each leading in leash a peacock whiter than snow. One only of these slaves – whose slender and graceful form was a delight to the eye – had no bird in leash, and kept her veil down.

"Why this eclipse?" said the Emir to Shaban.

"Lord," answered he, with joyful mien, "I am better than all your astrologers, for it is I who have discovered this lovely star. But do not imagine that she is yet within your reach; her father, the holy and venerable Iman Abzenderoud, will never consent to make you happy in the possession of her charms unless you perform your ablutions with greater regularity, and give the go-by to Sages and their hieroglyphics."

My father, without replying to Shaban, ran to snatch away the veil that hid the countenance of Ghulendi Begum – for such was the name of Abzenderoud's daughter – and he did so with such violence that he nearly crushed two peacocks, and overturned several baskets of flowers. To this sudden heat succeeded a kind of ecstatic stupor. At last he cried: "How beautiful she is, how divine! Go, fetch at once the Iman of Soussouf – let the nuptial chamber be got ready, and all necessary preparations for our marriage be complete within one hour!"

"But, lord," said Shaban, in consternation, "you have forgotten that Ghulendi Begum cannot marry you without the consent of her father, who makes it a condition that you should abandon . . ."

"What nonsense are you talking?" interrupted the vizier. "Do you think I am fool enough not to prefer this young virgin, fresh as the dew of the morning, to cartloads of hieroglyphics, mouldy and of the colour of dead ashes? As to Abzenderoud, go and fetch him if you like – but quickly, for I shall certainly not wait a moment longer than I please."

"Hasten, Shaban," said Ghulendi Begum modestly, "hasten; you see that I am not going to resist."

"It's my fault," mumbled the eunuch, as he departed, "but I shall do what I can to rectify my error."

Accordingly he flew to find Abzenderoud. But that faithful servant of Allah had gone from home very early in the morning, and sought the open fields in order to pursue his pious investigations into the growth of plants and the life of insects. A death-like pallor overspread his countenance when he saw Shaban swooping upon him like a raven of evil omen, and heard him tell, in broken accents, how the Emir had promised nothing, and how he himself might well arrive too late to exact the pious conditions he had so deeply pondered. Nevertheless, the Iman did not lose courage, and reached my father's palace in a very few moments; but unfortunately he was by this time so out of breath that he sank on to a sofa, and remained for over an hour panting and speechless.

While all the eunuchs were doing their best to revive the holy man, Shaban had quickly gone up to the apartment assigned to Abou Taher Achmed's pleasures; but his zeal suffered some diminution when he saw the door guarded

172

by two black eunuchs, who, brandishing their sabres, informed him that if he ventured to take one more step forward, his head would roll at his own feet. Therefore had he nothing better to do than to return to Abzenderoud, whose gaspings he regarded with wild and troubled eyes, lamenting the while over his own imprudence in bringing Ghulendi Begum within the Emir's power.

Notwithstanding the care my father was taking for the entertainment of the new sultana, he had heard something of the dispute between the black eunuchs and Shaban, and had a fair notion of what was going on. As soon, therefore, as he judged it convenient, he came to find Abzenderoud in the Hall of Golden Trellises, and presenting Ghulendi Begum to the holy man assured him that, while awaiting his arrival, he, the Emir, had made her his wife.

At these words, the Iman uttered a lamentable and piercing cry, which relieved the pressure on his chest; and, rolling his eyes in a fearful manner, he said to the new sultana: "Wretched woman, dost thou not know that rash and ill-considered acts lead ever to a miserable end? Thy father would have made thy lot secure; but thou has not awaited the result of his efforts, or rather it is Heaven itself that mocks all human previsions. I ask nothing more of the Emir; let him deal with thee, and with his hieroglyphics, as he deems best! I foresee untold evils in the future; but I shall not be there to witness them. Rejoice for a while, intoxicated with thy pleasures. As for me, I call to my aid the Angel of Death, and hope, within three days, to rest in peace in the bosom of our great Prophet!"

After saying these words, he rose to his feet, tottering. His daughter strove in vain to hold him back. He tore his robe from her trembling hands. She fell fainting to the ground, and while the distracted Emir was striving to bring her back to her senses, the obstinate Abzenderoud went muttering from the room.

At first it was thought that the holy man would not keep his vow quite literally, and would suffer himself to be comforted; but such was not the case. On reaching his own house, he began by stopping his ears with cotton wool, so as not to hear the clamour and adjurations of his friends; and then, having seated himself on the mats in his cell, with his legs crossed, and his head in his hands, he remained in that posture speechless, and taking no food; and finally, at the end of three days, expired according to his prayer. He was buried magnificently, and during the obsequies Shaban did not fail to manifest his grief by slashing his own flesh without mercy, and soaking the earth with little rivulets of his blood; after which, having caused balm to be applied to his wounds, he returned to the duties of his office.

Meanwhile, the Emir had no small difficulty in assuaging the despair of Ghulendi Begum, and often cursed the hieroglyphics which had been its first efficient cause. At last his attentions touched the heart of the sultana. She regained her ordinary equability of spirits, and became pregnant; and everything returned to its accustomed order.

The Emir, his mind always dwelling on the magnificence of the ancient Pharaohs, built, after their manner, a palace with twelve pavilions — proposing, at an early date, to install in each pavilion a son. Unfortunately, his wives brought forth nothing but daughters. At each new birth he grumbled, gnashed his teeth, accused Mahomet of being the cause of his mishaps, and would have been altogether unbearable, if Ghulendi Begum had not found means to moderate his ill temper. She induced him to come every night into her apartment, where, by a thousand ingenious devices, she succeeded in introducing fresh air, while, in other parts of the palace, the atmosphere was stifling.

During her pregnancy my father never left the dais on which she reclined. This dais was set in a large and long gallery overlooking the Nile, and so disposed as to seem about on a level with the stream, — so close, too, that anyone reclining upon it could throw into the water the grains of any pomegranate he might be eating. The best dancers, the most excellent musicians, were always about the place. Every night pantomimes were performed to the light of a thousand golden lamps – lamps placed upon the floor so as to bring out the fineness and grace of the performers' feet. The dancers themselves cost my father immense sums in golden fringed slippers and sandals a-glitter with jewellery; and, indeed, when they were all in motion together the effect was dazzling.

But notwithstanding this accumulation of splendours, the sultana passed very unhappy days on her dais. With the same indifference that a poor wretch tormented by sleeplessness watches the scintillation of the stars, so did she see pass before her eyes all this whirl of performers in their brilliancy and charm. Anon she would think of the wrath, that seemed almost prophetic, of her venerable father; anon she would deplore his strange and untimely end. A thousand times she would interrupt the choir of singers, crying: "Fate has decreed my ruin! Heaven will not vouchsafe me a son, and my husband will banish me from his sight!" The torment of her mind intensified the pain and discomfort attendant on her condition. My father, thereupon, was so greatly perturbed that, for the first time in his life, he made appeal to Heaven, and ordered prayers to be offered up in every mosque. Nor did he omit the giving of alms, for he caused it to be publicly announced that all beggars were to assemble in the largest court of the palace, and would there be served with rice, each according to his individual appetite. There followed such a crush every morning at the palace gates that the incomers were nearly suffocated. Mendicants swarmed in from all parts, by land, and by the river. Whole villages would come down the stream on rafts. And the appetites of all were enormous; for the buildings which my father had erected, his costly pursuit of hieroglyphics, and the maintenance of his Sages, had caused some scarcity throughout the land.

Among those who came from a very far distance was a man of an extreme age, and great singularity, by name Abou Gabdolle Guehaman, the hermit of the Great Sandy Desert. He was eight feet high, so ill proportioned, and of a leanness so extreme, that he looked like a skeleton, and hideous to behold. Nevertheless, this lugubrious and forbidding piece of human mechanism enshrined the most benevolent and religious spirit in the universe. With a voice of thunder he proclaimed the will of the Prophet, and said openly it was a pity that a prince who distributed rice to the poor, and in such great profusion, should be a determined lover of hieroglyphics. People crowded round him – the Imans, the Mullahs, the Muezins, did nothing but sing his praises. His feet, though ingrained with the sand of his native desert, were freely kissed. Nay, the very grains of the sand from his feet were gathered up, and treasured in caskets of amber.

One day he proclaimed the truth and the horror of the sciences of evil, in a voice so loud and resonant that the great standards set before the palace trembled. The terrible sound penetrated into the interior of the harem. The women and the eunuchs fainted away in the Hall of the Golden Trellises; the dancers stood with one foot arrested in the air; the mummers had not the courage to pursue their antics; the musicians suffered their instruments to fall to the ground; and Ghulendi Begum thought to die of fright as she lay on her dais.

Abou Taher Achmed stood astounded. His conscience smote him for his idolatrous proclivities, and during a few remorseful moments he thought that the Avenging Angel had come to turn him into stone – and not himself only but the people committed to his charge.

After standing for some time, upright, with arms uplifted, in the Gallery of the Daises, he called Shaban to him, and said: "The sun has not lost its brightness, the Nile flows peacefully in its bed, what means then this supernatural cry that has just resounded through my palace?"

"Lord," answered the pious eunuch, "this voice is the voice of Truth, and it is spoken to you through the mouth of the venerable Abou Gabdolle Guehaman, the Hermit of the Sandy Desert, the most faithful, the most zealous, of the servants of the Prophet, who has, in nine days, journeyed three hundred leagues to make proof of your hospitality, and to impart to you the knowledge with which he is inspired. Do not neglect the teachings of a man who in wisdom, in piety, and in stature, surpasses the most enlightened, the most devout, and the most gigantic of the inhabitants of the earth. All your people are in an ecstasy. Trade is at a standstill. The inhabitants of the city hasten to hear him, neglecting their wonted assemblies in the public gardens. The storytellers are without hearers at the edges of the public fountains. Jussouf himself was not wiser than he, and had no greater knowledge of the future."

At these last words, the Emir was suddenly smitten with the desire of consulting Abou Gabdolle with regard to his family affairs, and particularly with regard to the great projects he entertained for the future advantage of his sons, who were not yet born. He deemed himself happy in being thus able to consult a living prophet; for, so far, it was only in the form of mummies that he had been brought into relation with these inspired personages. He resolved, therefore, to summon into his presence, nay, into his very harem, the extraordinary being now in question. Would not the Pharaohs have so dealt with the necromancers of their time, and was not he determined, in all circumstances, to follow the Pharaoh's example? He therefore graciously directed Shaban to go and fetch the holy man.

Shaban, transported with joy, hastened to communicate this invitation to the hermit, who, however, did not appear to be as much charmed by the summons as were the people at large. These latter filled the air with their acclamations, while Abou Gabdolle stood still, with his hands clasped, and his eyes uplifted to heaven, in a prophetic trance. From time to time he uttered the deepest sighs, and, after remaining long rapt in holy contemplation, shouted out, in his voice of thunder: "Allah's will be done! I am but his creature. Eunuch, I am ready to follow thee. But let the doors of the palace be broken down. It is not meet for the servants of the Most High to bend their heads."

The people needed no second command. They all set hands to the work with a will, and in an instant the gateway, a piece of the most admirable workmanship, was utterly ruined.

At the sound of the breaking in of the doors, piercing cries arose within the harem. Abou Taher Achmed began to repent of his curiosity. Nevertheless, he ordered, though somewhat reluctantly, that the passages into the harem should be laid open to the holy giant, for he feared lest the enthusiastic adherents of the prophet should penetrate into the apartments occupied by the women, and containing the princely treasures. These fears were, however, vain, for the holy man had sent back his devout admirers. I have been assured that on their all kneeling to receive his blessing he said to them, in tones of the deepest solemnity: "Retire, remain peacefully in your dwellings, and be assured that, whatever happens, Abou Gabdolle Guehaman is prepared for every emergency." Then, turning towards the palace, he cried: "O domes of dazzling brilliancy, receive me, and may nothing ensue to tarnish your splendour."

Meanwhile, everything had been made ready within the harem. Screens had been duly ordered, the door-curtains had been drawn, and ample draperies hung before the daises in the long gallery that ran round the interior of the building – thus concealing from view the sultanas, and the princesses, their daughters.

Such elaborate preparations had caused a general ferment; and curiosity was at its height, when the hermit, trampling under foot the ruined fragments of the door-ways, entered majestically into the Hall of the Golden Trellises. The magnificence of the palace did not even win from him a passing glance, his eyes remained fixed, mournfully, on the pavement at his feet. At last he penetrated into the great gallery of the women. These latter, who were not at all accustomed to the sight of creatures so lean, gaunt, and gigantic, uttered piercing cries, and loudly asked for essences and cordials to enable them to bear up against the apparition of such a phantasm.

The hermit paid not the smallest heed to the surrounding tumult. He was gravely pursuing his way, when the Emir came forward, and, taking him by the skirt of his garment, led him, with much ceremony, to the dais of the gallery which looked out upon the Nile. Basins of comfits and orthodox liquors were at once served; but though Abou Gabdolle Guehaman seemed to be dying of hunger, he refused to partake of these refreshments, saying that for ninety years he had drunk nothing but the dew of heaven, and eaten only the locusts of the desert. The Emir, who regarded this diet as conformable to what might properly be expected of a prophet, did not press him further, but at once entered into the question he had at heart, saying how much it grieved him to be without an heir male, notwithstanding all the prayers offered up to that effect, and the flattering hopes which the Imans had given him. "But now," he continued, "I am assured that this happiness will at last be mine. The Sages, the mediciners, predict it, and my own observations confirm their prognostications. It is not, therefore, for the purpose of consulting you with regard to the future that I have caused you to be summoned. It is for the purpose of obtaining your advice upon the education I should give to the son whose birth I am expecting – or rather to the two sons, for, without doubt, heaven, in recognition of my alms, will accord to the Sultana Ghulendi Begum a double measure of fertility, seeing that she is twice as large as women usually are on such occasions."

Without answering a word, the hermit mournfully shook his head three times.

My father, greatly astonished, asked if his anticipated good fortune was in any wise displeasing to the holy man.

"Ah! too blind prince," replied the hermit, uttering a cavernous sigh that seemed to issue from the grave itself, "why importune heaven with rash prayers? Respect its decrees! It knows what is best for all men better than they do themselves. Woe be to you, and woe be to your son whom you will doubtless compel to follow in the perverse

179

ways of your own beliefs, instead of submitting himself humbly to the guidance of Providence. If the great of this world could only foresee all the misfortunes they bring upon themselves, they would tremble in the midst of their splendour. Pharaoh recognised this truth, but too late. He pursued the children of Moussa in despite of the divine decrees, and died the death of the wicked. What can alms avail when the heart is in rebellion? Instead of asking the Prophet for an heir, to be led by you into the paths of destruction, those who have your welfare at heart should implore him to cause Ghulendi Begum to die – yes, to die, before she brings into the world presumptuous creatures, whom your conduct will precipitate into the abyss! Once again I call upon you to submit. If Allah's angel threatens to cut short the days of the sultana, do not make appeal to your magicians to ward off the fatal blow: let it fall, let her die! Tremble not with wrath, Emir; harden not your heart! once again call to mind the fate of Pharaoh and the waters that swallowed him up!"

"Call them to mind yourself!" cried my father, foaming with rage, and springing from the dais to run to the help of the sultana, who, having heard all, had fainted away behind the curtains. "Remember that the Nile flows beneath these windows, and that thou hast well deserved that thy odious carcass should be hurled into its waters!"

"I fear not," cried the gigantic hermit in turn; "the prophet of Allah fears naught but himself," and he rose on the tips of his toes, and touched with his hands the supports of the dome of the apartment.

"Ha! ha! thou fearest nothing," cried all the women and eunuchs, issuing like tigers out of their den. "Accursed assassin, thou has just brought our beloved mistress to death's door, and yet fearest nothing! Go, and become food for the monsters of the river!" Screaming out these words they threw themselves, all at once, on Abou Gabdolle Guehaman, bore him down, strangled him without pity, and cast his body through a dark grating into the Nile, which there lost itself obscurely among piers of iron.

The Emir, astonished by an act at once so sudden and so atrocious, remained with his eyes fixed on the waters; but the body did not again come to the surface; and Shaban, who now appeared upon the scene, bewildered him with his cries. At last he turned to look upon the perpetrators of the crime; but they had scattered in every direction, and hidden behind the curtains of the gallery; each avoiding the other, they were overwhelmed with the thought of what they had done.

Ghulendi, who had only come to herself in time to witness this scene of horror, was now in mortal anguish. Her convulsions, her agonising cries, drew the Emir to her side. He bedewed her hand with tears. She opened her eyes wildly, and cried: "Oh Allah! Allah! put an end to a wretched creature who has already lived only too long, since she has been the cause of so terrible an outrage, and suffer not that she should bring into the world – –" "Stop, stop," interrupted the Emir, holding her hands which she was about to turn against herself, "thou shalt not die, and my children shall yet live to give the lie to that demented skeleton, worthy only of contempt. Let my Sages be summoned instantly. Let them use all their art to keep thy soul from flitting hence and to save from harm the fruit of thy body."

The Sages were convened accordingly. They demanded that one of the courts in the palace should be placed entirely at their disposal, and there began their operations, kindling a fire whose light penetrated into the gallery. The sultana rose from her couch, notwithstanding all the efforts made to restrain her, and ran to the balcony overlooking the Nile. The view from thence was lonely and dreary. Not a single boat showed upon the surface of the stream. In the distance were discernible stretches of sand, which the wind, from time to time, sent whirling into the air. The rays of the setting sun dyed the waters blood-red. Scarcely had the deepening twilight stretched over the horizon, when a sudden and furious wind broke the open lattice-work of the gallery. The sultana, beside herself, her heart beating, tried to plunge back into the interior of the apartment, but an irresistible power held her where she was, and forced her, against her will, to contemplate the mournful scene before her eyes. A great silence now reigned. Darkness had insensibly covered the earth. Then suddenly a streak of blue light furrowed the clouds in the direction of the pyramids. The princess could distinguish their enormous mass against the horizon as clearly as if it had been noonday. The spectacle thus suddenly revealed, chilled her with fear. Several times did she try to call her slaves, but her voice refused its office. She endeavoured to clap her hands, but in vain.

While she remained thus — as if in the grip of some horrible dream — a lamentable voice broke the silence, and uttered these words: "My latest breath has just been exhaled into the waters of the river; vainly have thy servants striven to stifle the voice of truth; it rises now from the abysses of death. O wretched mother! see whence issues that fatal light, and tremble!"

Ghulendi Begum endured to hear no more. She fell back senseless. Her women, who had been anxious about her, hurried up at this moment, and uttered the most piercing cries. The Sages approached, and placed into the hands of my father, who was in terrible perturbation, the powerful elixir they had prepared. Scarcely had a few drops fallen on the sultana's breast, when her soul, which had seemed about to follow the orders of Asrael, the Angel of Death, came back, as if in nature's despite, to reanimate her body. Her eyes re-opened to see, still illuminating the pyramids, the fatal furrow of blue light which had not yet faded from the sky. She raised her arms, and, pointing out to the Emir with her finger that dread portent, was seized with the pains of childbirth, and, in the paroxysm of an unspeakable anguish, brought into the world a son and a daughter: the two wretched beings you see before you here.

The Emir's joy in the possession of a male child was greatly dashed when he saw my mother die before his eyes. Notwithstanding his excessive grief, however, he did not lose his head, and at once handed us over to the care of his Sages. The nurses, who had been engaged in great number, wished to oppose this arrangement; but the ancient men, all muttering incantations simultaneously, compelled them to silence. The cabalistic lavers in which we were to be immersed stood all ready prepared; the mixture of herbs exhaled a vapour that filled the whole palace. Shaban, whose very stomach was turned by the unspeakable odour of these infernal drugs, had all the trouble in the world to restrain himself from summoning the Imans, and doctors of the law, in order to oppose the impious rites now in contemplation. Would to heaven he had had the courage to do so! Ah, how terrible has been the influence upon us of the pernicious immersions to which we were then subjected! In short, lord, we were plunged, both successively and together, into a hell-broth which was intended to impart to us a strength and intelligence more than human, but has only instilled into our veins the ardent elixir of a too exquisite sensibility, and the poison of an insatiable desire.

It was to the sound of brazen wands beating against the metal sides of the lavers, it was in the midst of thick fumes issuing from heaps of burning herbs, that invocations were addressed to the Jinns, and specially to those who preside over the pyramids, in order that we might be endowed with marvellous gifts. After this we were delivered over to the nurses, who scarcely could hold us in their arms, such was our liveliness and vivacity. The good women shed tears when they saw how our young blood boiled within us, and strove in vain to cool its effervescence, and to calm us by cleansing our bodies from the reeking mess with which they were still covered; but, alas! the harm was already done! Nay, if even, as sometimes happened in after days, we wished to fall into the ordinary ways of childhood, my father, who was determined, at all hazards, to possess children of an extraordinary nature, would brisk us up with heating drugs and the milk of negresses.

We thus became unendurably headstrong and mettlesome. At the age of seven, we could not bear contradiction. At the slightest restraint, we uttered cries of rage, and bit those who had us in charge till the blood flowed. Shaban came in for a large share of our attentions in this kind; sighing over us, however, in silence, for the Emir only regarded our spitefulness as giving evidence of a genius equal to that of Saurid and Charobé. Ah! how little did anyone suspect the real cause of our frowardness! Those who look too long into the light are soonest afflicted with blindness. My father had not yet remarked that we were never arrogant and overbearing towards one another, that each was ready to yield to the other's wishes, that Kalilah, my brother, was never at peace save in my arms, and that, as for me, my only happiness lay in overwhelming him with caresses.

Up to this time, we had in all things been educated together: the same book was always placed before the eyes of both, each turned over the leaves alternately. Though my brother was subjected to a course of study rigorous, and above his years, I insisted on sharing it with him. Abou Taher Achmed, who cared for nothing save the aggrandisement of his son, gave directions that in this I should be humoured, because he saw that his son would only fully exert himself when at my side.

We were taught not only the history of the most remote ages of antiquity, but also the geography of distant lands. The Sages never ceased to indoctrinate us with the abstruse and ideal moral code, which, as they pretended, lurked hidden in the hieroglyphics. They filled our ears with a magnificent verbiage about wisdom and foreknowledge, and the treasure houses of the Pharaohs, whom sometimes they compared to ants, and sometimes to elephants. They inspired us with a most ardent curiosity as to those mountains of hewn stone beneath which the Egyptian kings lie sepulchred. They compelled us to learn by heart the long catalogue of architects and masons who had laboured at the building of them. They made us calculate the quantity of provisions that would be required by the workmen employed, and how many threads went to every ell of silk with which Sultan Saurid had covered his pyramid. Together with all this rubbish, these most weariful old dotards bewildered our brains with a pitiless grammar of the language spoken of old by the priests in their subterranean labyrinths.

The childish games in which we were allowed to indulge, during our playtime, had no charms for us unless we played them alone together. The princesses, our sisters, wearied us to death. Vainly did they embroider for my brother the most splendid vests; Kalilah disdained their gifts, and would only consent to bind his lovely hair with the muslin that had floated over the breast of his beloved Zulkaïs. Sometimes they invited us to visit them in the twelve pavilions which my father, no longer hoping to have that number of sons, had abandoned to their use – erecting another, and of greater magnificence, for my brother, and for myself. This latter building, crowned by five domes, and situated in a thick grove, was, every night, the scene of the most splendid revels in the harem. My father would come thither, escorted by his most beautiful slaves – each holding in her hand a candlestick with a white taper. How many times has the light of these tapers, appearing through the trees, caused our hearts to beat in sad anticipation! Everything that broke in upon our solitude was in the highest degree distasteful. To hide among the leafage, and listen to its murmur, seemed to us sweeter far than attending to the sound of the lute and the song of the musicians. But these soft luxurious reveries of ours were highly offensive to my father; he would force us back into the cupoled saloons, and compel us to take part in the common amusements.

Every year the Emir treated us with greater sternness. He did not dare to separate us altogether for fear of the effect upon his son, but tried rather to win him from our languorous dalliance, by throwing him more and more into the company of young men of his own age. The game of reeds, so famous among the Arabs, was introduced into the courts of the palace. Kalilah gave himself up to the sport with immense energy; but this was only so as to bring the games to a speedier end, and then fly back to my side. Once reunited we would read together, read of the loves of Jussouf and Zelica, or some other poem that spoke of love – or else, taking advantage of our moments of liberty, we would roam through the labyrinth of corridors looking out upon the Nile, always with our arms intertwined, always with eyes looking into each other's eyes. It was almost impossible to track us in the mazy passages of the palace and the anxiety we inspired did but add to our happiness.

One evening when we were thus tenderly alone together, and running side by side in childish glee, my father appeared before us and shuddered. "Why," said he to Kalilah, "why are you here and not in the great courtyard, shooting with the bow, or else with the horse-trainers training the horses which are to bear you into battle? Must the sun, as it rises and sets, see you only bloom and fade like a weak narcissus flower? Vainly do the Sages try to move you by the most eloquent discourses, and unveil before your eyes the learned mysteries of an older time; vainly do they tell you of warlike and magnanimous deeds. You are now nearly thirteen, and never have you evinced the smallest ambition to distinguish yourself among your fellow-men. It is not in the lurking haunts of effeminacy that great characters are formed; it is not by reading love poems that men are made fit to govern nations! Princes must act; they must show themselves to the world. Awake! Cease to abuse my patience which has too long allowed you to waste your hours by the side of Zulkaïs. Let her, tender creature that she is, continue to play among her flowers, but you should cease to haunt her company from dawn till eve. I see well enough that it is she who is perverting you."

Having spoken these words, which he emphasised by angry and threatening gestures, Abou Taher Achmed took my brother by the arm, and left me in a very abyss of bitterness. An icy numbness overcame me. Though the sun still shed its fullest rays upon the water, I felt as if it had disappeared below the horizon. Stretched at length upon the ground, I did nothing but kiss the sprays of orange flowers that Kalilah had gathered. My sight fell upon the drawings he had traced, and my tears fell in greater abundance. "Alas!" said I, "all is over. Our blissful moments will return no more. Why accuse me of perverting Kalilah? What harm can I do him? How can our happiness offend my father? If it was a crime to be happy, the Sages would surely have given us warning."

My nurse Shamelah found me in this condition of languor and dejection. To dissipate my grief she immediately led me to the grove where the young girls of the harem were playing at hide-and-seek amid the golden aviaries of which the place was full. I derived some little solace from the song of the birds, and the murmur of the rillets of clear water that trickled round the roots of the trees, but when the hour came at which Kalilah was wont to appear these sounds did but add to my sufferings.

Shamelah noticed the heavings of my breast; she drew me aside, placed her hand upon my heart, and observed me attentively. I blushed, I turned pale, and that very visibly. "I see very well," said she, "that it is your brother's absence that so upsets you. This is the fruit of the strange education to which you have been subjected. The holy reading of the Koran, the due observance of the Prophet's laws, confidence in the known mercies of Allah, these are as milk to cool the fever heat of human passion. You know not the soft delight of lifting up your soul to heaven, and submitting without a murmur to its decrees. The Emir, alas! would forestall the future; while, on the contrary, the future should be passively awaited. Dry your tears, perchance Kalilah is not unhappy though distant from your side."

"Ah!" I cried, interrupting her with a sinister look, "if I were not fully convinced that he is unhappy, I should myself be far more miserable."

Shamelah trembled at hearing me speak thus. She cried: "Would to heaven that they had listened to my advice, and the advice of Shaban, and instead of handing you over to the capricious teaching of the Sages, had left you, like true believers, at peace in the arms of a blissful and quiet ignorance. The ardour of your feelings alarms me in the very highest degree. Nay, it excites my indignation. Be more calm; abandon your soul to the innocent pleasures that surround you, and do so without troubling yourself whether Kalilah shares in those pleasures or not. His sex is made for toil and manly hardship. How should you be able to follow him in the chase, to handle a bow, and to dart reeds in the Arab game? He must look for companions manly and worthy of himself, and cease to fritter away his best days here at your side amid bowers and aviaries."

This sermon, far from producing its desired effect, made me altogether beside myself. I trembled with rage, and, rising to my feet like one bereft of reason, I rent my veil into ten thousand pieces, and, tearing my breast, cried with a loud voice that my nurse had mishandled me.

The games ceased. Everyone crowded about me; and though the princesses did not love me overmuch, because I was Kalilah's favourite sister, yet my tears, and the blood that flowed from my self-inflicted wounds, excited their indignation against Shamelah. Unfortunately for the poor woman, she had just awarded a severe punishment to two young slaves who had been guilty of stealing pomegranates; and these two little vipers, in order to be revenged, bore testimony against her, and confirmed all I said. They ran, and retailed their lies to my father, who, not having Shaban at his side, and being, moreover, in a good temper because my brother had just thrown a javelin into a crocodile's eye, ordered Shamelah to be tied to a tree, and whipped without mercy.

Her cries pierced my heart. She cried without ceasing: "O you, whom I have carried in my arms, whom I have fed from my breast, how can you cause me to suffer thus? Justify me! Declare the truth! It is only because I tried to save you from the black abyss, into which your wild and unruly desires cannot fail to precipitate you in the end, that you are thus causing this body of mine to be torn to shreds."

I was about to ask that she should be released and spared further punishment, when some demon put into my mind the thought that it was she who, conjointly with Shaban, had inspired my father with the desire of making a hero of Kalilah. Whereupon, I armed myself against every feeling of humanity, and cried that they should go on whipping her till she confessed her crime. Darkness at last put an end to this horrible scene. The victim was unloosed. Her friends, and she had many, endeavoured to close her wounds. They asked me, on their knees, to give them a sovereign balm which I possessed, a balm which the Sages had prepared. I refused. Shamelah was placed before my eyes on a litter, and, of set purpose, kept for a moment in front of the place where I stood. That breast, on which I had so often slept, streamed with blood. At this spectacle, at the memory of the tender care she had taken of my infancy, my heart at last was moved − I burst into tears; I kissed the hand she feebly extended to the monster she had nourished in her bosom; I ran to fetch the balm; I applied it myself, begging her, at the same time, to forgive me, and declaring openly that she was innocent, and I alone guilty.

This confession caused a shudder to pass among all who surrounded us. They recoiled from me with horror. Shamelah, though half dead, perceived this, and stifled her groans with the skirt of her garment so as not to add to my despair and the baleful consequences of what I had done. But her efforts were in vain. All fled, casting upon me looks that were evil indeed.

The litter was removed, and I found myself alone. The night was very dark. Plaintive sounds seemed to issue from the cypresses that cast their shadow over the place. Seized with terror, I lost myself amid the black foliage, a prey to the most harrowing remorse. Delirium laid its hand upon me. The earth seemed to yawn before my feet, and I to fall headlong into an abyss which had no bottom. My spirit was in this distraught condition, when, through the thick underwood, I saw shine the torches of my father's attendants. I noticed that the cortège stopped suddenly. Someone issued from the crowd. A lively presentiment made my heart beat. The footsteps came nearer; and, by the light of a faint and doleful glimmer, such as prevails in the place where we now are, I saw Kalilah appear before me.

"Dear Zulkaïs," cried he, intermingling words and kisses, "I have passed an age without seeing you, but I have spent it in carrying out my father's wishes. I have fought with one of the most formidable monsters of the river. But what would I not do when, for recompense, I am offered the bliss of spending a whole evening with you alone? Come! Let us enjoy the time to the full. Let us bury ourselves among these trees. Let us, from our retreat, listen, disdainful, to the tumultuous sound of music and dances. I will cause sherbet and cakes to be served on the moss that borders the little porphyry fountain. There I shall enjoy your sweet looks, and charming converse, till the first dawn of the new day. Then, alas! I must plunge once more into the world's vortex, dart accursed reeds, and undergo the interrogatories of Sages."

Kalilah said all this with such volubility that I was unable to put in a word. He drew me after him, scarce resisting. We made our way through the leafage to the fountain. The memory of what Shamelah had said concerning my excessive tenderness for my brother, had, in my own despite, produced a strong impression upon me. I was about to withdraw my hand from his, when, by the light of the little lamps that had been lit on the margin of the fountain, I saw his charming face reflected in the waters, I saw his large eyes dewy with love, I felt his looks pierce to the very bottom of my heart. All my projects of reform, all my agony of remorse, made way for a ferment of very different feelings. I dropped on to the ground by Kalilah's side, and, leaning his head upon my breast, gave a free course to my tears. Kalilah, when he saw me thus crying passionately, eagerly asked me why I wept. I told him all that had passed between myself and Shamelah, without omitting a single particular. His heart was at first much moved by the picture I drew of her sufferings; but, a moment after, he cried: "Let the officious slave perish! Must the heart's soft yearnings ever meet with opposition! How should we not love one another, Zulkaïs? Nature caused us to be born together. Has not nature, too, implanted in us the same tastes, and a kindred ardour? Have not my father and his Sages made us partakers in the same magic baths? Who could blame a sympathy all has conspired to create? No, Zulkaïs, Shaban and our superstitious nurse may say what they please. There is no crime in our loving one another. The crime would rather be if we allowed ourselves, like cowards, to be separated. Let us swear – not by the Prophet, of whom we have but little knowledge, but by the elements that sustain man's existence – let us swear that, rather than consent to live the one without the other, we will take into our veins the soft distillation of the flowers of the stream, which the Sages have so often vaunted in our hearing. That essence will lull us painlessly to sleep in each other's arms, and so bear our souls imperceptibly into the peace of another existence!"

These words quieted me. I resumed my ordinary gaiety, and we sported and played together. "I shall be very valiant to-morrow," Kalilah would say, "so as to purchase such moments as these, for it is only by the promise of such a prize that my father can induce me to submit to his fantastic injunctions."

"Ha, ha!" cried Abou Taher Achmed, issuing from behind some bushes, where he had been listening, "is that your resolve! We will see if you keep to it! You are already fully paid this evening for the little you have done during the day. Hence! And as to you, Zulkaïs, go and weep over the terrible outrage you have committed against Shamelah."

In the greatest consternation we threw ourselves at his feet; but, turning his back upon us, he ordered the eunuchs to conduct us to our separate apartments.

It was no scruple with regard to the kind and quality of our love that exercised the Emir. His sole end was to see his son become a great warrior, and a potent prince, and with regard to the character of the means by which that end was to be obtained, he cared not one tittle. As for me, he regarded me only as an instrument that might have its use; nor would he have felt any scruples concerning the danger of inflaming our passion by the alternation of obstacles and concessions. On the other hand, he foresaw that indolence and pleasure, too constantly indulged in, must necessarily interfere with his designs. He deemed it necessary, therefore, to adopt with us a harsher and more decided line of conduct than he had hitherto done; and in an unhappy moment he carried that resolution into effect. Alas! without his precautions, his projects, his accursed foresight, we should have remained in innocence, and never been brought to the horror of this place of torment!

The Emir, having retired to his apartments, caused Shaban to be summoned, and imparted to him his fixed resolve to separate us for a certain time. The prudent eunuch prostrated himself immediately, with his face to the ground, and then, rising to his feet, said: "Let my lord forgive his slave if he ventures to be of a different opinion. Do not let loose upon this nascent flame the winds of opposition and absence, lest the final conflagration should be such as you are unable to master. You know the prince's impetuous disposition; his sister has to-day given proofs, only too signal, of hers. Suffer them to remain together without contradiction; leave them to their childish propensities. They will soon grow tired of one another; and Kalilah, disgusted with the monotony of the harem, will beg you on his knees to remove him from its precincts!"

"Have you done talking your nonsense?" interrupted the Emir impatiently. "Ah, how little do you know the genius of Kalilah! I have carefully studied him, I have seen that the operations of my Sages have not been void of their effect. He is incapable of pursuing any object with indifference. If I leave him with Zulkaïs, he will be utterly drowned in effeminacy. If I remove her from him, and make their reunion the price of the great things I require at his hands, there is nothing of which he will not prove himself capable. Let the doctors of our law dote as they please! What can their idle drivel matter so long as he becomes what I desire him to be? Know besides, O eunuch, that when he has once tasted the delights of ambition, the idea of Zulkaïs will evaporate in his mind as a light morning mist absorbed into the rays of the noonday sun – the sun of glory. Therefore enter to-morrow morning into the chamber of Zulkaïs, forestall her awakening, wrap her up in these robes, and convey her, with her slaves, and all that may be necessary to make her life pleasant, to the borders of the Nile, where a boat will be ready to receive you. Follow the course of the stream for twenty-nine days. On the thirtieth you will disembark at the Isle of Ostriches. Lodge the princess in the palace which I have had built for the use of the Sages who roam those deserts – deserts replete with ruins and with wisdom. One of these Sages you will find there, called the Palm-tree-climber, because he pursues his course of contemplation upon the tops of the palm-trees. This ancient man knows an infinite number of stories, and it will be his care to divert Zulkaïs, for I know very well that, next to Kalilah, stories are the chief object of her delight."

Shaban knew his master too well to venture upon any further opposition. He went, therefore, to give the necessary orders, but sighed heavily as he went. He had not the slightest desire to undertake a journey to the Isle of Ostriches, and had formed a very unfavourable opinion of the Palm-tree-climber. He was himself a faithful Mussulman, and held the Sages and all their works in abomination.

Everything was made ready all too soon. The agitation of the previous day had greatly fatigued me, so that I slept very heavily. I was taken from my bed so quietly, and carried with such skill, that I never woke till I was at a distance of four leagues from Cairo. Then the noise of the water gurgling round the boat began to alarm me. It filled my ears strangely, and I half fancied I had drunk of the beverage spoken of by Kalilah, and been borne beyond the confines of our planet. I lay thus, bewildered with strange imaginings, and did not dare to open my eyes, but stretched out my arms to feel for Kalilah. I thought he was by my side. Judge of the feelings of hateful surprise to which I was doomed, when, instead of touching his delicate limbs, I seized hold of the horny hand of the eunuch who was steering the boat, and was even older, and more grotesquely ugly, than Shaban himself. I sat up and uttered piercing cries. I opened my eyes, and saw before me a vast stretch of sky, and of water bounded by bluish banks. The sun was shining in its fullness. The azure heavens caused all nature to rejoice. A thousand river birds played around amid the water-lilies, which the boat shore through at every moment, their large yellow flowers shining like gold, and exhaling a sweet perfume. But all these objects of delight were lost upon me, and, instead of rejoicing my heart, filled me with a sombre melancholy.

Looking about me, I saw my slaves in a state of desolation, and Shaban who, with an air at once of discontent and authority, was making them keep silence. The name of Kalilah came at every moment to the tip of my tongue. At last I spoke it aloud, with tears in my eyes, and asked where he was, and what they intended to do with me. Shaban, instead of replying, ordered his eunuchs to redouble their exertions, and to strike up an Egyptian song, and sing in time to the cadence of their oars. Their accursed chorus rang out so potently that it brought an even worse bewilderment in my brain. We shot through the water like an arrow. It was in vain that I begged the rowers to stop, or at least to tell me where I was going. The barbarous wretches were deaf to my entreaties. The more insistent I was, the louder did they roar out their detestable song so as to drown my cries. Shaban, with his cracked voice, made more noise than the rest.

Nothing can express the torments I endured, and the

horror I felt at finding myself so far from Kalilah, and on the waters of the fearful Nile. My terrors increased with nightfall. I saw, with an inexpressible anguish, the sun go losing itself in the waters – its light, in a thousand rays, trembling upon their surface. I brought to mind the quiet moments which, at that same hour, I had passed with Kalilah, and, hiding my head in my veil, I gave myself up to my despair.

Soon a soft rustling became audible. Our boat was shearing its way through banks of reeds. A great silence succeeded to the song of the rowers, for Shaban had landed. He came back in a few moments, and carried me to a tent, erected a few paces from the river's bank. I found there lights, mattresses stretched on the ground, a table covered with various kinds of food, and an immense copy of the Koran, unfolded. I hated the holy book. The Sages, our instructors, had often turned it into ridicule, and I had never read it with Kalilah. So I threw it contemptuously to the ground. Shaban took upon himself to scold me; but I flew at him, and endeavoured to reduce him to silence. In this I proved successful, and the same treatment retained its efficacy during the whole course of the long expedition. Our subsequent experiences were similar to those of the first day. Endlessly did we pass banks of water-lilies, and flocks of birds, and an infinite number of small boats that came and went with merchandise.

At last we began to leave behind us the plain country. Like all who are unhappy and thus led to look forward, I kept my eyes continually fixed on the horizon ahead of us, and one evening I saw, rising there, great masses of much greater height, and of a form infinitely more varied, than the pyramids. These masses proved to be mountains. Their aspect inspired me with fear. The terrible thought occurred to me that my father was sending me to the woeful land of the Negro king, so that I might be offered up as a sacrifice to the idols, who, as the Sages pretended, were greedy of princesses. Shaban perceived my increasing distress, and at last took pity upon me. He revealed our ultimate destination; adding that though my father wished to separate me from Kalilah, it was not for ever, and that, in the meanwhile, I should make the acquaintance of a marvellous personage, called the Palm-tree-climber, who was the best story-teller in the universe.

This information quieted me to some extent. The hope, however distant, of seeing Kalilah again, poured balm into my soul, and I was not sorry to hear that I should have stories to my liking. Moreover, the idea of a realm of solitude, such as the Ostrich Isle, flattered my romantic spirit. If I must be separated from him whom I cherished more than life itself, I preferred to undergo my fate rather in some savage spot than amid the glitter and chatter of a harem. Far from all such impertinent frivolities, I purposed to abandon my whole soul to the sweet memories of the past, and give a free course to the languorous reveries in which I could see again the loved image of my Kalilah.

Fully occupied with these projects, it was with heedless eyes that I saw our boat approaching nearer and nearer to the land of mountains. The rocks encroached more and more upon the borders of the stream, and seemed soon about to deprive us of all sight of the sky. I saw trees of immeasurable height whose intertwisted roots hung down into the water. I heard the noise of cataracts, and saw the boiling eddies flash in foam and fill the air with a mist thin as silver gauze. Through this veil I perceived, at last, a green island of no great size, on which the ostriches were gravely promenading. Still further forward I discerned a domed edifice standing against a hill all covered with nests. This palace was utterly strange of aspect, and had, in truth, been built by a noted cabalist. The walls were of yellow marble, and shone like polished metal, and every object reflected in them assumed gigantic proportions. I trembled as I saw what a fantastic figure the ostriches presented as seen in that strange mirror; their necks seemed to go losing themselves in the clouds, and their eyes shone like enormous balls of iron heated red in a furnace. My terrors were observed by Shaban, who made me understand the magnifying qualities of the palace walls, and assured me that even if the birds were really as monstrous as they appeared, I might still trust, in all security, to their good manners, since the Palm-tree-climber had been labouring for over a hundred years to reduce their natural disposition to an exemplary mildness. Scarcely had he furnished me with this information, when I landed at a spot where the grass was green and fresh. A thousand unknown flowers, a thousand shells of fantastic shape, a thousand oddly fashioned snails, adorned the shore. The ardour of the sun was tempered by the perpetual dew distilled from the falling waters, whose monotonous sound inclined to slumber.

Feeling drowsy, I ordered a penthouse to be affixed to one of the palm-trees of which the place was full; for the Palm-tree-climber, who always bore at his girdle the keys of the palace, was at that hour pursuing his meditations at the other end of the island.

While a soft drowsiness took possession of my senses, Shaban ran to present my father's letters to the man of wisdom. In order to do this he was compelled to attach the missives to the end of a long pole, as the Climber was at the top of a palm-tree, fifty cubits high, and refused to come down without knowing why he was summoned. So soon as he had perused the leaves of the roll, he carried them respectfully to his forehead, and slipped down like a meteor; and indeed he had somewhat the appearance of a meteor, for his eyes were of flame, and his nose was a beautiful blood-red.

Shaban, amazed by the rapidity of the old man's descent, uninjured, from the tree, was somewhat outraged when asked to take him on his back; but the Climber declared that he never so far condescended as to walk. The eunuch, who loved neither Sages nor their caprices, and regarded both as the plagues of the Emir's family, hesitated for a moment; but, bearing in mind the positive order he had received, he conquered his aversion, and took the Palm-tree-climber on his shoulders saying: "Alas, the good hermit, Abou Gabdolle Guehaman, would not have behaved after this manner, and would, moreover, have been much more worthy of my assistance." The Climber heard these words in high dudgeon, for he had aforetime had pious squabbles with the hermit of the Sandy Desert; so he administered a mighty kick on to the small of Shaban's back, and thrust a fiery nose into the middle of his countenance. Shaban, on this, stumbled, but pursued his way without uttering a syllable.

I was still asleep. Shaban came up to my couch, and, throwing his burden at my feet, said, and his voice had a certain ring in it so that it awoke me without difficulty: "Here is the Climber! Much good may he do you!"

At the sight of such an object, I was quite unable, notwithstanding all my sorrows, to help bursting out into a fit of uncontrollable laughter. The old man did not change countenance, notwithstanding; he jingled his keys with an air of importance, and said to Shaban, in grave tones: "Take me again upon your back; let us go to the palace, and I will open its doors, which have never, hitherto, admitted any member of the female sex save my great egg-layer, the queen of the ostriches."

I followed. It was late. The great birds were coming down from the hills, and surrounded us in flocks, pecking at the grass and at the trees. The noise they made with their beaks was such that I seemed to be listening to the feet of an army on the march. At last I found myself before the shining walls of the palace. Though I knew the trick of them, my own distorted figure terrified me, as also the figure of the Climber on the shoulders of Shaban.

We entered into a vaulted apartment, lined with black marble starred with golden stars, which inspired a certain feeling of awe – a feeling to which, however, the old man's grotesque and amusing grimaces afforded some relief. The air was stifling, and nearly made me sick. The Climber, perceiving this, caused a great fire to be lit, and threw into it a small aromatic ball which he drew from his bosom. Immediately a vapour, rather pleasant to the smell, but very penetrating, diffused itself through the room. The eunuch fled, sneezing. As for me, I drew near to the fire, and sadly stirring the ashes, began to form in them the cipher of Kalilah.

The Climber did not interfere. He praised the education I had received, and approved greatly of our immersions, just after birth, by the Sages, adding maliciously that nothing so sharpened the wits as a passion somewhat out of the common. "I see clearly," he continued, "that you are absorbed in reflections of an interesting nature; and I am well pleased that it should be so. I myself had five sisters; we made very light of Mahomet's teaching, and loved one another with some fervour. I still, after the lapse of a hundred years, bear this in my memory with pleasure, for we scarcely ever forget early impressions. This my constancy has greatly commended me to the Jinns whose favourite I am. If you are able, like myself, to persevere in your present sentiments, they will probably do something for you. In the meanwhile, place your confidence in me. I shall not prove surly or unsympathetic as a guardian and keeper. Don't get it into your head that I am dependent on the caprice of your father, who has a limited outlook, and prefers ambition to pleasure. I am happier amid my palms, and my ostriches, and in the enjoyment of the delights of meditation, than he in his divan, and in all his grandeur. I don't mean to say that you yourself cannot add to the pleasures of my life. The more gracious you are to me, the more shall I show civility to you, and make you the partaker in things of beauty. If you seem to be happy in this place of solitude, you will acquire a great reputation for wisdom, and I know, by my own experience, that under the cloak of a great reputation it is possible to hide whole treasures of folly. Your father in his letters has told me all your story. While people think that you are giving heed to my instructions, you can talk to me about your Kalilah, as much as you like, and without offending me in any way. On the contrary, nothing affords me greater pleasure than to to observe the movements of a heart abandoning itself to its youthful inclinations, and I shall be glad to see the bright colours of a first love mantling on young cheeks."

While listening to this strange discourse, I kept my eyes on the ground; but the bird of hope fluttered in my bosom. At last I looked at the Sage, and his great red nose, that shone like a luminous point in that room of black marble, seemed to me less disagreeable. The smile accompanying my glance was of such significance that the Climber easily perceived I had swallowed his bait. This pleased him so mightily that he forgot his learned indolence, and ran to prepare a repast of which I stood greatly in need.

Scarcely had he departed, when Shaban came in, holding in his hand a letter, sealed with my father's seal, which he had just opened. "Here," said he, "are the instructions I was only to read when I reached this place; and I have read them only too clearly. Alas! how wretched it is to be the slave of a prince whose head has been turned by much learning. Unhappy princess! I am compelled, much against my will, to abandon you here. I must re-embark with all who have followed me hither, and only leave in your service the lame Mouzaka, who is deaf and dumb. The wretched Climber will be your only helper. Heaven alone knows what you will gain from his companionship. The Emir regards him as a prodigy of learning and wisdom; but as to this he must suffer a faithful Mussulman to have his doubts." As he spoke these words, Shaban touched the letter three times with his forehead, and then, leaping backward, disappeared from my sight.

The hideous manner in which the poor eunuch wept on leaving me, amused me much. I was far indeed from making any attempt to keep him back. His presence was odious to me, for he always avoided all conversation about the only subject that filled my heart. On the other hand, I was enchanted at the choice of Mouzaka as my attendant. With a deaf and dumb slave, I should enjoy full liberty in imparting my confidences to the obliging old man, and in following his advice, if so be that he gave me advice of which I approved.

All my thoughts were thus assuming a somewhat rosy hue, when the Climber returned, smothered up in carpets and cushions of silk, which he stretched out upon the ground; and he then proceeded, with a pleasant and contented air, to light torches, and to burn pastilles in braziers of gold. He had taken these sumptuous articles from the palace treasury, which, as he assured me, was well worthy of exciting my curiosity. I told him I was quite ready to take his word for it at that particular time, the smell of the excellent viands which had preceded him, having very agreeably whetted my appetite. These viands consisted chiefly of slices of deer spiced with fragrant herbs, of eggs prepared after divers recipes, and of cakes more dainty and delicate than the petals of a white rose. There was besides a ruddy liquor, made of date juice, and served in strange translucent shells, and sparkling like the eyes of the Climber himself.

We lay down to our meal together in a very friendly fashion. My amazing keeper greatly praised the quality of his wine, and made very good use of it, to the intense surprise of Mouzaka, who, huddled up in a corner, indulged in indescribable gestures, which the polished marble reflected on all sides. The fire burnt gaily, throwing out sparks, which, as they darkened, exhaled an exquisite perfume. The torches gave a brilliant light, the braziers shone brightly, and the soft warmth that reigned in the apartment inclined to a voluptuous indolence.

The situation in which I found myself was so singular, the kind of prison in which I was confined was so different from anything I could have imagined, and the ways of my keeper were so grotesque, that from time to time I rubbed my eyes to make sure that the whole thing was not a dream. I should even have derived amusement from my surroundings, if the thought that I was so far from Kalilah had left me for a single moment. The Climber, to distract my thoughts, began the marvellous story of the Giant Gebri, and the artful Charodé, but I interrupted him, and asked him to listen to the recital of my own real sorrows, promising that, afterwards, I should give ear to his tales. Alas, I never kept that promise. Vainly, at repeated intervals, did he try to excite my curiosity: I had none save with regard to Kalilah, and did not cease to repeat: "Where is he? What is he doing? When shall I see him again?"

The old man, seeing me so headstrong in my passion, and so well resolved to brave all remorse, became convinced that I was a fit object for his nefarious purposes, for, as my hearers will doubtless have already understood, he was a servant of the monarch who reigns in this place of torment. In the perversity of his soul, and that fatal blindness which makes men desire to find an entrance here, he had vowed to induce twenty wretches to serve Eblis, and he exactly wanted my brother and myself to complete the number. Far indeed was he, therefore, from really trying to stifle the yearnings of my heart; and though, in order to fan the flame that consumed me, he seemed, from time to time, to be desirous of telling me stories, yet, in reality, his head was filled with quite other thoughts.

I spent a great part of the night in making my criminal avowals. Towards morning I fell asleep. The Climber did the same, at a few paces' distance, having first, without ceremony, applied to my forehead a kiss, that burned me like a red-hot iron. My dreams were of the saddest. They left but a confused impression on my mind; but, so far I can recollect, they conveyed the warnings of heaven, which still desired to open before me a door of escape and of safety.

So soon as the sun had risen, the Climber led me into his woods, introduced me to his ostriches, and gave me an exhibition of his supernatural agility. Not only did he climb to the tremulous tops of the tallest and most slender palms, bending them beneath his feet like ears of corn, but he would dart like an arrow from one tree to another. After the display of several of these gymnastic feats, he settled on a branch, told me he was about to indulge in his daily meditations, and advised me to go with Mouzaka and bathe by the border of the stream, on the other side of the hill.

The heat was excessive. I found the clear waters cool and delicious. Bathing pools, lined with precious marbles, had been hollowed out in the middle of a little level mead over which high rocks cast their shadow. Pale narcissuses and gladioluses grew on the margin, and, leaning towards the water, waved over my head. I loved these languid flowers, they seemed an emblem of my fortunes, and for several hours I allowed their perfume to intoxicate my soul.

On returning to the palace, I found that the Climber had made great preparations for my entertainment. The evening passed like the evening before; and from day to day, pretty nearly after the same manner, I spent four months. Nor can I say that the time passed unhappily. The romantic solitude, the old man's patient attention, and the complacency with which he listened to love's foolish repetitions, all seemed to unite in soothing my pain. I should perhaps have spent whole years in merely nursing those sweet illusions that are so rarely realised, have seen the ardour of my passion gradually dwindle and die, have become no more than the tender sister and friend of Kalilah, if my father had not, in pursuit of his wild schemes, delivered me over to the impious scoundrel who sat daily watching at my side to make me his prey. Ah! Shaban, ah! Shamelah, you, my real friends, why was I torn from your arms? Why did you not, from the very first, perceive the germs of a too passionate tenderness existing in our hearts, germs which ought then and there to have been extirpated, since the day would come when neither fire nor steel would be of any avail!

One morning when I was steeped in sad thoughts, and expressing in even more violent language than usual my despair at being separated from Kalilah, the old man fixed upon me his piercing eyes, and addressed me in these words: "Princess, you, who have been taught by the most enlightened of Sages, cannot doubtless be ignorant of the fact that there are Intelligences, superior to the race of man, who take part in human affairs, and are able to extricate us from the greatest difficulties. I, who am telling you this, have had experience, more than once, of their power; for I had a right to their assistance, having been placed, as you yourself have been, under their protection from my birth. I quite see that you cannot live without your Kalilah. It is time, therefore, that you should apply for aid to such helpful Spirits. But will you have the strength of mind, the courage to endure the approach of Beings so different from mankind? I know that their coming produces certain inevitable effects, as internal tremors, the revulsion of the blood from its ordinary course; but I also know that these terrors, these revulsions, painful as they undoubtedly are, must appear as nothing compared with the mortal pain of separation from an object loved greatly and exclusively. If you resolve to invoke the aid of the Jinn of the Great Pyramid, who, as I know, presided at your birth, if you are willing to abandon yourself to his care, I can, this very evening, give you speech of your brother, who is nearer than you imagine. The Being in question, so renowned among the Sages, is called Omoultakos; he is, at present, in charge of the treasure which the ancient cabalist kings have placed in this desert. By means of the other spirits under his command, he is in close touch with his sister, whom, by the by, he loved in his time just as you now love Kalilah. He will, therefore, enter into your sorrows, just as much as I do myself, and will, I have no doubt, do all he can to further your desires."

At these last words my heart beat with unspeakable violence. The possibility of seeing Kalilah once again excited a transport in my breast. I rose hastily, and ran about the room like a mad creature. Then, coming back to the old man's side, I embraced him, called him my father, and, throwing myself at his knees, I implored him, with clasped hands, not to defer my happiness, but to conduct me, at whatever hazard, to the sanctuary of Omoultakos.

The crafty old scoundrel was well pleased, and saw with a malicious eye into what a state of delirium he had thrown me. His only thought was how to fan the flame thus kindled. For this purpose he resumed a cold and reserved aspect, and said, in tones of great solemnity: "Be it known to you, Zulkaïs, that I have my doubts, and cannot help hesitating, in a matter of such importance, great as is my desire to serve you. You evidently do not know how dangerous is the step you propose to take; or, at least, you do not fully appreciate its extreme rashness. I cannot tell how far you will be able to endure the fearful solitude of the immeasurable vaults that you must traverse, and the strange magnificence of the place to which I must conduct you. Neither can I tell in what shape the Jinn will appear. I have often seen him in a form so fearful that my senses have long remained numbed; at other times he has shown himself under an aspect so grotesque that I have been scarcely able to refrain from choking laughter, for nothing can be more capricious than beings of that nature. Omoultakos, perhaps, will spare your weakness; but it is right to warn you that the adventure on which you are bound is perilous, that the moment of the Jinn's apparition is uncertain, that while you are waiting in expectation you must show neither fear, nor horror, nor impatience, and that, at the sight of him, you must be very sure not to laugh, and not to cry. Observe, moreover, that you must wait in silence, and the stillness of death, and with your hands crossed over your breast, until he speaks to you, for a gesture, a smile, a groan, would involve not only your own destruction, but also that of Kalilah, and my own."

"All that you tell me," I replied, "carries terror into my bosom; but, impelled by such a fatal love as mine, what would one not venture!"

"I congratulate you on your sublime perseverance," rejoined the Climber, with a smile of which I did not then appreciate the full significance and wickedness. "Prepare yourself. As soon as darkness covers the earth, I will go and suspend Mouzaka from the top of one of my highest palm-trees, so that she may not be in our way. I will then lead you to the door of the gallery that leads to the retreat of Omoultakos. There I shall leave you, and myself, according to my custom, go and meditate at the top of one of the trees, and make vows for the success of your enterprise."

I spent the interval in anxiety and trepidation. I wandered aimlessly amid the valleys and hillocks on the island. I gazed fixedly into the depths of the waters. I watched the rays of the sun declining over their surface, and looked forward, half in fear, and half in hope, to the moment when the light should abandon our hemisphere. The holy calm of a serene night at last overspread the world.

I saw the Climber detach himself from a flock of ostriches that were gravely marching to drink at the river. He came to me with measured steps. Putting his finger to his lips, he said: "Follow me in silence." I obeyed. He opened a door, and made me enter, with him, into a narrow passage, not more than four feet high, so that I was compelled to walk half doubled up. The air I breathed was damp and stifling. At every step I caught my feet in viscous plants that issued from certain cracks and crevices in the gallery. Through these cracks the feeble light of the moon's rays found an entrance, shedding light, every here and there, upon little wells that had been dug to right and left of our path. Through the black waters in these wells I seemed to see reptiles with human faces. I turned away my eyes in horror. I burned with desire to ask the Climber what all this might mean, but the gloom and solemnity of his looks made me keep silence. He appeared to progress painfully, and to be pushing aside with his hands something to me invisible. Soon I was no longer able to see him at all. We were going, as it seemed, round and round in complete darkness; and, so as not to lose him altogether in that frightful labyrinth, I was compelled to lay hold upon his robe. At last we reached a place where I began to breathe a freer and fresher air. A solitary taper of enormous size, fixed upright in a block of marble, lighted up a vast hall, and discovered to my eyes five staircases, whose banisters, made of different metals, faded upwards into the darkness. There we stopped, and the old man broke the silence, saying: "Choose between these staircases. One only leads to the treasury of Omoultakos. From the others, which go losing themselves in cavernous depths, you would never return. Where they lead you would find nothing but hunger, and the bones of those whom famine has aforetime destroyed." Having said these words, he disappeared, and I heard a door closing behind him.

Judge of my terror, you who have heard the ebony portals, which confine us for ever in this place of torment, grind upon their hinges! Indeed I dare to say that my position was, if possible, even more terrible than yours, for I was alone. I fell to the earth at the base of the block of marble. A sleep, such as that which ends our mortal existence, overcame my senses. Suddenly a voice, clear, sweet, insinuating like the voice of Kalilah, flattered my ears. I seemed, as in a dream, to see him on the staircase of which the banisters were of brass. A majestic warrior, whose pale front bore a diadem, held him by the hand. "Zulkaïs," said Kalilah, with an afflicted air, "Allah forbids our union. But Eblis, whom you see here, extends to us his protection. Implore his aid, and follow the path to which he points you."

I awoke in a transport of courage and resolution, seized the taper, and began, without hesitation, to ascend the stairway with the brazen banister. The steps seemed to multiply beneath my feet; but my resolution never faltered; and, at last, I reached a chamber, square and immensely spacious, and paved with a marble that was of flesh colour, and marked as with the veins and arteries of the human body. The walls of this place of terror were hidden by huge piles of carpets of a thousand kinds, and a thousand hues, and these moved slowly to and fro, as if painfully stirred by human creatures stifling beneath their weight. All around were ranged black chests, whose steel padlocks seemed encrusted with blood. . . .